I0650260

The Price of Things

Elinor Glyn

Contents

THE PRICE OF THINGS

BY

Elinor Glyn

THE PRICE OF THINGS
BY ELINOR GLYN
1919

FOREWORD

I wrote this book in Paris in the winter of 1917-18--in the midst of bombs, and raids, and death. Everyone was keyed up to a strange pitch, and only primitive instincts seemed to stand out distinctly.

Life appeared brutal, and our very fashion of speaking, the words we used, the way we looked at things, was more realistic--coarser--than in times of peace, when civilization can re-assert itself again. This is why the story shocks some readers. I quite understand that it might do so; but I deem it the duty of writers to make a faithful picture of each phase of the era they are living in, that posterity may be correctly informed about things, and get the atmosphere of epochs.

The story is, so to speak, rough hewn. But it shows the danger of breaking laws, and interfering with fate--whether the laws be of God or of Man.

It is also a psychological study of the instincts of two women, which the strenuous times brought to the surface. "Amaryllis," with all her breeding and gentleness, reacting to nature's call in her fierce fidelity to the father of her child--and "Harietta," becoming in herself the epitome of the age-old prostitute.

I advise those who are rebuffed by plain words, and a ruthless analysis of the result of actions, not to read a single page.

Elinor Glyn

THE PRICE OF THINGS
CHAPTER I

"If one consciously and deliberately desires happiness on this plane," said the Russian, "one must have sufficient strength of will to banish all thought. The moment that one begins to probe the meaning of things, one has opened Pandora's box and it may be many lives before one discovers hope lying at the bottom of it."

"What do you mean by thought? How can one not think?" Amaryllis Ardayre's large grey eyes opened in a puzzled way. She was on her honeymoon in Paris at a party at the Russian Embassy, and until now had accepted things and not speculated about them. She had lived in the country and was as good as gold.

She was accepting her honeymoon with her accustomed calm, although it was not causing her any of the thrills which Elsie Goldmore, her school friend, had assured her she should discover therein.

Honeymoons! Heavens! But perhaps it was because Sir John was dull. He looked dull, she thought, as he stood there talking to the Ambassador. A fine figure of an Englishman but--yes--dull. The Russian, on the contrary, was not dull. He was huge and ugly and rough-hewn--his eyes were yellowish-green and slanted upwards and his face was frankly Calmuck. But you knew that you were talking to a personality--to one who had probably a number of unknown possibilities about him tucked away somewhere.

John had none of these. One could be certain of exactly what he would do on any given occasion--and it would always be his duty. The Russian was observing this charming English bride critically; she was such a perfect specimen of that estimable race--well-shaped, refined and healthy. Chock full of temperament too, he reflected--when she should discover herself. Temperament and romance and even passion, and there were shrewdness and commonsense as well.

"An agreeable task for a man to undertake her education," and he wished that he had time.

Amaryllis Ardayre asked again:

"How can one not think? I am always thinking."

He smiled indulgently.

"Oh! no, you are not--you only imagine that you are. You have questioned nothing--you do right generally because you have a nice character and have been well brought up, not from any conscious determination to uplift the soul. Yes--is it not so?"

She was startled.

"Perhaps."

"Do you ever ask yourself what things mean? What we are--where we are going? What is the end of it all? No--you are happy; you live from day to day--and yet you cannot be a very young ego, your eyes are too wise--you have had many incarnations. It is merely that in this one life the note of awakening has not yet been struck. You certainly must have needed sleep."

"Many lives? You believe in that theory?"

She was not accustomed to discuss unorthodox subjects. She was interested.

"But of course--how else could there be justice? We draw the reflex of every evil action and of every good one, but sometimes not until the next incarnation, that is why the heedless ones cannot grasp the truth--they see no visible result of either good or evil--evil, in fact, seems generally to win if there is a balance either way."

"Why are we not allowed memory then, so that we might profit by our lessons?"

"We should in that case improve from self-interest and not have our faults eliminated by suffering. We are given no conscious memory of our last life, so we go on fighting for whatever desire still holds us until its achievement brings such overwhelming pain that the desire is no more."

"Why do you say that for happiness we must banish thought--that seems a paradox."

She was a little disturbed.

"I said if one ***consciously*** and deliberately desired happiness, one must ban-ish thought to bring oneself back to the condition of hundreds of people who are happy; many of them are even elementals without souls at all. They are permit-ted happiness so that they may become so attached to the earth plane that they willingly return and gradually obtain a soul. But no one who is allowed to think is allowed any continued happiness; there would be no progress. If so, we should remain as brutes."

"Then how cruel of you to suggest to me to think. I want to be happy--perhaps I do not want to obtain a soul."

"That was born long ago--my words may have awakened it once more, but the sleep was not deep."

Amaryllis Ardayre looked at the crowds passing and re-passing in those stately rooms.

"Tell me, who is that woman over there?" she asked. "The very pretty one with the fair hair in jade green--she looks radiantly happy."

"And is--she is frankly an animal--exquisitely preserved, damnably selfish, completely devoid of intellect, sugar manners, the senses of a harem houri--and the tenacity of a rat."

"You are severe."

"Not at all. Harietta Boleski is a product of that most astonishing nation across the Atlantic--none other could produce her. It is the hothouse of the world as regards remarkable types. Here for immediate ancestry we have a mother, from heaven knows what European refuse heap, arrived in an immigrant ship--father of the 'pore white trash' of the south--result: Harietta, fine points, beautiful, quite a lady for ordinary purposes. The absence of soul is strikingly apparent to any or-dinary observer, but one only discovers the vulgarity of spirit if one is a student of evolution--or chances to catch her when irritated with her modiste or her maid. Other nations cannot produce such beings. Women with the attributes of Harietta, were they European, would have surface vulgarity showing--and so be out of the running, or they would have real passion which would be their undoing--passion is glorious--it is aroused by something beyond the physical. Observe her nostril! There is simple, delightful animal sensuality for you! Look also at the convex curve below the underlip--she will bite off the cherry whether it is hers by right or another's, and devour it without a backward thought."

"Boleski--that is a Russian name, is it not?"

"No, Polish--she secured our Stanislass, a great man in his country--last year in Berlin, having divorced a no longer required, but worthy German husband who had held some post in the American Consulate there."

"Is that old man standing obediently beside her your Stanislass?--he looks quite cowed."

"A sad sight, is it not? Stanislass, though, is not old, barely forty. He had a *beguin* for her. She put his intelligence to sleep and bamboozled his judgment with a continuous appeal to the senses; she has vampired him now. Cloying all his will with her sugared caprices, she makes him scenes and so keeps him in subjection. He was one of the Council de l'Empire for Poland; the aims of his country were his earnest work, but now ambition is no more. He is tired, he has ceased to struggle; she rules and eats his soul as she has eaten the souls of others. Shall I present her to you? As a type, she is worthy of your attention."

"It sounds as if she had the evil eye, as the Italians say," Amaryllis shuddered.

"Only for men. She is really an amiable creature--women like her. She is so frankly simple, since for her there are never two issues--only to be allowed her own desires--a riot of extravagance, the first place--and some one to gratify certain instincts without too many refinements when the mood takes her. For the rest, she is kind and good-natured and 'jolly,' as you English say, and has no notion that she is a road to hell. But they are mostly dead, her other spider mates, and cannot tell of it."

"I am much interested. I should like to talk to her. You say that she is happy?"

"Obviously--she is an elemental--she never thinks at all, except to plan some further benefit for herself. I do not believe in this life that she can obtain a soul--her only force is her tenacious will."

"Such force is good, though?"

"Certainly. Even bad force is better than negative Good. One must first be strong before one can be serene."

"You are strong."

"Yes, but not good. Hardly a fit companion for sweet little English brides with excellent husbands awaiting them."

"I shall judge of that."

"*Tiens!* So emancipated!"

"If you are bad, how does your theory work that we pay for each action? Since by that you must know that it cannot be worth while to be bad."

"It is not--I am aware of it, but when I am bad I am bad deliberately, knowing that I must pay."

"That seems stupid of you."

He shrugged his shoulders.

"I take very severe exercise when I begin to think of things I should not and I become savage when I require happiness--now is our chance for making you acquainted with Harietta, she is moving our way."

Madame Boleski swept towards them on the arm of an Austrian Prince and the Russian Verisschenzko said, with suave politeness:

"Madame, let me present you to Lady Ardayre. With me she has been admiring you from afar."

The two women bowed, and with cheery, disarming simplicity, the American made some gracious remarks in a voice which sounded as if she smoked too much; it was not disagreeable in tone, nor had she a pronounced American accent.

Amaryllis Ardayre found herself interested. She admired the superb attention to detail shown in Madame Boleski's whole person. Her face was touched up with the lightest art, not overdone in any way. Her hair, of that very light tone bordering on gold, which sometimes goes with hazel eyes, was quite natural and wonderfully done. Her dress was perfection--so were her jewels. One saw that her corsetiere was an artist, and that everything had cost a great deal of money. She had taken off one glove and Amaryllis saw her bare hand--it was well-shaped, save that the thumb turned back in a remarkable degree.

"So delighted to meet you," Madame Boleski said. "We are going over to London next month and I am just crazy to know more of you delicious English people."

They chatted for a few moments and then Madame Boleski swept onwards. She was quite stately and graceful and had a well-poised head. Amaryllis turned to the Russian and was startled by the expression of fierce, sardonic amusement in his yellow-green eyes.

"But surely, she can see that you are laughing at her?" she exclaimed, astonished.

"It would convey nothing to her if she did."

"But you looked positively wicked."

"Possibly--I feel it sometimes when I think of Stanislass; he was a very good friend of mine."

Sir John Ardayre joined them at this moment and the three walked towards the supper room and the Russian said good-night.

"It is not good-bye, Madame. I, too, shall be in your country soon and I also hope that I may see you again before you leave Paris."

They arranged a dinner for the following night but one, and said au revoir.

An hour later the Russian was seated in a huge English leather chair in the little salon of his apartment in the rue Cambon, when Madame Boleski very softly entered the room and sat down upon his knee.

"I had to come, darling Brute," she said. "I was jealous of the English girl," and she fitted her delicately painted lips to his. "Stanislass wanted to talk over his new scheme for Poland, too, and as you know that always gets on my nerves."

But Verisschenzko threw his head back impatiently, while he answered roughly.

"I am not in the mood for your chastisement to-night. Go back as you came, I am thinking of something real, something which makes your body of no use to me--it wearies me and I do not even desire your presence. Begone!"

Then he kissed her neck insolently and pushed her off his knee.

She pouted resentfully. But suddenly her eyes caught a small case lying on a table near--and an eager gleam came into their hazel depths.

"Oh, Stepan! Is it the ruby thing! Oh! You beloved angel, you are going to give it to me after all! Oh! I'll rush off at once and leave you, if you wish it! Good-night!"

And when she was gone Verisschenzko threw some incense into a silver burner and as the clouds of perfume rose into the air:

"Wough!" he said.

CHAPTER II

"What are you doing in Paris, Denzil?"

"I came over for a bit of racing. Awfully glad to see you. Can't we dine togeth-er? I go back to-morrow." Verisschenzko put his arm through Denzil Ardayre's and drew him in to the Cafe de Paris, at the door of which they had chanced to meet.

"I had another guest, but she can be consoled with some of Midas' food, and I want to talk to you; were you going to eat alone?"

"A fellow threw me over; I meant to have just a snack and go on to a theatre. It is good running across you--I thought you were miles away!"

Verisschenzko spoke to the head waiter, and gave him directions as to the disposal of the lovely lady who would presently arrive, and then he went on to his table, rather at the top, in a fairly secluded corner.

The few people who were already dining--it was early on this May night--looked at Denzil Ardayre--he was such a refreshing sight of health and youth, so tall and fit and English, with his brown smooth head and fearless blue eyes, gay and debonnaire. One could see that he played cricket and polo, and any other game that came along, and that not a muscle of his frame was out of condition. He had "sol-dier" written upon him--young, gallant, cavalry soldier. Verisschenzko appreciated him; nothing complete, human or inanimate, left him unconscious of its meaning. They knew one another very well--they had been at Oxford and later had shot bears together in the Russian's far-off home.

They talked for a while of casual things, and then Verisschenzko said:

"Some relations of yours are here--Sir John Ardayre and his particularly attrac-tive bride. Shall we eat what I had ordered for Collette, or have you other fancies after the soup?"

Denzil paid only attention to the first part of the speech--he looked surprised and interested.

"John Ardayre here! Of course, he married about ten days ago--he is the head of the family as you are aware, but I hardly even know him by sight. He is quite ten years older than I am and does not trouble about us, the poor younger branch--" and he smiled, showing such good teeth. "Besides, as you know, I have been for such a long time in India, and the leaves were for sport, not for hunting up relations."

Verisschenzko did not press the matter of his guest's fancies in food, and they continued the menu ordered for Collette without further delay.

"I want to hear all that you know about them, the girl is an exquisite thing with immense possibilities. Sir John looks--dull."

"He is really a splendid character though," Denzil hastened to assure him. "Do you know the family history? But no, of course not, we were too busy in the old days enjoying life to trouble to talk of such things! Well, it is rather strange in the last generation--things very nearly came to an end and John has built it all up again. You are interested in heredity?"

"Naturally--what is the story?"

"Our mutual great-grandfather was a tremendous personage in North Somerset--the place Ardayre is there. My father was the son of the younger son, who had just enough to do him decently at Eton, and enable him to scrape along in the old regiment with a pony or two to play with. My mother was a Willowbrook, as you know, and a considerable heiress, that is how I come out all right, but until John's father, Sir James, squandered things, the head of the family was always very rich and full of land--and awfully set on the dignity of his race. They had turned the cult of it into regular religion."

"The father of this man made a *gaspillage*, then--well?"

"Yes, he was a rotter--a hark-back to his mother's relations; she was a Cranmote--they ruin any blood they mix with. I am glad that I come from the generation before."

Denzil helped himself to a Russian salad, and went on leisurely. "He fortunately married Lady Mary de la Paule--who was a saint, and so John seems to have righted, and takes after her. She died quite early, she had had enough of Sir James, I expect, he had gambled away everything he could lay hands upon. Poor John was brought up with a tutor at home, for some reason--hard luck on a man. He was only about thirteen when she died and at seventeen went straight into the city. He was determined to make a fortune, it has always been said, and redeem the mortgages on Ardayre--very splendid of him, wasn't it?"

"Yes--well all this is not out of the ordinary line--what comes next?"

Denzil laughed--he was not a good raconteur.

"The poor lady was no sooner dead than the old boy married a Bulgarian snake charmer, whom he had picked up in Constantinople! You may well smile"--for Verisschenzko had raised his eyebrows in a whimsical way--this did sound such a highly coloured incident!

"It was an unusual sort of thing to do, I admit, but the tale grows more lurid still, when I tell you that five months after the wedding she produced a son by the Lord knows who, one of her own tribe probably, and old Sir James was so infatuated with her that he never protested, and presently when he and John quarrelled like hell he pretended the little brute was his own child--just to spite John."

Verisschenzko's Calmuck eyes narrowed.

"And does this result of the fusion of snake charmers figure in the family history? I believe I have met him--his name is Ferdinand, is it not, and he is, or was, in some business in Constantinople?"

"That is the creature--he was brought up at Ardayre as though he were the heir, and poor John turned out of things. He came to Eton three years before I left, but even there they could not turn him into the outside semblance of a gentleman. I loathed the little toad, and he loathed me--and the sickening part of the thing is that if John does not have a son, by the English law of entail Ferdinand comes into Ardayre, and will be the head of the family. Old Sir James died about five years ago, always protesting this bastard was his own child, though every one knew it was a lie. However, by that time John had made enough in the city to redeem Ardayre twice over. He had tremendous luck after the South African War, so he came into possession and lives there now in great state--I do really hope that he will have a son."

"You, too, have the instinct of the family, then--this pride in it--since it cannot benefit you either way."

"I believe it is born in us, and though I have never seen Ardayre, I should hate this mongrel to have it. I was brought up with a tremendous reverence for it, even as a second cousin."

"Well, the new Lady Ardayre looks young enough and of a health to have ten sons!"

"Y-es," Denzil acquiesced in a tentative tone.

"Not so?" Verisschenzko glanced up surprised, and then gave his attention to the waiter who had brought some Burgundy and was pouring it out into his glass.

"Not so you would say?"

"I don't know, I have never seen her--but in the family it is whispered that John--poor devil--he had an accident hunting two or three years ago. However, it may not any of it be true--here, let us drink to the Ardayre son!"

"To the Ardayre son!" and Verisschenzko filled his friend's glass with the decanted wine and they both drank together.

"Your cousin is like you," he said presently. "A fatiguing likeness, but the same height and make--and voice--strange things these family reproductions of an exact type. I have no family, as you know--we are of the people, arisen by trade to riches. Could I go beyond my immediate parents, could I know cousins and uncles and brothers, should I find this same peculiar stamp of family among us all? Who knows? I think not."

"I suppose there is something in it. My father has told me that in the picture gallery at Ardayre they are as like as two pins the whole way down."

"The concentration upon the idea causes it. In people risen like my father and myself, we only resemble a group--a nation; if I have children they will resemble me. It is strength in the beginning when an individual rises beyond the group, which produces a type. One says 'English' to look at you, and then, if one knows, one says 'Ardayre' at once; one gets as far as 'Calmuck' with me, that is all, but in years to come it will have developed into 'Verisschenzko.'"

"How you study things, Stepan; you are always putting new ideas into my head whenever I see you. Life would be just a routine, for all the joy of sport, if one did not think. I am going to finish my soldiering this autumn and stand for Parliament. It seems waste of time now, with no wars in prospect, sticking to it; I want a vaster field."

"You think there can be no wars in prospect--no? Well, who can prophesy? There are clouds in the Southeast, but for the moment we will not speculate about them--and they may affect my country and not yours. And so you will settle down and become a reputable member of Parliament?" Then, as Denzil would have spoken perhaps upon the subject of war clouds, Verisschenzko hastily continued:

"Will you dine to-morrow night at the Ritz to meet your cousin and his wife?

They are honouring me."

"I wish I could, but I am off in the morning. What is she like?"

Verisschenzko paid particular attention to the selection of a quail, and then he answered:

"She is of the same type as the family, Denzil,--that is, a good skeleton--bones in the right place, firm white flesh, colouring as yours--well bred, balanced, un-awakened as yet. Was she a relation?"

"Yes, I believe so--a cousin of a generation even before mine. I wish I could have dined, I would awfully like to have met them; I shall have to make a chance in England. It is stupid not to know one's own family, but our fathers quarrelled and we have never had a chance of mending the break."

"They were at the Russian Embassy last night; the throng admired Lady Ardayre very much."

"And what are you doing in Paris, Stepan? The last I heard of you, you were on your yacht in the Black Sea."

"I was cruising near countries whose internal affairs interest me for the moment. I returned to my *appartement* in Paris to see a friend of mine, Stanislass Boleski--he also has a lovely wife. Look, she has just come in with him. She is in the devil of a temper--observe her. If I sit back, the pillar hides me--I do not wish them to see me yet."

Denzil glanced down the room; two people were taking their seats by the wall. The mask was off Harietta Boleski's face for the moment; it looked silly with its raised eyebrows and was full of ill temper and spite. The husband had an air of extreme worry on his clever, intellectual face, but that he was solicitous to gratify his wife's caprices, any casual observer could have perceived.

"You mean the woman with the wonderful *cigrettes*--she is good-looking, isn't she? I wonder who it is she has caught sight of now, though? Look at the eagerness which has come into her eyes--you can see her in the mirror if you want to."

But Verisschenzko had missed nothing, and he bent forward to endeavour to identify the person upon whom Madame Boleski's gaze had turned. There was nothing to distinguish any individual--the company were of several nations--German and Austrian and Balkan and Russian scattered about here and there among the French and American *habitues*. The only plan would be to continue to watch

Harietta--but although he did this throughout the dinner, not a flicker of her eye-lids gave him any further clue.

Denzil was interested--he felt something beyond what appeared on the surface was taking place, so he waited for his friend to speak.

Verisschenzko was silent for a little, and then he casually gave a resume of the character and place of Madame Boleski and her husband, a good deal more baldly expressed, but in substance much the same as he had given to Amaryllis at the Russian Embassy the night before.

He spoke lightly, but his yellow green eyes were keen.

"Look at her well--she is capable of mischief. Her extreme stupidity--only the brain of a rodent or a goat--makes her more difficult to manipulate than the cleverest diplomat, because you can never be sure whether the blank want of understanding which she displays is real or simulated. She is a perfect actress, but very often is quite natural. Most women are either posing all the time, or not at all. Harietta's miming only comes into action for self-preservation, or personal gain, and then it is of such a superb quality that she leaves even me--I, who am no poor diviner--confused as to whether she is telling a lie or the truth."

"What an exceptional character!" Denzil was thrilled.

"An absence of all moral sense is her great power," Verisschenzko continued, while he watched her narrowly, "because she never has any of the prickings of conscience which even most rogues experience at times, and so draws no demagnetising nervous uncertain currents. If it were not for an insatiable extravagance, and a capricious fancy for different jewels, she would be impossible to deal with. She has information, obtained from what source I do not as yet know, which is of vital importance to me. Were it not for that, one could simply enjoy her as a mistress and take delight in studying her idiosyncrasies."

"She has lovers?"

"Has had many; her role now is that of a great lady and so all is of a respectability! She is so stupid that if that instinct of self-preservation were not so complete as to be like a divine guide, she would commit betises all the time. As it is, when she takes a lover it is hidden with the cunning of a fox."

"Who did you say the first husband was--?"

"A German of the name of Von Wendel--he used to beat her with a stick, it is said--so naturally such a nature adored him. I did not meet her until she had got rid of him and he had disappeared. She would sacrifice any one who stood in her way."

"Your friend, the present husband, looks pretty epuise--one feels sorry for the poor man."

Then, as ever, at the mention of the debacle of Stanislass, Verisschenzko's eyes filled with a fierce light.

"She has crushed the hope of Poland--for that, indeed, one day she must pay."

"But I thought you Russians did not greatly love the Poles?" Denzil remarked.

"Enlightened Russians can see beyond their old prejudices--and Stanislass was a lifetime friend. One day a new dawn will come for our Northern world."

His eyes grew dreamy for an instant, and then resumed their watch of Harietta. Denzil looked at him and did not speak for a while. He had always been drawn to Stepan, from a couple of terms at Oxford before the Russian was sent down for a mad freak, and did not return. He was such a mixture of idealism and brutal commonsense, a brain so alert and the warm heart of a generous child--capable of every frenzy and of every sacrifice. They had planned great things for their afterlives before the one joined his regiment, and learned discipline, and the other wandered over many lands--and as they sat there in the Cafe de Paris, the thoughts of both wandered back to old days gapping the encounters for sport in Russia and in India between.

"They were glorious times, Denzil, weren't they?" Verisschenzko said presently, aware by that wonderfully delicately attuned faculty of his of what his friend was thinking. "We had thought to conquer the sun, moon and stars--and who knows, perhaps we will yet!"

"Who knows? I feel my real life is only just beginning. How old are we, Stepan? Twenty-nine years old!"

Afterwards, as they went out, they passed the Boleskis close, and the two rose and spoke to Verisschenzko, with empressement. He introduced Captain Ardayre and they talked for a few minutes, Harietta Boleski all smiles and flattering cajoleries now--and then they said good-night and went out.

But as Stepan passed, a man half hidden behind a pillar leaned forward and looked at him, and in his light blue eyes there burned a jealous hate.

"Ah, Gott in Himmel!" he growled to himself. "It is he whom she loves--not the pig-fool who we gave her to--one day I shall kill him--" and he raised his glass of Rhine wine and murmured "Der Tag!"

That evening Sir John Ardayre had taken his bride to dine in the Bois, and they were sitting listening to the Tziganes at Armenonville. Amaryllis was conscious that the evening lacked something. The circumstances were interesting--a bride of ten days, and the environment so illuminating--and yet there was John smoking an expensive cigar and not saying *anything!* She did not like people who chattered--and she could even imagine a delicious silence wrought with meaning. But a stolid respectable silence with Tziganes playing moving airs and the romantic background of this Paris out-of-door joyous night life, surely demanded some show of emotion!

John loved her she supposed--of course he did--or he never would have asked her to marry him, rich as he was and poor as she had been. She could not help going over all their acquaintance; the date of its beginning was only three months back!

They had met at a country house and had played golf together, and then they had met again a month later at another house, in March, but she could not remember any love-making--she could not remember any of those warm looks and those surreptitious hand-clasps when occasion was propitious, which Elsie Goldmore had told her men were so prodigal of in demonstrating when they fell in love. Indeed, she had seen emotion upon the faces of quite two or three young men, for all her secluded life and restricted means, since she had left the school in Dresden, where a worldly maiden aunt had pinched to send her, German officers had looked at her there with interest in the street, and the clergyman's three sons and the Squire's two, when she returned home. Indeed, Tom Clarke had gone further than this! He had kissed her cheek coming out of the door in the dark one evening, and had received a severe rebuff for his pains.

She had read quantities of novels, ancient and modern. She knew that love was a wonderful thing; she knew also that modern life and its exigencies had created a new and far more matter-of-fact point of view about it than that which was obtained in most books. She did not expect much, and had indulged in none of those visions of romantic bliss which girls were once supposed to spend their time in constructing. But she did expect *something*, and here was nothing--just nothing!

The day John had asked her to marry him he had not been much moved. He had put the question to her simply and calmly, and she had not dreamed of refusing him. It was obviously her duty, and it had always been her intention to marry well, if the chance came her way, and so leave a not too congenial home.

She had been to a few London balls with the maiden aunt, a personage of some prestige and character. But invitations do not flow to a penniless young woman from the country, nor do partners flock to be presented to strangers in those days, and Amaryllis had spent many humiliating hours as a wall-flower and had grown to hate balls. She was not expansive in herself and did not make friends easily, and pretty as she was, as a girl, luck did not come her way.

When she had said "Yes" in as matter-of-fact a voice as the proposal of marriage had been made to her, Sir John had replied: "You are a dear," and that had seemed to her a most ordinary remark. He had leaned over--they were climbing a steep pitch in search of a fugitive golf ball--and had taken her hand respectfully, and then he had kissed her forehead--or her ear--she forgot which--nothing which mattered much, or gave her any thrill!

"I hope I shall make you happy," he had added. "I am a dull sort of a fellow, but I will try."

Then they had talked of the usual things that they talked about, the most every-day,--and they had returned to the house, and by the evening every one knew of the engagement, and she was congratulated on all sides, and petted by the hostess, and she and John were left ostentatiously alone in a smaller drawing-room after dinner, and there was not a grain of excitement in the whole conventional thing!

There was always a shadow, too, in John's blue eyes. He was the most reserved creature in this world, she supposed. That might be all very well, but what was the good of being so reserved with the woman you liked well enough to make your wife, if it made you never able to get beyond talking on general subjects!

This she had asked herself many times and had determined to break down the reserve. But John never changed and he was always considerate and polite and perfectly at ease. He would talk quietly and with commonsense to whoever he was placed next, and very seldom a look of interest flickered in his eyes. Indeed, Amaryllis had never seen him really interested until he spoke of Ardayre--then his very voice altered.

He spoke of his home often to her during their engagement, and she grew to know that it was something sacred to him, and that the Family and its honour, and its traditions, meant more to him than any individual person could ever do.

She almost became jealous of it all.

Her trousseau was quite nice--the maiden aunt had seen to that. Her niece had done well and she did not grudge her pinchings.

Amaryllis felt triumphant as she walked up the aisle of St. George's, Hanover Square, on the arm of a scapegrace sailor uncle--she would not allow her stepfather to give her away.

Every one was so pleased about the wedding! An Ardayre married to an Ardayre! Good blood on both sides and everything suitable and rich and prosperous, and just as it should be! And there stood her handsome, stolid bridegroom, serenely calm--and the white flowers, and the Bishop--and her silver brocade train--and the pages, and the bridesmaids. Oh! yes, a wedding was a most agreeable thing!

And could she have penetrated into the thoughts of John Ardayre, this is the prayer she would have heard, as he knelt there beside her at the altar rails: "Oh, God, keep the axe from falling yet, give me a son."

The most curious emotions of excitement rose in her when they went off in the smart new automobile en route for that inevitable country house "lent by the bridegroom's uncle, the Earl de la Paule, for the first days of the honeymoon."

This particular mansion was on the river, only two hours' drive from her aunt's Charles Street door. Now that she was his wife, surely John would begin to make love to her, real love, kisses, claspings, and what not. For Elsie Goldmore had presumed upon their schoolgirl friendship and been quite explicate in these last days, and in any case Amaryllis was not a miss of the Victorian era. The feminine world has grown too unrefined in the expression of its private affairs and too indiscreet for any maiden to remain in ignorance now.

It is true John did kiss her once or twice, but there was no real warmth in the embrace, and when, after an excellent dinner her heart began to beat with wonderment and excitement, she asked herself what it meant. Then, all confused, she murmured something about "Good-night," and retired to the magnificent state suite alone.

When she had left him John Ardayre drank down a full glass of Benedictine and followed her up the stairs, but there was no lover's exaltation, but an anguish almost of despair in his eyes.

Amaryllis thought of that night--and of other nights since--as she sat there at Armenonville, in the luminous sensuous dusk.

So this was being married! Well, it was not much of a joy--and why, why did John sit silent there? Why?

Surely this is not how the Russian would have sat--that strange Russian!

CHAPTER III

It was nearing sunset in the garden below the Trocadero. A tall German officer waited impatiently not far from the bronze of a fierce bull in a secluded corner under the trees; he was plainly an officer although he was clothed in mufti of English make. He was a singularly handsome creature in spite of his too wide hips. A fine, sensual, brutal male.

He swore in his own language, and then, through the glorious light, a woman came towards him. She wore an unremarkable overcoat and a thick veil.

"Hans!" she exclaimed delightedly, and then went on in fluent German with a strong American accent.

He looked round to be sure that they were alone, and then he clasped her in his arms. He held her so tightly that she panted for breath; he kissed her until her lips were bruised, and he murmured guttural words of endearment that sounded like an animal's growl.

The woman answered him in like manner. It was as though two brute beasts had met.

Then presently they sat upon a seat and talked in low tones. The woman protested and declaimed; the man grumbled and demanded. An envelope passed between them, and more crude caresses, and before they parted the man again held her in close embrace--biting the lobe of her ear until she gave a little scream.

"Yes--if there was time--" she gasped huskily. "I should adore you like this--but here--in the gardens--Oh! do mind my hat!"

Then he let her go--they had arranged a future meeting. And left alone, he sat down upon the bench again and laughed aloud.

The woman almost ran to the road at the bottom and jumped into a waiting taxi, and once inside she brought out a gold case with mirror and powder puff, and red greases for her lips.

"My goodness! I can't say that's a mosquito!" and she examined her ear. "How tiresome and imprudent of Hans! But Jingo, it was good!--if there only had been time--"

Then she, too, laughed as she powdered her face, and when she alighted at the door of the Hotel du Rhin, no marks remained of conflict except the telltale ear.

But on encountering her maid, she was carrying her minute Pekinese dog in her arms and was beating him well.

"Regardez, Marie! la vilaine bete m'a mordu l'oreil!"

"Tiens!" commented the affronted Marie, who adored Fou-Chou. "Et le cher petit chien de Madame est si doux!"

*   *   *   *   *

Stanislass Boleski was poring over a voluminous bundle of papers when his wife, clad in a diaphanous wrap, came into his sitting room. They had a palatial suite at the Rhin. The affairs of Poland were not prospering as he had hoped, and these papers required his supreme attention--there was German intrigue going on somewhere underneath. He longed for Harietta's sympathy which she had been so prodigal in bestowing before she had secured her divorce from that brute of a Teutonic husband, whom she hated so much. Now she hardly ever listened, and yawned in his face when he spoke of Poland and his high aims. But he must make allowances for her--she was such a child of impulse, so lovely, so fascinating! And here in Paris, admired as she was, how could he wonder at her distraction!

"Stanislass! my old Stannie," she cooed in his ear, "what am I to wear to-night for the Montivacchini ball? You will want me to look my best, I know, and I just love to please you."

He was all attention at once, pushing the documents aside as she put her arms around his neck and pulled his beard, then she drew his head back to kiss the part where the hair was growing thin on the top--her eyes fixed on the papers.

"You don't want to bother with those tiresome old things any more; go and get into your dressing-gown, and come to my room and talk while I am polishing my nails,--we can have half an hour before I must dress. I'll wait for you here--I must be petted to-night, I am tired and cross."

Stanislass Boleski rose with alacrity. She had not been kind to him for days--fretful and capricious and impossible to please. He must not lose this chance--if it could only have been when he was not so busy--but--

"Run along, do!" she commanded, tapping her foot.

And putting the papers hastily in a drawer with a spring lock, he went gladly from the room.

Her whole aspect changed; she lit a cigarette and hummed a tune, while she fingered a key which dangled from her bracelet.

No one eclipsed Madame Boleski in that distinguished crowd later on. Her clinging silver brocade, and the one red rose at the edge of the extreme decolletage, were simply the perfection of art. She did not wear gloves, and on her beautifully manicured hands she wore no rings except a magnificent ruby on the left little finger. It was her caprice to refuse an alliance. "Wedding rings!" she had said to Stanislass. "Bosh! they spoil the look. Sometimes it is chic to have a good jewel on one finger, sometimes on another, but to be tied down to that band of homely gold! Never!"

Stanislass had argued in those early days--he seldom argued now.

"My love!" he cried, as she burst upon his infatuated vision, when ready for the ball, "let me admire you!"

She turned about; she knew that she was perfection.

Her husband kissed her fingers, and then he caught sight of the ruby ring. He examined it.

"I had not seen this ruby before," he exclaimed in a surprised voice, "and I thought I knew all your jewel case!"

She held out her hand while her big, stupid, appealing hazel eyes expressed childish innocence.

"No--I'd put it away, it was of other days--but I do love rubies, and so I got it out to-night, it goes with my rose!"

He had perceived this. Had he not become educated in the subtleties of a woman's apparel? For was it not his duty often, and his pleasure sometimes, to have to assist at her toilet, and to listen for hours to discussions of garments, and if they could suit or not. He was even accustomed now to waiting in the hot salons in the Rue de la Paix, while these stately perfections were being essayed. But the ruby ring worried him. Why had she asked him to give her just such a one only last month, if she already possessed its fellow?... He had refused because her extravagance had grown fantastic, but he had meant to cede later. Every pleasure of the senses he always had to secure by bribes.

"I do not understand why?--" he began, but she put her hand over his mouth and then kissed him voluptuously before she turned and shrilly cried to Marie to bring her ermine cloak.

The maid's eyes were round and sullen with resentment; she had not forgotten the beating of Fou-Chou! "As for the ear of Madame!" she said, clasping the tiny dog to her heart, as she watched her mistress go towards the lift from the sitting-room, "as for that maudite ear, thy teeth are innocent, my angel! But I wish that he who is guilty had bitten it off!" Then she laughed disdainfully.

"And look at the old fool! He dreams of nothing! And if he dreamed, he would not believe--such *insenses* are men!"

Meanwhile the Boleskis had arrived at the hotel of the Duchesse di Montivac-chini, that rich and ravishing American-Italian, who gave the most splendid and exclusive entertainments in Paris. So, too, had arrived Sir John and Lady Ardayre, brought on from the dinner at the Ritz by Verisschenzko.

Denzil had left that morning for England, or he would have had the disagree-able experience of meeting his *soi-disant* cousin, to whom he had applied the epi-thet "toad." For Ferdinand Ardayre had just reached the gay city from Constanti-nople, and had also come to the ball with a friend in the Turkish Embassy.

He happened to be standing at the door when the Boleskis were announced, and his light eyes devoured Harietta--she seemed to him the ideal of things fem-inine--and he immediately took steps to be presented. Assurance was one of his strongest cards. He was a fair man--with the fairness of a Turk not European--and there was something mean and chetive in his regard. He would have looked over-dressed and un-English in a London ball-room, but in that cosmopolitan company he was unremarkable. He had been his mother's idol and Sir James had left him everything he could scrape from his highly mortgaged property. But certain tastes of his own made a Continental life more congenial to him, and he had chosen early to enter a financial house which took him to the East and Constantinople. He was about twenty-seven years old at this period and was considered by himself and a number of women to be a creature of superlative charm.

The one burning bitterness in his spirit was the knowledge that Sir John Ardayre had never recognised him as a brother. During Sir James' lifetime there had been silence upon the matter, since John had no legal reason for denying the relationship, but once he had become master of Ardayre he had let it be known that he refused to believe Ferdinand to be his father's son. On the rare occasions when he had to be mentioned, John called him "the mongrel" and Ferdinand was aware of this. A silent, intense hatred filled his being--more than shared by his mother who, until the day of her death, two years before, had always plotted vengeance-- without being able to accomplish anything. Either mother or son would willingly have murdered John if a suitable and safe method had presented itself. And now to know that John had married a beautiful far-off cousin and might have children, and so forever preclude the possibility of his--Ferdinand's--own inheritance of Ardayre was a further incentive to hate! If only some means could be discovered to remove John, and soon! But while Ferdinand thought these things, watching his so-called brother from across the room, he knew that he was impotent. Poisons and daggers were not weapons which could be employed in civilised Paris in the twentieth century! If they would only come to Constantinople!

Amaryllis Ardayre had never seen a Paris ball before. She was enchanted. The sumptuous, lofty rooms, with their perfect Louis XV gilt *boiseries*, the marvellous clothes of the women, the gaiety in the air! She was accustomed to the new weird dances in England, but had not seen them performed as she now saw them.

"This orgie of mad people is a wonderful sight," Verisschenzko said, as he stood by her side. "Paris has lost all good taste and sense of the fitness of things. Look! the women who are the most expert in the wriggle of the tango are mostly over forty years old! Do you see that one in the skin-tight pink robe? She is a grandmother! All are painted--all are feverish--all would be young! It is ever thus when a country is on the eve of a cataclysm--it is a dance Macabre."

Amaryllis turned, startled, to look at him, and she saw that his eyes were full of melancholy, and not mocking as they usually were.

"A dance Macabre! You do not approve of these tangoes then?"

He gave a small shrug of his shoulders, which was his only form of gesticulation.

"Tangoes--or one steps--I neither approve nor disapprove--dancing should all have its meaning, as the Greek Orchises had. These dances to the Greeks would have meant only one thing--I do not know if they would have wished this to take place in public, they were an aesthetic and refined people, so I think not. We Russians are the only so-called civilised nation who are brutal enough for that; but we are far from being civilised really. Orgies are natural to us--they are not to the French or the English. Savage sex displays for these nations are an acquired taste, a proof of vicious decay, the middle note of the end."

"I learned the tango this Spring--it is charming to dance," Amaryllis protested. She was a little uncomfortable--the subject, much as she was interested in the Russian's downright views, she found was difficult to discuss.

"I am sure you did--you counted time--you moved your charming form this way and that--and you had not the slightest idea of anything in it beyond anxiety to keep step and do the thing well! Yes--is it not so?"

Amaryllis laughed--this was so true!

"What an incredibly false sham it all is!" he went on. "Started by niggers or Mexicans for what it obviously means, and brought here for respectable mothers, and wives, and girls to perform. For me a woman loses all charm when she cheapens the great mystery-ceremonies of love--"

"Then you won't dance it with me?" Amaryllis challenged smilingly--she would not let him see that she was cast down. "I do so want to dance!"

His eyes grew fierce.

"I beg of you not! I desire to keep the picture I have made of you since we met--later I shall dance it myself with a suitable partner, but I do not want you mixed with this tarnished herd."

Amaryllis answered with dignity:

"If I thought of it as you do I should not want to dance it at all." She was aggrieved that her expressed desire might have made him hold her less high--"and you have taken all the bloom from my butterfly's wing--I will never enjoy dancing it again--let us go and sit down."

He gave her his arm and they moved from the room, coming almost into conflict with Madame Boleski and her partner, Ferdinand Ardayre, whose movements would have done honour to the lowest nigger ring.

"There is your friend, Madame Boleski--she dances--and so well!"

"Harietta is an elemental--as I told you before--it is right that she should express herself so. She is very well aware of what it all means and delights in it. But look at that lady with the hair going grey--it is the Marquise de Saint Vrilliere--of the bluest blood in France and of a rigid respectability. She married her second daughter last week. They all spend their days at the tango classes, from early morning till dark--mothers and daughters, grandmothers and demi-mondaines, Russian Grand Duchesses, Austrian Princesses--clasped in the arms of incredible scum from the Argentine, half-castes from Mexico, and farceurs from New York--decadent male things they would not receive in their ante-chambers before this madness set in!"

"And you say it is a dance Macabre? Tell me just what you mean."

They had reached a comfortable sofa by now in a salon devoted to bridge, which was almost empty, the players, so eager to take part in the dancing, that they had deserted even this, their favourite game.

"When a nation loses all sense of balance and belies the traditions of its whole history, and when masses of civilised individuals experience this craze for dancing and miming, and sex display, it presages some great upheaval--some calamity. It was thus before the revolution of 1793, and since it is affecting England and America and all of Europe it seems, the cataclysm will be great."

Amaryllis shivered. "You frighten me," she whispered. "Do you mean some war--or some earthquake--or some pestilence, or what?"

"Events will show. But let us talk of something else. A cousin of your husband's, who is a very good friend of mine, was here yesterday. He went to England to-day, you have not met him yet, I believe--Denzil Ardayre?"

"No--but I know all about him--he plays polo and is in the Zingari."

"He does other things--he will even do more--I shall be curious to hear what you think of him. For me he is the type of your best in England. We were at Oxford together; we dreamed dreams there--and perhaps time will realise some of them. Denzil is a beautiful Englishman, but he is not a fool."

A sudden illumination seemed to come into Amaryllis' brain; she felt how limited had been all her thoughts and standpoints in life. She had been willing to drift on without speculation as to the goal to be reached. Indeed, even now, had she any definite goal? She looked at the Russian's strong, rugged face, his inscrutable eyes narrowed and gazing ahead--of what was he thinking? Not stupid, ordinary things--that was certain.

"It is the second evening, amidst the most unlikely surroundings, that you have made me speculate about subjects which never troubled me before. Then you leave me unsatisfied--I want to know--definitely to know!"

"Searcher after wisdom!" and he smiled. "No one can teach another very much. Enlightenment must come from within; we have reached a better stage when we realise that we are units in some vast scheme and responsible for its working, and not only atoms floating hither and thither by chance. Most people have the brains of grasshoppers; they spring from subject to subject, their thoughts are never under control. Their thoughts rule them--it is not they who rule their thoughts."

They were seated comfortably on their sofa, and Verisschenzko leaning forward from his corner, looked straight into her eyes.

"You control your thoughts?" she asked. "Can you really only let them wander where you choose?"

"They very seldom escape me, but I consciously allow them indulgences."

"Such as?"

"Visions--day dreams--which I know ought not to materialise."

Something disturbed her in his regard; it was not easy to meet, so full of magnetic emanation. Amaryllis was conscious that she no longer felt very calm--she longed to know What his dreams could be.

"Yes--but if I told you, you would send me away."

It seemed that he could read her desire. "I shall order myself to be gone presently, because the interest which you cause me to feel would interfere with work which I have to do."

"And your dreams? Tell them first?" she knew that she was playing with fire.

He looked down now, and she saw that he was not going to gratify her curiosity.

"My noblest dream is for the regeneration of a nation--on that I have ordered my thoughts to dwell. For the others, the time is not yet for me to tell you of them--

it may never come. Now answer me, have you yet seen your new home, Ardayre?"

"No, but why should you be interested in that? It seems strange that you, a Russian, should even know that there is such a place as Ardayre!"

"Continue--I know that it is a wonderful place, and that your husband loves it more than his life."

Amaryllis pouted slightly.

"He does indeed! Perhaps I shall grow to do so also when I know it; it is the family creed. Sir James--my late father-in-law--was the only exception to this rule."

"You must uphold the idea then, and live to do fine things."

"I will try--if only--" then she paused, she could not say "if only John would be human and unfreeze to me, and love me, and let us go on the road together hand in hand!"

"It is quite useless for a family merely to continue from generation to generation piling up possessions, and narrowing its interests. It must do this for a time to become solid, and then it should take a vaster view, and begin to help the world. Nearly everything is spoiled in all civilisation because of this inability to see beyond the nose, this poor and paltry outlook."

"People rave vaguely," Amaryllis argued, "about one's duty and vast outlooks and those things, but it is difficult to get any one to give concrete advice--what would you advise me to do, for instance?"

"I would advise you first to begin asking yourself the reason of everything, each day, since Pandora's box has been opened for you in any case. 'What caused this? What caused that?' Search for causes--then eradicate the roots, if they are not good, do not waste time on trying to ameliorate the results! Determine as to why you are put into such and such a place, and accomplish what you discover to be the duty of the situation. But how serious we have become! I am not a priest to give you guidance--I am a man fighting a tremendously strong desire to take you in my arms--so come, we will return to the ball room, and I will deliver you to your husband."

Amaryllis rose and stood facing him, her heart was beating fast. "If I try to do well--to climb the straight road of the soul's advancement, will you give me counsel should I need it by the way?"

"Yes, this I will do when I have complete control, but for the moment you are causing me emotions, and I wish to keep you a thing apart--of the spirit. Hermits and saints subdue the flesh by abstinence and fasting; they then become useless to the world. A man can only lead men while he remains a man, with a man's passions, so that he should not fight in this beyond his strength--only he should **never sully the wrong thing**. Come! Return to the husband--and I shall go for a while to hell."

And presently Amaryllis, standing safely with John, saw Verisschenzko dancing the maddest one-step with Madame Boleski, their undulations outdoing all others in the room!

CHAPTER IV

The day after the wonderful rejoicing which the homecoming of Amaryllis had been the occasion of at Ardayre, she was sitting waiting for her husband in that exquisite cedar parlour which led from her room.

They would breakfast cosily there, she had arranged, and nothing was wanting in the setting of a love scene. The bride wore the most alluring cap and daintiest Paris neglige, and her fair and pure skin gleamed through the diaphanous stuff.

How she longed for John to notice it all, and make love to her! She had apprehended a number of delightful possibilities in Paris, none of which had materialised, alas! in her case.

John was the same as ever--quiet, dignified, polite and unmoved. She had taken to turning out the light before he came to her at night, to hide the disappointment and chagrin which she felt might show in her eyes. It would be so humiliating if he should see this. There would soon be nothing left for her to do but pretend that she was as cold as he was, if this last effort of *froufrous* left him as stolid as usual.

She smoothed out the pale chiffon draperies with a tender hand. She got up and looked at herself in the mirror. It was fortunate that the reflection of snowy nose and throat and chin, and the pink velvet cheeks, required no art to perfect them; it was all natural and quite nice, she felt. What a bore it must be to have to touch up like Madame Boleski!

But what was the meaning of all the imputations she had read of in those interesting French novels in Paris?--the languors and lassitudes and tremors of breakfasting love! There was just such a scene as this in one she had devoured on the boat.

A *dejeuner* of *amants*--certainly they had not been married, there was that want of resemblance, but surely this could not matter? For a fortnight, three weeks, a month, surely even a husband could be as a lover--especially to a mistress who took such pains to please his eye!

Would Elsie Goldmore spend such dull breakfasts when she espoused Harry Kahn? Elsie Goldmore was a Jewess, perhaps that made the difference, perhaps Jews were more expansive--But the people in the novels were not Jews. Of course, though, they were French, that must be it! Could it be that all Englishmen, to their wives, were like John? This she must presently find out.

Meanwhile she would try--oh, try so hard to entice him to be lovely to her! He was her own husband; there was absolutely no harm in doing this. And how glorious it would be to turn him into a lover! Here in this perfectly divine old house! John was so good-looking, too, and had the most attractive deep voice, but heavens! the matter-of-factness of everything about him!

How long would it all go on?

John came in presently with *The Times* under his arm. He was immaculately dressed in a blue serge suit. Amaryllis had hoped to see him in that subduedly gorgeous dressing gown she had persuaded him to order at Charvets during their first days. It would have been so suitable and intimate and lover-like. But no! there was the blue serge suit--and *The Times*.

A shadow fell upon her mood. Her own pink chiffons almost seemed out of place!

John glanced at them, and at the glowing, living, delicious bit of young womanhood which they adorned. He saw the rebellious ripe cherry of a mouth, and the warm, soft tenderness in the grey eyes, and then he quickly looked out of the window--his own blue ones expressionless, but the hand which held the newspaper clenched rather hard.

"Amn't I a pet!" cooed Amaryllis, deliberately subduing the chill of her first disappointment. "Dearest, see I have kept this last and loveliest set of garments for the morning of our home-coming--and for you!" and she crept close to him and laid her cheek against his cheek.

He encircled her with his arm and kissed her calmly.

"You look most beautiful, darling," he said. "But then, you always do, and your frills are perfection. Now I think we ought to have breakfast; it is most awfully late."

She sat down in her place and she felt stupid tears rise in her eyes.

She poured out the tea and buttered herself some toast, while John was apparently busy at a side table where dwelt the hot dishes.

He selected the daintiest piece of sole for her, and handed her the plate.

"I am not hungry," she protested, "keep it for yourself."

He did not press the matter, but took his place and began to talk quietly upon the news of the day--in a composed fashion between glances at **The Times** and mouthfuls of sole.

Amaryllis controlled herself. She was too proud and too just to make a foolish scene. If this was John's way and her little effort at enticement was a failure, she must put up with it. Marriage was a lottery she had always heard, and it might be her luck to have drawn a blank. So she choked down the rising emotion and answered brightly, showing interest in her husband's remarks--and she even managed to eat some omelette, and when the business of breakfast was quite over she went to the window and John followed her there.

The view which met their eyes was exquisite.

Beyond the perfect stately garden, with its quaint clipped yews and masses of spring flowers and velvet lawns, there stretched the vast park with its splendid oaks and browsing deer. It was a possession which any man could feel proud to own.

John slipped his arm round her waist and drew her to him.

"Amaryllis," he said, and his voice vibrated, "to-day I am going to show you everything I love here at Ardayre--because I want you to love it all, too. You are of the family, so it must mean something to you, dear."

Amaryllis kindled with re-awakening hope.

"Indeed, it will mean everything to me, John."

He kissed her forehead and murmured something about her dressing quickly, and that he would wait for her there in the cedar room. And when she returned in about a quarter of an hour in the neatest country clothes, he placed her hand on his arm and led her down the great stairs and on through the hall into the picture gallery.

It was a wonderful place of green silk and chestnut wainscoting, and all the walls of its hundred feet of length were hung with canvases of value--portraits principally of those Ardayres who had gone on. Face after face looked down on Amaryllis of the same type as John's and her own--the brown hair and eyes of grey or blue. Some were a little fairer, some a little darker, but all unmistakably stamped "Ardayre."

John pointed out each individual to her, while she hung fondly on his arm, from some doubtful crude fourteenth century wooden panels of Johns and Denzils, on to Benedict in a furred Henry VII. gown. Then came Henrys and Denzils in Elizabethan armour and puffed white satin, and through Stuart and Commonwealth to Stuart again, and so to William and Mary numbers of Benedicts, and lastly to powdered Georgian James' and Regency Denzils and Johns. And the name Amaryllis recurred more than once in stately dame or damsel, called after that fair Amaryllis of Elizabeth's days who had been maid of honour to the virgin Queen, and had sonnets written to her nut brown locks by the gallants of her time.

"How little the women they married seem to have altered the type!" the young living Amaryllis exclaimed, when they came nearly to the end. "It goes on Ardayre, Ardayre, Ardayre, ever since the very first one. Oh! John, if we ever have a son he ought to be even more so--you and I being of the same blood--" and then she hesitated and blushed crimson. This was the first time she had ever spoken of such a thing.

John held her arm very tightly to his side for a second, and his voice was uncertain as he answered:

"Amaryllis, that is the profound desire of my heart, that we should have a son."

A strange feeling of exaltation came over Amaryllis, half-innocent, wholly ignorant as she was.

She had been stupid--French novels were all nonsense. Marriages in real life were always like this--of course they must be--since John said plainly and with such deep feeling that his profoundest desire was that they should have a son! That meant that she would surely have one. This was perfectly glorious, and it must simply be those silly books and Elsie Goldmore's too uxorious imagination which had given her some ridiculously romantic exaggerated ideas of what love hours would be. She would now be contented and never worry again. She nestled closer to her husband and looked up at him with eyes sweet and fond, the brown, curly lashes wet with tender dew.

"Oh!--darling, when, when do you think we shall have a son?"

Then, for the first time in their lives, John Ardayre clasped her in his arms passionately and held her to his heart.

"Ah, God," he whispered hoarsely, as he kissed her fresh young lips. "Pray for that, Amaryllis--pray for that, my own."

Then he restrained himself and drew her on to the four last pictures at the end of the room. They were of his grandfather and grandmother, and his father and mother. And then there was a blank space, and the brighter colour of the damask showed that a canvas had been removed.

"Who hung there, John?"

"The accursed snake charmer woman whom my father disgraced the family with by bringing home. She was his wife by the law, and a Frenchman painted her. It was a fine picture with the bastard Ferdinand in her arms--the proof of our shame. I had it taken down and burnt the day the place was mine."

Amaryllis was receiving surprises to-day--John's face was full of emotion, his eyes were sparkling with hate as he spoke. How he must love everything connected with his home, and its honour, and its name--he could not be so very cold after all!

She thought of the Russian's words about a family--the uselessness of its going on for generations, piling up possessions and narrowing its interests. What had the aims been of all these handsome men? She knew the earlier history a little, for even though she was of a distant branch they had been proud of the connection, and treasured the traditions belonging to it. But these were just dry facts of history which she knew, so now she asked:

"John, what did any of them do? Did they accomplish great deeds?"

He took her back to the beginning again and began to tell her of the achievements of each one. There would be three perhaps, one after another, who had filled high posts in the State, and indeed had been worthy of the name. Then would come one or two quiet plodding ones, who seemed to have done little but sit still and hold on.

Then Denzil Ardayre, knight of Elizabeth's time, pleased Amaryllis most of all--though there had been greater soldiers, and more able politicians than he later on, culminating in Sir John Ardayre of George IV. days, who had hammered against pocket boroughs and corruption until he died an old man, the hour the Reform Bill swept aside abuses and the road to freedom was won.

"How strange it seems that different ages produce more accentuated stamps of breeding than others," Amaryllis said, "even in the same families where the blood is all blue. Look, John! that Denzil and the rest of the Elizabethans are the most refined, aristocratic creatures you could imagine, in their little ruffs. Absolutely intellectual and cultivated faces and of old race--and then comes a James period, less intelligent, more round featured. And a Cavalier one, gay and gallant, aristocratic and chiselled also, but not nearly so clever looking as the Elizabethan. Then we get cadaverous William and Mary ones, they might be lawyers or business men, not that look of great gentlemen, and the Anne's and the first George's are really bucolic! And then that wonderfully refined, cultivated, intellectual finish seems to crop up in the later eighteenth century again. Have you noticed this, John? You can see it in every collection of miniatures and portraits even in the museums."

John responded interestedly:

"The Elizabethans were supremely cultivated gentlemen--no wonder that they look as they do--and their lives were always in their hands which gives them that air of insouciance."

When the history of the family achievements had been told her down to John's father, she paused, still clinging to his arm, and said:

"I am so glad that they did splendid things, aren't you? And we shall not drift either. You must teach me to be the most perfect mistress of Ardayre, and the most perfect wife for the greatest of them all--because your achievement is the finest, John, to have won it all back and redeemed it by the work of your own brain."

He pressed the hand on his arm.

"It was hard work--and the home times were ugly in those days, Amaryllis, though the goal was worth it, and now we must carry on...." And then his reserve seemed to fall upon him again, and he took her through the other rooms, and kept to solid facts, and historic descriptions, and his bride had continuously the impression that he was mastering some emotion in himself, and that this stolidity was a mask.

When lunch time came the usual relations of obvious and commonplace good-fellowship had been fully restored between them, and that atmosphere of aloofness which seemed impossible to banish enveloped John once more.

Amaryllis sighed--but it was too soon to despair she thought, after the hope of John's words, and with her serene temperament she decided to leave things as they were for the present and trust to time.

But as her maid brushed out the soft brown hair that night, an unrest and longing for something came over her again--what she knew not, nor could have put into words. She let herself re-live that one moment when John had pressed herewith passion to his heart. Perhaps, perhaps that was the beginning of a change in him--perhaps--presently--

But the clock in the long gallery had chimed two, and there was yet no sound of John in the dressing-room beyond.

Amaryllis lay in the great splendid gilt bed in the warm darkness, and at last tears trickled down her cheeks.

What could keep him so long away from her? Why did he not come?

The large Queen Anne windows were wide open, and soft noises of the night floated in with the zephyrs. The whole air seemed filled with waiting expectancy for something tender and passionate to be.

What was that? Steps upon the terrace--measured steps--and then silence, and then a deep sigh. It must be John--out there alone!--when she would have loved to have stayed with him, to have woven sweet fancies in the luminous darkness, to have taken and given long kisses, to have buried her face in the honeysuckle which grew there, steeped in dew. But he had said to her after their stately dinner in the great dining-hall:

"Play to me a little, Amaryllis, and then go to bed, child--you must be tired out."

And after that he had not spoken more, but pushed her gently towards the door with a solemn kiss on the forehead, and just a murmur of "Good-night." And she had deceived herself and thought that it meant that he would come quickly, and so she had run up the stairs.

But now it was after two in the morning, and would soon be growing towards dawn--and John was out there sighing alone!

She crept to the window and leaned upon the sill. She thought that she could distinguish his tall figure there by the carved stone bench.

"John!" she called softly, "I am, so lonely--John, dearest--won't you come?"

Then she felt that her ears must be deceiving her, for there was the sound of a faint suppressed sob, and then, a second afterwards, her husband's voice answering cheerily, with its usual casual note:

"You naughty little night bird! Go back to bed--and to sleep--yes--I am coming immediately now!"

But when he did steal in silently from the dressing-room an hour later in a grey dawn, Amaryllis, worn out with speculation and disappointment, had fallen asleep.

He looked down upon her charming face--the long, curly brown lashes sweeping the flushed cheek, and at the rounded, beautiful girlish form--all his very own to clasp and to kiss and to hold in his arms--and two scalding tears gathered in his blue eyes, and he took his place beside her without making a sound.

CHAPTER V

"Here are the papers, Hans, but I think the whole thing stupid nonsense. What does it matter to any one what Poland wants? What a nuisance all these old boring political things are! They always spoiled our happiness since the beginning--and now if it wasn't for them we could have a glorious time here together. I would love managing to come out to meet you under Stanislass' nose. None of the others I have ever had are as good in the way of a lover as you."

The man swore in German under his breath.

"Of a lightness always, Harietta! No ***devouement***, no patriotism.... Should I have agreed to the divorce, loving your body as I do, had it not been a serious matter? The pig-dog who now owns you must be sucked dry of information--and then I shall take you back again."

A cunning look came into Madame Boleski's hazel eyes. She had not the slightest intention of permitting this--to go back to Hans! To the difficulty of making both ends meet! Even though he did cause every inch of her well-preserved body to tingle! They had suggested her getting the divorce for their own stupid political ends, to be able to place her in the arms of Stanislass Boleski, and there she meant to stay! It was infinitely more agreeable to be a grande dame in Paris, and presently in London, than to be the spouse of Hans in Berlin, where, whatever his secret power might be with the authorities, he could give her no great social position; and social position was the goal of all Harietta Boleski's desires!

She could attract lovers in any class of life--that had never been her difficulty. Her trouble had been that she could never force herself into good American society, even after she had married Hans, and they had dwelt there for a year or more. Her own compatriots would have none of her, and so she wanted triumph in other lands. She hated to remember her youth of humiliation, trying to play a social game on the earnings of any work that she could pick up, between discreet outings with--friends who failed to suggest matrimony. Hans, on some secret mission to San Francisco, where she had gone as companion to a friend, had seemed a veritable Godsend and Prince Charming, when, in her thirtieth year, he actually offered legal marriage, completely overcome by her great physical charm. But although she loved Hans with whatever of that emotion such a nature could be capable of, five years of him and more or less genteel poverty had been enough, and now she was free of that, and could still enjoy surreptitiously the pleasure of his passion, and reign as a *persona grata* wife of one of the richest men in Poland at the same time. That those in authority who had arranged the divorce required of her certain tiresome obligations in return for their services, was one of those annoying parts of life! She took not the slightest interest in the affairs of any country. Nothing really mattered to her, but herself. Her whole force was concentrated upon the betterment of the position and physical pleasure of Harietta Boleski.

It was this instinct alone which had prompted her to acquire a smattering of education--and with the quick, adaptive faculty of a monkey she had been able to use this to its utmost limits, as well as her histrionic talent--no mean one--to gain her ends. She was now playing the role of a lady, and playing it brilliantly she knew--and here was Hans back again, and suggesting that when she had secured all the information that he required from Stanislass she should return to him!

"Tra la la!" she said to herself, there in the room at the Hotel Astoria, where she had gone to meet him, "think this if it pleases you! It will keep you quiet and won't hurt me!"

For the moment she wanted Hans--the man, and was determined to waste no further time on useless discussion. So she began her blandishments, taking pride in showing him her beautiful garments, and her string of big pearls; each thing exhibited between her voluptuous kisses, until Hans grew intoxicated with desire, and became as clay in her hands.

"It is not thy pig-dog of a husband I wish to kill!" he said, after one hour had gone by in inarticulate murmurings. "Him I do not fear--it is the Russian, Verisschenzko, who fills me with hate--we have regard of him, he does not go unobserved, and if you allure him also among the rest, beyond the instructions which you had, then there will be unpleasantness for you, my little cat--thy Hans will twist his bear's neck, and thine also, if need be!"

"Verisschenzko!" laughed Harietta, "why, I hardly know him; he don't amount to a row of pins! He's Stanislass' friend--not mine."

Then she smoothed back Hans' rather fierce, fair moustache from his lips and kissed him again--her ruby ring flashing in a ray of sunlight.

"Look! isn't this a lovely jewel, Hans! My old Stannie gave it to me only some days ago--it is my new toy--see--"

Hans examined it:

"Thou art a creature of the devil, Harietta, there is not one of thy evil qualities of greed and extortion which I do not know. Thou liest to me and to all men--the only good thing in thee is thy body--and for that all men let thee lie."

Harietta pouted.

"I can't understand when you talk like that, Hans--it's all warbash, as we said out West. What are qualities? What is there but the body anyway? Great sakes! that's enough for me, and the devil is only in story books to frighten children--I'm just like every other woman and I want to have a good time."

"I hear that you are going to London soon," said Hans, dropping the tutoyage and growing brutally severe, "to conquer new lovers and to wear more dresses? But there you will be of great use to me. Your instructions will be all ready in cypher by Tuesday night, when you must meet me at whatever point is convenient to you, after nine o'clock--here, perhaps?"

Harietta frowned--she had other views for Tuesday night.

"What shall I gain by coming, or by going on with this spying on Stan? I'm tired of it all; it breaks my head trying to take in your horrid old cypher. I don't think I'll do it any more."

The Prussian's face grew livid and his mouth set like an iron spring. He looked at her straight between the eyes, as a lion tamer might have done, and he took a cane from where it laid on a bureau near.

"Until you are black and blue, I will beat you, woman," he said, "as I have done before--if you fail us in a single thing--and do not think we are powerless! It shall be that you are exposed and degraded, and so lose your game. Now tell me, will you go on?"

Harietta crouched in fear, just animal, physical fear--she had felt that stick, it was a nightmare to her, as it might have been to a child. She knew that Hans would keep his word. His physical strength had been one of the things she had adored in him--but to be degraded and exposed, as well as beaten, touched her sensibilities, after all the trouble she had taken to become a lady of the world! This was too much. No! Tiresome as all these old papers were, she would have to go on--but since he threatened her she would pay him out! The Russian should have papers as well! And so there was good in all things, since now material advantage would come from both sides. Was it not right that you looked to yourself, especially when menaced with a stick?

She laughed softly; this was humorous and she could appreciate such kind of humour.

Hans crushed her in his arms.

"Answer!" he ordered gutturally. "Answer, you fiend!"

Harietta became cajoling--no one could have looked more frank or simple, as simple as she looked to all great ladies when she would disarm them and win her way. She would look up at them gently, and ask their advice, and say that of course she was only a newcomer and very ignorant, not clever like they!

"Hans, darling, I was only joking, am I not devoted to your interests and always ready to serve you and the higher powers whom you serve? Of course, I will come on Tuesday night and, of course, I will go on."

She let her lip tremble and her eyes fill with tears; they were quite real tears. She felt the hardship of having to weary her brain with a new cypher, and self-pity inflames the lachrymose glands.

"To business then, ***mein liebchen***--attend carefully to every word. In England you must be received by Royalty itself, and you must go into the highest circles of the diplomatic and political world. The men are indiscreet there; they trust their women and tell them secret things. It is the women you must please. The English are a race of fools; numbers are aristocrats in all classes and therefore too stupid to suspect craft, and those who are not are trying to appear to be, and too conceited to use their wits. You can be of enormous use to our country, Harietta, my wife," and he walked up and down the room in his excitement, his hands clasped behind him--he would have been a very handsome man but for his too wide hips.

Marietta looked at him out of the corner of her eye; she did not notice this defect in him, for her he was a splendid male, with a delightful quality of savagery in love which she had found in no other man except Verisschenzko--Verisschenzko! Her thoughts hesitated when they came to him--Verisschenzko was adorable, but he was a man to be feared--much more than Hans. Him she could always cajole if she used passion enough, but she had the uncomfortable feeling that Verisschenzko gave way to her only when--and because--he wanted to, not for the reason that she had conquered him.

"Of great use to our country, Harietta, my wife," Hans murmured again, clearing his throat.

"I am not your wife, my pretty Hans!" and she raised her eyebrows, and curled one corner of her upper lip. "You gave me up at the bidding of the higher command--I am your mistress now and then, when I feel inclined--but I am Stanislass' wife. I like a man better when I am his mistress; there are no tiresome old duties along with it."

Hans growled, he hated to realise this.

"You must be more careful with your speech, Harietta. When you get to England you must not say 'along with it'--after the pains I have taken with your grammar, too! You can use Americanisms if they are apt, and even a literal translation of another language--but bad grammar--common phrases--pah! that is to give the show away!"

Harietta reddened--her vanity disliked criticism.

"I take very good care of my language when it is necessary in the world--I am considered to have a lovely voice--but when I'm with you I guess I can enjoy a holiday--it's kind of a rest to let yourself go," her pronunciation lapsed into the broadest American, just to irritate him, and she stood and laughed in his face.

He caught her in his arms. She never failed to appeal to his senses; she had won him by that force and so held his brute nature even after five years. This was always the reason of whatever success she secured. A man had no smallest doubt as to why he was drawn; it was a direct appeal to the most primitive animal nature in him. The birth of Love is ever thus if we would analyse it truly, but the spirit fortunately so wraps things in illusion that generally both participants really believe that the mutual attraction is because of higher emotions of the mind, and so they are doomed to disappointment when passion is sated, unless the mind fulfills the ideal. But if the reality fails to make good, the refined spirit turns in disgust from the material, unconsciously resentful in that it has suffered deception. With Harietta this disappointment could never occur, since she created no illusion that she was appealing to the mind at all, and so a man if he were attracted faced no unknown quality, but was aware that it was only the animal in him which was drawn, and if his senses were his masters, not his servants, her victory was complete.

After some more fierce caresses had come to an end--there was no delicacy about Harietta--Hans continued his discourse.

"There has come here to Paris a young man of the name of Ardayre--Ferdinand Ardayre--he is slippery, but he can be of the greatest value to us. See that you become friends--you can reach him through Abba Bey. He hates his brother who is the head of the family and he hates his brother's wife--for family reasons which it is not necessary to waste time in telling you. I knew him in Constantinople. Underneath I believe he hates the English--there is a slur on him."

"I have already met him," and Harietta's eyes sparkled. "I hate the wife also for my own reasons--yes--how can I help you with this?"

"It is Ferdinand you must concentrate on; I am not concerned with the brother or his wife, except in so far as his hate for them can be used to our advantage. Do not embark upon this to play games of your own for your hate--you may be foolish then and upset matters."

"Very well." The two objects could go together, Harietta felt; she never wasted words. It would be a pleasure one day, perhaps, to be able to injure that girl whom

Verisschenzko certainly respected, if he was not actually growing to love her. Harietta did not desire the respect of men in the abstract; it could be a great bore--what
they thought of her never entered her consideration, since she was only occupied
with her own pleasure in them and how they affected herself. Respect was one of
the adjuncts of a good social position; and of value merely in that aspect. But as
Verisschenzko respected no one else, as far as she knew, that must mean something
annoyingly important.

Seven o'clock struck; she had thoroughly enjoyed being with Hans, he satisfied
her in many ways, and it was also a relaxation, as she need not act. But the joys of
the interview were over now, and she had others prepared for later on, and must go
back to the Rhin to dress. So she kissed Hans and left, having arranged to meet him
on the Tuesday night here in his rooms, and having received precise instructions as
to the nature of the information to be obtained from Ferdinand Ardayre.

Life would be a paradise if only it were not for these ridiculous and tiresome
political intrigues. Harietta had no taste for actual intrigue, its intricacies were a
weariness to her. If she could have married a rich man in the beginning, she always
told herself, she would never have mixed herself up in anything of the kind, and
now that she *had* married a rich man, she would try to get out of the nuisance as
soon as possible. Meanwhile, there was Ferdinand--and Ferdinand was becoming in
love with her--they had met three times since the Montivacchini ball.

"He'll be no difficulty," she decided, with a sigh of relief. It would not be as it
had been with Verisschenzko, whom she had been directed to capture. For in Verisschenzko she had found a master--not a dupe.

When she reached the beautiful Champs-Elysees, she looked at her diamond
wrist watch. It was only ten minutes past seven, the dinner at the Austrian Embassy
was not until half-past eight. Dressing was a serious business to Harietta, but she
meant to cut it down to half an hour to-night, because there was a certain apartment in the Rue Cambon which she intended to visit for a few minutes.

"What an original street to have an apartment in!" people always said to Verisschenzko. "Nothing but business houses and model hotels for travellers!" And the
shabby looking *porte-cochere* gave no evidence of the old Louis XV. mansion within, converted now into a series of offices, all but the top flooring looking on to the
gardens of the *Ministere*.

Verisschenzko had taken it for its situation and its isolation, and had converted it into a thing of great beauty of panelling and rare pictures and the most comfortable chairs. There was absolute silence, too, there among the tree tops.

Madame Boleski ascended leisurely the shallow stairs--there was no lift--and rang her three short rings, which Peter, the Russian servant, was accustomed to expect. The door was opened at once, and she was taken through the quaint square hall into the master's own sitting-room, a richly sombre place of oak boiserie and old crimson silk.

Verisschenzko was writing and just glanced up while he murmured Napoleon's famous order to Mademoiselle George--but Harietta Boleski pushed out her full underlip and sat down in a deep armchair.

"No--not this evening, I have only a moment. I have merely come, Stepan, you darling, to tell you that I have something interesting to say."

"Not possible!" and he carefully sealed down a letter he had been writing and put it ready to be posted. Then he came over and took some cigarettes from a Faberger enamel box and offered her one.

Harietta smoked most of the day but she refused now.

"You have come, not for pleasure, but to talk! Sapristi! I am duly amazed!"

Another woman would have been insulted at the tone and the insinuation in the words, but not so Harietta. She did not pretend to have a brain, that was one of her strong points, and she understood and appreciated the crudest methods, so long as their end was for the pleasure of herself.

She nodded, and that was all.

Verisschenzko threw himself into the opposite chair, his yellow-green eyes full of a mocking light.

"I have seen a brooch even finer than the ruby ring at Cartier's just now--I thought perhaps if I were very pleased with you, it might be yours."

Harietta bounded from her chair and sat upon his knee.

"You perfect angel, Stepan, I adore you!" she said. He did not return the caresses at all, but just ordered:

"Now talk."

She spoke rapidly, and he listened intently. He was weighing her words and searching into their truth. He decided that for some reason of her own she was not lying--and in any case it did not matter if she were not, because he had resources at his command which would enable him to test the information, and if it were true it would be worth the brooch.

"She has been wounded in some way, probably physically, since nothing less material would affect her. Physically and in her vanity--but who can have done it?" the Russian asked himself. "Who is her German correspondent? This I must discover--but since it is the first time she has knowingly given me information, it proves some revenge in her goat's brain. Now is the time to obtain the most."

He encircled her with his arm and kissed her with less contemptuous brutality than usual, and he told her that she was a lovely creature, and the desire of all men--while he appeared to attach little importance to the information she vouchsafed, asking no questions and re-lighting a cigarette. This forced her to be more explicit, and at last all that she meant to communicate was exposed.

"You imagine things, my child," he scoffed. "I would have to have proof--and then if it all should be as you say. Why, that brooch must be yours--for I know that it is out of real love for me that you talk, and I always pay lavishly for--love."

"Indeed, you know that I adore you, Stepan--and that brooch is just what I want. Stanislass has been niggardly beyond words to me lately, and I am tired of all my other things."

"Bring me some proof to the reception to-night. I am not dining, but I shall be there by eleven for a few moments."

She agreed, and then rose to go--but she pouted again and the convex *obstine* curve below her under lip seemed to obtrude itself.

"She has gone back to England--your precious bride--I suppose?"

"She has."

"We shall all meet there in a week or so--Stanislass is going to see some of his boring countrymen in London--the conference you know about--and we have taken a house in Grosvenor Square for some months. I do not know many people yet--will you see to it that I do?"

"I will see that you have as many of these handsome Englishmen as will completely keep your hands full."

She laughed delightedly.

"But it is women I want; the men I can always get for myself."

"Fear nothing, your reception will be great."

Then she flung herself into his arms and embraced him, and then moved towards the door.

"I will telephone to Cartier in the morning," and Verisschenzko opened the door for her, "if you bring me some interesting proof of your love for me--to-night."

And when she had gone he took up his letter again and looked at the address, **To** Lady Ardayre, ***Ardayre Chase, North Somerset, Angleterre***.

"I must keep to the things of the spirit with you, precious lady. And when I cannot subdue it, there is Harietta for the flesh--wough! but she sickens me--even for that!"

CHAPTER VI

Denzil Ardayre could not get any more leave for a considerable time and remained quartered in the North, where he played cricket and polo to his heart's content, but the head of the family and his charming wife went through the feverish season of 1914 in the town house in Brook Street. Ardayre was too far away for week-end parties, but they had several successful London dinners, and Amaryllis was becoming quite a capable hostess, and was much admired in the world.

Very fine of instinct and apprehension at all times she was developing by contact with intelligent people--for John had taken care that she only mixed with the most select of his friends. The de la Paule family had been more than appreciative of her and had guided her and supervised her visiting list with care.

Everything was too much of a rush for her to think and analyse things, and if she had been asked whether she was happy, she would have thought that she was replying with honesty when she affirmed that she was. John was not happy and knew it, but none of his emotions ever betrayed themselves, and the mask of his stolid content never changed.

They had gone on with their matter-of-fact relations, and when they returned to London after a week at Ardayre, all had been much easier, because they were seldom alone--and at last Amaryllis had grown to accept the situation, and try not to speculate about it. She danced every night at balls and continued the usual round, but often at the Opera, or the Russian ballet, or driving back through the park in the dawn, some wild longing for romance would stir in her, and she would nestle close to John. And John would perhaps kiss her quietly and speak of ordinary things. He went everywhere with her though, and never failed in the kindest consideration. He seldom danced himself, and therefore must often have been weary, but no suggestion of this ever reached Amaryllis.

"What does he talk to his friends about, I wonder?" she asked herself, watching him from across a room, in a great house after dinner one night.

John was seated beside the American Lady Avonwier, a brilliant person who did not allow herself to be bored. He appeared calm as usual, and there they sat until it was time to go on to a ball.

Everything he said was so sensible, so well informed--perhaps that was a nice change for people--and then he was very good-looking and--but oh! what was it-- what was it which made it all so disappointing and tame!

A week after they had come up to Brook Street, the Boleskis arrived at the Mount Lennard House which they had taken in Grosvenor Square, armed with every kind of introduction, and Harietta immediately began to dazzle the world.

Her dresses and jewels defied all rivalry; they were in a class alone, and she was frank and stupid and gracious--and fitted in exactly with the spirit of the time.

She restrained her movements in dancing to suit the less advanced English taste; she gave to every charity and organized entertainments of a fantastic extravagance which whetted the appetite of society, grown jaded with all the old ways. The men of all ages flocked round her, and she played with them all--ambassadors, politicians, guardsmen, all drawn by her own potent charm, and she disarmed criticism by her stupidity and good nature, and the lavish amusements she provided for every one--while the chef they had brought over with them from Paris would have insured any hostess's success!

Harietta had never been so happy in all the thirty-six years of her life. This was her hour of triumph. She was here in a country which spoke her own language--for her French was deplorably bad--she had an unquestioned position, and all would have been without flaw but for this tiresome information she was forced to collect.

Verisschenzko had been detained in Paris. The events of the twenty-eighth of

June at Serajevo were of deep moment to him, and it was not until the second week in July that he arrived at the Ritz, full of profound preoccupation.

Amaryllis had been to Harietta's dinners and dances, and now the Boleskis had been asked down to Ardayre in return for the three days at the end of the month, when the coming of age of the young Marquis of Bridgeborough would give occasion for great rejoicings, and Amaryllis herself would give a ball.

"You cannot ask people down to North Somerset in these days just for the pleasure of seeing you, my dear child," Lady de la Paule had said to her nephew's wife. "Each season it gets worse; one is flattered if one's friends answer an invitation to dinner even, or remain for half an hour when it is done. I do not know what things are coming to, etiquette of all sorts went long ago--now manners, and even decency have gone. We are rapidly becoming savages, openly seizing whatever good thing is offered to us no matter from whom, and then throwing it aside the instant we catch sight of something new. But one must always go with the tide unless one is strong enough to stem it, and frankly *I* am not. Now Bridgeborough's coming of age will make a nice excuse for you to have a party at Ardayre. How many people can you put up? Thirty guests and their servants at least, and seven or eight more if you use the agent's house."

So thus it had been arranged, and John expressed his pleasure that his sweet Amaryllis should show what a hostess she could be.

None but the most interesting people were invited, and the party promised to be the greatest success.

Two or three days before they were to go down, Amaryllis coming in late in the afternoon, found Verisschenzko's card.

"Oh! John!" she cried delightedly, "that very thrilling Russian whom we met in Paris has called. You remember he wrote to me some time ago and said he would let us know when he arrived. Oh! would not it be nice to have him at our party--let us telephone to him now!"

Verisschenzko answered the call himself, he had just come in; he expressed himself as enchanted at the thought of seeing her--and yes--with pleasure he would come down to Ardayre for the ball.

"We shall meet to-night, perhaps, at Carlton House Terrace at the German Embassy," he said, "and then we can settle everything."

Amaryllis wondered why she felt rather excited as she walked up the stairs--she had often thought of Verisschenzko, and hoped he would come to England. He was vivid and living and would help her to balance herself. She had thought while she dressed that her life had been one stupid rush with no end, since that night when they had talked of serious things at the Montivacchini hotel. She had need of the counsel he had promised to give her, for this heedless racket was not adding lustre to her soul.

Verisschenzko seemed to find her very soon--he was not one of those persons who miss things by vagueness. His yellow-green eyes were blazing when they met hers, and without any words he offered her his arm, foreign fashion, and drew her out on to the broad terrace to a secluded seat he had apparently selected beforehand, as there was no hesitancy in his advance towards this goal.

He looked at her critically for an instant when they were seated in the soft gloom.

"You are changed, Madame. Half the soul is awake now, but the other half has gone further to sleep."

"--Yes, I felt you would say that--I do not like myself," and she sighed.

"Tell me about it."

"I seem to be drifting down such a useless stream--and it is all so mad and aimless, and yet it is fun. But every one is tired and restless and nobody cares for anything real--I am afraid I am not strong enough to stand aside from it though, and I wonder sometimes what I shall become."

Verisschenzko looked at her earnestly--he was silent for some seconds.

"Fate may alter the atmosphere. There are things hovering, I fear, of which you do not dream, little protected English bride. Perhaps it is good that you live while you can."

"What things?"

"Sorrows for the world. But tell me, have you seen Harietta Boleski in her London role?"

"Yes--she is the greatest success--every one goes to her parties; she is coming to mine at Ardayre."

Verisschenzko raised his eyebrows, and nothing could have been more sardonically whimsical than his smile.

"I saw Stanislass this morning--he is almost *gaga* now--a mere cypher--she has destroyed his body, as well as his soul."

"They are both coming on the twenty-third."

"It will be an interesting visit I do not doubt--and I shall see the Family house!"

"I hope you will like it--I shall love to show it to you, and the pictures. It means so much to John."

"Have you met your cousin Denzil yet?".

Verisschenzko was studying her face; it had gained something, it was a little finer--but it had lost something too, and there was a shadow in her eyes.

"Denzil Ardayre? No--What made you mention him now?"

"I shall be curious as to what you think of him, he is so like--your husband, you know."

The subject did not interest Amaryllis; she wanted to hear more of the Russian's unusual views.

"You know London well, do you not?" she asked.

"Yes--I often came up from Oxford when I was there, and I have revisited it since. It is a sane place generally, but this year it would seem to be almost as *desequilibre* as the rest of the world."

"You give me an uneasy feeling, as though you knew that something dreadful was going to happen. What is it? Tell me."

"One can only speculate how soon a cauldron will boil over, one cannot be certain in what direction the liquid will fly. The whole world seems feverish; the spirit of progress has awakened after hundreds of years of sleep, and is disturbing everything. In all boilings the scum rises to the top; we are at the period when this has occurred--we can but wait--and watch."

"If we had a new religion?"

"It will come presently, the reign of mystical make-believe is past."

"But surely it is mysticism and idealism which make ordinary things divine!"

"Certainly when they are emplanted upon a true basis. I said 'make-believe'-- that is what kills all good things--make-believe. Most of the present-day leaders are throwing dust in their followers' eyes--or their own. Priests and politicians, lawyers and financiers--all of them are afraid of the truth. Every one lives in a stupid atmosphere of self-deception. The religion of the future will teach each individual to be true to himself, and when that is accomplished the sixth root race will be born. Look at that man over there talking to a woman with haggard eyes--can you see them in the gloom? They have all the ugly entities around them, the spirits of morphine and nicotine--drawing misfortune and bodily decay. Every force has to have its congenial atmosphere, or it cannot exist; fishes cannot breathe on land."

Amaryllis looked at the pair; they were well-known people, the man celebrated in the literary and artistic section of the world of fashion--the woman of high rank and of refined intelligence.

Verisschenzko looked also. "I do not know either of their names," he said, "I am simply judging by the obvious deductions to be made by their appearances to any one who has developed intuition."

"How I wish I could learn to have that!"

"Read Voltaire's 'Zadig.' Deductive methods are shown in it useful to begin upon--observe everything about people, and then having seen results, work back to causes, and then realise that all material things are the physical expression of an etheric force, and as we can control the material, we need thus only attract what etheric waves we desire."

Amaryllis looked again at the pair--both were smoking idly, and she remembered having heard that they both "took drugs." It was a phrase which had meant nothing to her until now.

"You mean that because they smoke all the time, and it is said they take morphine *piqures*, that they are not only hurting their bodies, but drawing spiritual ills as well."

"Obviously. They have surrounded themselves with the drab demagnetising current which envelops the body when human beings give up their wills. It would be very difficult for anything good to pierce through such ambience. Have you ever remarked the strange ends of all people who take drugs? They seldom die natural, ordinary deaths. The evil entities which they have drawn round them by their own weakness, destroy them at last."

"I do not like the idea that there are these 'entities,' as you call them, all around us."

"There are not, they cannot come near us unless we allow them--have I not told you that the atmosphere must be congenial? Our own wills can create an armour through which nothing demagnetising can pass. It is weakness and drifting which are inexorably punished; they draw currents suitable for the vampires beyond to exist on."

"All this does sound so weird to me." Amaryllis was interested and yet repelled.

"Have you ever thought about Marconigrams and their etheric waves? No--not often. People just accept such things as facts as soon as they become commercial commodities--and only a few begin to speculate upon what such discoveries suggest, and the other possibilities which they could lead to. Nothing is supernatural; it is only that we are so ignorant. Some day I will take you to my laboratory in my home in Russia and show you the result of my experiments with vibrations and coloured lights."

"I should love that--but just now you troubled me--you seemed to include smoking in the things which brought evil--I smoke sometimes."

"So do I--will you have a Russian cigarette?"

He took out his case and offered her one, which she accepted. "Will it bring something bad?"

"Not more than a glass of wine," and he opened his lighter and bent nearer to her. "One glass of wine might be good for you, but twenty would make you very drunk and me very quarrelsome!"

They laughed softly and lit their cigarettes.

"I feel when I am with you that I am enveloped in some strong essence," and Amaryllis lay back with a satisfied sigh--"as though I were uplifted and awakened--it is very curious because you have such a wicked face, but you make me feel that I want to be good."

His queer, husky voice took on a new note.

"We have met of course in a former life--then probably I tempted you to break all vows--it was my fault. So in this life you are to tempt me--it may be--but my will has developed--I mean to resist. I want to place you as my joy of the spirit this time--something which is pure and beautiful apart from earthly things."

Into Amaryllis' mind there flashed the thought that if she saw him often, her emotions for him might not keep at that high level! Her eyes perhaps expressed this doubt, for Verisschenzko bent nearer.

"Another must fulfil that which must be denied to me. You are too young to remain free from emotion. Hold yourself until the right time comes."

Amaryllis wondered why he should speak as though it were an understood thing that she could feel no emotion for John. She resented this.

"I have my husband," she answered with dignity and a sweetly conventional air.

Verisschenzko laughed.

"You are delicious when you say things like that--loyal, and English, and proud. But listen, child--it is waste of time to have any dissimulation with me, we finished all those things when we were lovers in our other life. Now we must be frank and learn of each other. Shall it not be so?"

Amaryllis felt a number of things.

"Yes, you are right, we will always speak the truth."

"You see," he went on, "if you represent anything you must never injure it; you must destroy yourself if necessary in its service. You represent an ideal, the ideal of the perfect wife of the Ardayres. You must fulfil this role. I represent a leader of certain thought in my country. My soul is given to this--I must only indulge in through which nothing demagnetising can pass. It is weakness and drifting which are inexorably punished; they draw currents suitable for the vampires beyond to exist on."

"All this does sound so weird to me." Amaryllis was interested and yet repelled.

"Have you ever thought about Marconigrams and their etheric waves? No--not often. People just accept such things as facts as soon as they become commercial commodities--and only a few begin to speculate upon what such discoveries suggest, and the other possibilities which they could lead to. Nothing is supernatural; it is only that we are so ignorant. Some day I will take you to my laboratory in my home in Russia and show you the result of my experiments with vibrations and coloured lights."

"I should love that--but just now you troubled me--you seemed to include smoking in the things which brought evil--I smoke sometimes."

"So do I--will you have a Russian cigarette?"

He took out his case and offered her one, which she accepted. "Will it bring something bad?"

"Not more than a glass of wine," and he opened his lighter and bent nearer to her. "One glass of wine might be good for you, but twenty would make you very drunk and me very quarrelsome!"

They laughed softly and lit their cigarettes.

"I feel when I am with you that I am enveloped in some strong essence," and Amaryllis lay back with a satisfied sigh--"as though I were uplifted and awakened--it is very curious because you have such a wicked face, but you make me feel that I want to be good."

His queer, husky voice took on a new note.

"We have met of course in a former life--then probably I tempted you to break all vows--it was my fault. So in this life you are to tempt me--it may be--but my will has developed--I mean to resist. I want to place you as my joy of the spirit this time--something which is pure and beautiful apart from earthly things."

Into Amaryllis' mind there flashed the thought that if she saw him often, her emotions for him might not keep at that high level! Her eyes perhaps expressed this doubt, for Verisschenzko bent nearer.

"Another must fulfil that which must be denied to me. You are too young to remain free from emotion. Hold yourself until the right time comes."

Amaryllis wondered why he should speak as though it were an understood thing that she could feel no emotion for John. She resented this.

"I have my husband," she answered with dignity and a sweetly conventional air.

Verisschenzko laughed.

"You are delicious when you say things like that--loyal, and English, and proud. But listen, child--it is waste of time to have any dissimulation with me, we finished all those things when we were lovers in our other life. Now we must be frank and learn of each other. Shall it not be so?"

Amaryllis felt a number of things.

"Yes, you are right, we will always speak the truth."

"You see," he went on, "if you represent anything you must never injure it; you must destroy yourself if necessary in its service. You represent an ideal, the ideal of the perfect wife of the Ardayres. You must fulfil this role. I represent a leader of certain thought in my country. My soul is given to this--I must only indulge in that over which I am master. Indulgences are our recompenses, our rights, when we have obtained dominion and they have become our slaves; to be enjoyed only when, and for so long as, our wills permit. When you say a thing is *'plus fort que vous'*--then you had better throw up the sponge--you have lost the fight, and your indulgence will scourge you with a scorpion whip.”

“You say this, and yet you are so far from being an ascetic!”

“As far as possible, I hope! They are self-acknowledged failures; they dare not permit themselves the smallest indulgence, they are weaklings afraid to enter the arena at all. To me they are at a stage further back than the sensualists--what are they accomplishing? They have withered nature, they are things of nought! A man or woman should realise what plane he or she is living on, and try to live to the highest of the best of the physical, mental and moral life on that plane, but not try to alter all its workings, and live as though in a different sphere altogether, where another scheme of nature obtained. It is colossal presumption in human beings to give examples to be followed, which, should they be followed, would end the human race. The Supreme Being will end it in His own time; it is not for us to usurp authority.”

“You reason in this in the same way that you did about the smoking.”

“Naturally--that is the only form of sensible reasoning. You must keep your judgment perfectly balanced and never let it be obscured by prejudice, tradition, custom, or anything but the actual common-sense view of the case.”

“I think we English like that better than any other quality in people--common sense.”

Verisschenzko looked away from her to a new stream of guests who had come out on the terrace--a splendid-looking group of tall young men and exquisite women.

“With all your faults you are a great nation, because although these latter years seem often to have destroyed the sense of duty in the individual in regard to his own life, the ingrained sense of it had become a habit and the habit still continues in regard to the community--you are not likely to have upheavals of great magnitude here. Now all other countries are moved by different spirits, some by patriotism and gallantry like the French, some by superstition and ignorance worked on by mystic religion, as in my country--some by ruthless materialism like Germany; but that dull, solid sense of duty is purely English--and it is really a glorious thing."

Amaryllis thought how John represented it exactly!

"I feel that I want to do my duty," she said softly, "but..."

"Continue to feel that and Fate will show you the way. Now I must take you back to your husband whom I see in the distance there--he is with Harietta Boleski. I wonder what he thinks of her?"

"I have asked him! He says that she is so obvious as to be innocuous, and that he likes her clothes!"

Verisschenzko did not answer, and Amaryllis wondered if he agreed with John!

They had to pass along a corridor to reach the staircase, upon the landing of which they had seen Sir John and Madame Boleski leaning over the balustrade, and when they got there they had moved on out of sight, so Verisschenzko, bowing, left Amaryllis with Lady de la Paule.

As he retraced his steps later on he saw Sir John Ardayre in earnest conversation with Lemon Bridges, the fashionable rising surgeon of the day. They stood in an alcove, and Verisschenzko's alert intelligence was struck by the expression on John Ardayre's face--it was so sad and resigned, as a brave man's who has received death sentence. And as he passed close to them he heard these words from John: "It is quite hopeless then--I feared so--"

He stopped his descent for a moment and looked again--and then a sudden illumination came into his yellow-green eyes, and he went on down the stairs.

"There is tragedy here--and how will it affect the Lady of my soul?"

He walked out of the House and into Pall Mall, and there by the Rag met Denzil Ardayre!

"We seem doomed to have unexpected meetings!" cried that young man delightedly. "Here I am only up for one night on regimental business, and I run into you!"

They walked on together, and Denzil went into the Ritz with Verisschenzko and they smoked in his sitting-room. They talked of many things for a long time--of the unrest in Europe and the clouds in the Southeast--of Denzil's political aims--of things in general--and at last Verisschenzko said:

"I have just left your cousin and his wife at the German Embassy; they have now gone on to a ball. He makes an indulgent husband--I suppose the affair is going well?"

"Very well between them, I believe. That sickening cad Ferdinand is circulating rumours--that they can never have any children--but they are for his own ends. I must arrange to meet them when I come up next time--I hear that the family are enchanted with Amaryllis--"

"She is a thing of flesh and blood and flame--I could love her wildly did I think it were wise."

Denzil glanced sharply at his friend. He had not often known him to hesitate when attracted by a woman--

"What aspect does the unwisdom take?"

"Certain absorption--I have other and terribly important things to do. The husband is most worthy--one wonders what the next few years will bring. Their temperaments must be as the poles.

"No one seems to think of temperament when he marries, or heredity, or anything, but just desire for the woman--or her money--or something quite outside the actual fact." Denzil lit another cigarette. "Marriage appears a perfect terror to me--how could one know one was going to continue to feel emotion towards some one who might prove to be the most awful physical or mental disappointment on intimate acquaintance? I believe *affaires de convenance* selected with thought-out reasoning are the best."

Verisschenzko shrugged his shoulders.

"That is not necessary. If the brain is disciplined, it is in a condition to use its judgment, even when in love, and ought therefore to be able to resist the desire to mate if the woman's character or tendencies are unsuitable, but most men's brains are only disciplined in regard to mental things, and have no real control over their physical desires. I have been this morning with Stanislass Boleski--there is a case and a warning. Stanislass was a strong man with a splendid brain and immense ambition, but no dominion over his senses, so that Succubus has completely annihilated all force in him. He should have strangled her after the first *etreinte* as I should have done, had I felt that she could ever have any power over me!"

Denzil smiled--Stepan was such a mixture of tenderness and complete savagery.

"I always thought the Russian character was the most headstrong and undisciplined in the world, and took what it desired regardless of costs. But you belie it, old boy!"

"I early said to myself on looking at my countrymen--and especially my countrywomen--these people are half genius, half fool; they have all the qualities and ruin most of them through being slaves, not masters to their own desires. If with his qualities a Russian could be balanced and deductive, and rule his vagrant thoughts, to what height could he not attain!"

"And you have attained."

"I am on the road, but did not affairs of vital importance occupy me at the moment I might be capable of ancient excess!"

"It is as well for the head of the Ardayre family that you are occupied then!" and Denzil smiled, and then he said, his thoughts drifting back to what interested him most:

"You think Europe will be blazing soon, Stepan? I have wondered myself in the last month if this hectic peace could continue."

"It cannot. I am here upon business with great issues, but I must not speak of facts, and what I say now is not from my knowledge of current events, but from my study of etheric currents which the thoughts and actions of over-civilised generations have engendered. You do not cram a shell with high explosives and leave it among matches with impunity."

The two men looked at one another significantly, and then Denzil said:

"I think I will not retire from the old regiment yet--I shall wait another year."

"Yes--I would if I were you."

They smoked silently for a moment--Verisschenzko's Calmuck face fixed and inscrutable and Denzil's debonnaire English one usually grave.

"Some one told me that your friend, Madame Boleski, was having a tremendous success in London. I wish I could have got leave, I should like to have seen the whole thing."

"Harietta is enjoying her luck-moment; she is in her zenith. She has baffled me as to where she receives her information from--she is capable of betraying both sides to gain some material, and possibly trivial, end. She is worth studying if you do come up, for she is unique. Most criminals have some stable point in immorality; Harietta is troubled by nothing fixed, no law of God or man means anything to her, she is only ruled by her sense of self-preservation. Her career is picturesque."

"Had she ever any children?"

Verisschenzko crossed himself.

"Heaven forbid! Think of watching Harietta's instincts coming out in a child! Poor Stanislass is at least saved that!"

"What a terrible thought that would be to one! But no man thinks of such things in selecting a wife!"

"You will not marry yet--no?"

"Certainly not, there is no necessity that I should. Marriage is only an obligation for the heads of families, not for the younger branches."

"But if Sir John Ardayre has no son, you are--in blood--the next direct heir."

"And Ferdinand is the next direct heir-in-law--that makes one sick--"

Verisschenzko poured his friend out a whisky and soda and said smiling:

"Then let us drink once more to the Ardayre son!"

CHAPTER VII

Lady de la Paule really felt proud of her niece; the party at Ardayre was progressing so perfectly. The guests had all arrived in time for the ball at Bridgeborough Castle on the twenty-third of July and had assisted next day at the garden party, and then a large dinner at Ardayre, and now on the last night of their stay Amaryllis' own ball was to take place.

All the other big country houses round were filled also, and nothing could have been gayer or more splendidly done than the whole thing.

John Ardayre had been quite enthusiastic about all the arrangements, taking the greatest pride in settling everything which could add lustre to his Amaryllis' success as a hostess.

The quantities of servants, the perfectly turned-out motors--the wonderful chef--all had been his doing, and when most of the party had retired to their rooms for a little rest before dinner on the twenty-fifth, the evening of the ball, Lady de la Paule and John's friend, Lady Avonwier, congratulated him, as he sat with them, the last ladies remaining, under the great copper beech tree on the lawn which led down to the lake.

"Everything has been perfect, has it not, Mabella?" Lady Avonwier said. "I have even been converted about your marvellous Madame Boleski! I confess I have avoided her all the season, because we Americans are far more exclusive than you English people in regard to whom we know of our own countrywomen, and no one would receive such a person in New York, but she is so luridly stupid, and such a decoration, that I quite agree you were right to invite her, John."

"She seems to me charming," Lady de la Paule confessed. "Not the least pretension, and her clothes are marvellous. You are abominably severe, Etta. I am quite sure if she wanted to she could succeed in New York."

"Mabella, you simple creature! She just cajoles you all the time--she has specialised in cajoling important great ladies! No American would be taken in by her, and we resent it in our country when an outsider like that barges in. But here, I admit, since she provides us with amusement, I have no objection to accepting her, as I would a new nigger band, and shall certainly send her a card for my fancy ball next week."

John Ardayre chuckled softly.

"That sound indicates?"--and Etta Avonwier flashed at him her lovely clever eyes.

John Ardayre did not answer in words, but both women joined in his smile.

"Yes, we are worldlings," Lady Avonwier admitted, "just measuring people up for what they can give us, it is the only way though when the whole thing is such a rush!"

"I am so sorry for the poor husband," and Lady de la Paule's fat voice was kindly. "He does look such a wretched, cadaverous thing, with that black beard and those melancholy black eyes, and emaciated face. Do you think she beats him when they are alone?"

"Who knows? She is so primitive, she may be capable even of that!"

"Her clothes are not primitive," and John Ardayre lighted a cigarette. "I don't think she really can be such a fool."

"I never suggested that she was a fool at all!" Lady Avonwier was decisive. "No one can be a fool who is as tenacious as she is--fools are vague people, who let things go. She is merely illiterate and stupid as an owl."

"I like your distinction between stupidity and foolishness!" John Ardayre often argued with Lady Avonwier; they were excellent friends.

"A stupid person is often a great rest and arrives--a fool makes one nervous and loses the game. But who is that walking with Amaryllis at the other side of the lake?"

John Ardayre looked up, and on over the water to the glory of the beech trees on the rising slope of the park, and there saw moving at the edge of them his wife and Verisschenzko, accompanied by two of the great tawny dogs.

"Oh! it is the interesting Russian whom we met in Paris, where all the charming ladies were supposed to be in love with him. He was to have come down for the whole three days. I suppose these Russian and Austrian rumours detained him, he has only arrived for to-night."

*   *   *   *   *

And across the lake Amaryllis was saying to Verisschenzko in her soft voice, deep as all the Ardayre voices were deep:

"I have brought you here so that you may get the best view of the house. I think, indeed, that it is very beautiful from over the water, do not you?"

Verisschenzko remained silent for a moment. His face was altered in this last week; it looked haggard and thinner, and his peculiar eyes were concentrated and intense.

He took in the perfect picture of this English stately home, with its Henry VII centre and watch towers, and gabled main buildings, and the Queen Anne added Square--all mellowed and amalgamated into a whole of exquisite beauty and dignity in the glow of the setting sun.

"How proud you should be of such possessions, you English. The accumulation of centuries, conserved by freedom from strife. It is no wonder you are so arrogant! You could not be if you had only memories, as we have, of wooden barracks up to a hundred and fifty years ago, and drunkenness and orgies, and beating of serfs. This is the picture our country houses call up--any of the older ones which have escaped being burnt. But here you have traditions of harmony and justice and obligations to the people nobody fulfilled." And then he took his hat off and looked up into the golden sky:

"May nothing happen to hurt England, and may we one day be as free."

A shiver ran through Amaryllis--but something kept her silent; she divined that her friend's mood did not desire speech from her yet. He spoke again and earnestly a moment or two afterwards.

"Lady of my soul--I am going away to-morrow into a frenzied turmoil. I have news from my country, and I must be in the centre of events; we do not know what will come of it all. I come down to-day at great sacrifice of time to bid you farewell. It may be that I shall never see you again, though I think that I shall; but should I not, promise me that you will remain my star unsmirched by the paltriness of the world, promise me that you will live up to the ideal of this noble home--that you will develop your brain and your intuition, that you will be forceful and filled with common sense. I would like to have moulded your spiritual being, and brought you to the highest, but it is not for me, perhaps, in this life--another will come. See that you live worthily."

Amaryllis was deeply moved.

"Indeed, I will try. I have seen so little of you, but I feel that I have known you always, and--yes--even I feel that it is true what you said," and she grew rosy with a sweet confusion--"that we were--lovers--I am so ignorant and undeveloped, not advanced like you, but when you speak you seem to awaken memories; it is as though a transitory light gleamed in dark places, and I receive flashes of understanding, and then it grows obscured again, but I will try to seize and hold it--indeed, I will try to do as you would wish."

They both looked ahead, straight at the splendid house, and then Amaryllis looked at Verisschenzko and it seemed as though his face were transfigured with some inward light.

"Strange things are coming, child, the cauldron has boiled over, and we do not know what the stream may engulf. Think of this evening in the days which will be, and remember my words."

His voice vibrated, but he did not look at her, but always across the lake at the house.

"Whenever you are in doubt as to the wisdom of a decision between two courses--put them to the test of which, if you follow it, will enable you to respect your own soul. Never do that which the inward You despises."

"And if both courses look equally good and it is merely a question of earthly benefit?"

Verisschenzko smiled.

"Never be vague. There is an Arab proverb which says: Trust in God but tie up your camel."

The setting sun was throwing its last gleams upon the windows of the high tower. Nothing more beautiful or impressive could have been imagined than the scene. The velvet lawn sloping down to the lake, with a group of trees to the right among which nestled the tiny cruciform ancient church, while in the distance, on all sides, stretched the vast, gloriously timbered park.

Verisschenzko gazed at the wonder of it, and his yellow-green eyes were wide with the vision it created in his brain.

No--this should never go to the bastard Ferdinand, whose life in Constantinople was a disgrace. This record of fine living and achievement of worthy Ardayres should remain the glory of the true blood.

He turned and looked at Amaryllis at his side, so slender, and strong, and young--and he said:

"It is necessary above all things that you cultivate a steadiness and clearness of judgment, which will enable you to see the great aim in a thing, and not be hampered by sentimental jingo and convention, which is a danger when a nature is as good and true, but as undeveloped, as yours. Whatever circumstance should arise in your life, in relation to the trust you hold for this family and this home, bring the keenest common sense to bear upon the matter, and keep the end, that you must uphold it and pass it on resplendent, in view."

Amaryllis felt that he was transmitting some message to her. His eyes were full of inspiration and seemed to see beyond.

What message? She refrained from asking. If he had meant her to understand more fully he would have told her plainly. Light would come in its own time.

"I promise," was all she said.

They looked at the great tower; the sun had left some of the windows and in one they could see the figure of a woman standing there in some light dressing-gown.

"That is Harietta Boleski," Verisschenzko remarked, his mood changing, and that penetrating and yet inscrutable expression growing in his regard. "It is almost too far away to be certain, but I am sure that it is she. Am I right? Is that window in her room?"

"Yes--how wonderful of you to be able to recognise her at that distance!"

"Of what is she thinking?--if one can call her planning thoughts! She does not gaze at views to appreciate the loveliness of the landscape; figures in the scene are all which could hold her attention--and those figures are you and me."

"Why should we interest her?"

"There are one or two reasons why we should. I think after all you must be very careful of her. I believe if she stays on in England you had better not let the acquaintance increase."

"Very well." Amaryllis again did not question him; she felt he knew best.

"She has been most successful here, and at the Bridgeborough ball she amused herself with a German officer, and left the other women's men alone. He was brought by the party from Broomgrove and was most *empresse;* he got introduced to her at once--just after we came in. I expect they will bring him to-night. He and she looked such a magnificent pair, dancing a quadrille. It was quite a serious ball to begin with! None of those dances of which you disapprove, and all the Yeomanry wore their uniforms and the German officer wore his too."

"He was a fine animal, then?"

"Yes--but?"

"You said *a pair*--only an animal could make a pair with Harietta! Describe him to me. What was he like? And what uniform did he wear?"

Amaryllis gave a description, of height, and fairness, and of the blue and gold coat.

"He would have been really good-looking, only that to our eyes his hips are too wide."

"It sounds typically German--there are hundreds such there--some ordinary Prussian Infantry regiment, I expect. You say he was introduced to Harietta? They were not old friends--no?"

"I heard him ask Mrs. Nordenheimer, his hostess, who she was, in his guttural voice, and Mrs. Nordenheimer came up to me and presented him and asked me to introduce him to my guest. So I did. The Nordenheimers are those very rich German Jews who bought Broomgrove Park some years ago. Every one receives them now."

"And how did Harietta welcome this partner?"

"She looked a little bored, but afterwards they danced several times together."

"Ah!"--and that was all Verisschenzko said, but his thoughts ran: "An infantry officer--not a large enough capture for Harietta to waste time on in a public place--when she is here to advance herself. She danced with him because *she was obliged to*. I must ascertain who this man is."

Amaryllis saw that he was preoccupied. They walked on now and round through the shrubbery on the left, and so at last to the house again. Amaryllis could not chance being late.

Verisschenzko recovered from his abstraction presently and talked of many things--of the friendship of the soul, and how it can only thrive after there has been in some life a physical passionate love and fusion of the bodies.

"I want to think that we have reached this stage, Lady mine. My mission on this plane now is so fierce a one, and the work which I must do is so absorbing, that I must renounce all but transient physical pleasures. But I must keep some radiant star as my lodestone for spiritual delights, and ever since we met and spoke at the Russian Embassy it seems as though step by step links of memory are awakening and comforting me with knowledge of satisfied desire in a former birth, so that now our souls can rise to rarer things. I can even see another in the earthly relation which once was mine, without jealousy. Child, do you feel this too?"

"I do not know quite what I feel," and Amaryllis looked down, "but I will try to show you that I am learning to master my emotions, by thinking only of sympathy between our spirits."

"It is well--"

Then they reached the house and entered the green drawing-room in the Queen Anne Square, by one of the wide open windows, and there Amaryllis held out her two slim hands to Verisschenzko.

"Think of me sometimes, even amidst your turmoil," she whispered, "and I shall feel your ambience uplifting my spirit and my will."

"Lady of my Soul!" he cried, exalted once more, and he bent as though to kiss her hands, but straightened himself and threw them gently from him.

"No! I will resist all temptations! Now you must dress and dine, and dance, and do your duty--and later we will say farewell."

Harietta Boleski stamped across her charming chintz chamber in the great tower. She was like an angry wolf in the Zoo, she burst with rage. Verisschenzko had never walked by lakes with her, nor bent over with that air of devotion.

"He loves that hateful bit of bread and butter! But I shall crush her yet--and Ferdinand Ardayre will help me!"

Then she rang her bell violently for Marie, while she kicked aside Fou-Chow, who had travelled to England as an adjunct to her beauty, concealed in a cloak. His minute body quivered with pain and fear, and he looked up at her reproachfully with his round Chinese idol's eyes, then he hid under a chair, where Marie found him trembling presently and carried him surreptitiously to her room.

"My angel," she told him as they went along the passage, "that she-devil will kill thee one day, unless happily I can place thee in safety first. But if she does, then I will murder for myself! What has caused her fury tonight, some one has spoilt her game."

In the oak-panelled smoking room, deserted by all but these two, Verisschenzko spoke to Stanislass, hastily, and in his own tongue.

"The news is of vital importance, Stanislass. You must return with me to London; of all things you must show energy now and hold your men together. I leave in the morning. You hesitate!--impossible!--Harietta keeps you! Bah!--then I wash my hands of you and Poland. Weakling! to let a woman rule you. Well; if you choose thus, you can go by yourself to hell. I have done with you." And he strode from the room, looking more Calmuck and savage than ever in his just wrath. And when he had gone the second husband of Harietta leant forward and buried his head in his hands.

*   *   *   *   *

The picture Gallery made a brilliant setting for that gallant company! A collection of England's best, dancing their hardest to a stirring band, which sang when the tune of some popular Revue chorus came in.

"The Song of the Swan," Verisschenzko thought as he observed it all in the last few minutes before midnight. He must go away soon. A messenger had arrived in hot haste from London, motoring beyond the speed limit, and as soon as his servant had packed his things he must return and not wait for the morning. All relations between Austria and Servia had been broken off, the conflagration had begun, and no time must be wasted further. He must be in Russia as soon as it was possible to get there. He blamed himself for coming down.

"And yet it was as well," he reflected, because he had become awakened in regard to possible double dealing in Harietta. But where were his host and hostess--he must bid them farewell.

John Ardayre was valsing with Lady Avonwier and Harietta Boleski undulated in the arms of the tall German who had come with the party from Broomgrove--but Amaryllis for the moment was absent from the room.

"If I could only know who the beast is before I go, and where she has met him previously!" Verisschenzko's thoughts ran. "It is more than ever necessary that I master her--and there is so little time."

He waited for a few seconds, the dance was almost done, and when the last notes of music ceased and the throng of people swept towards him, he fixed Harietta with his eye.

Her evening so far had not been agreeable. She had not been able to have a word with Stepan, who had been far from her at the banquet before the ball. She was torn with jealousy of Amaryllis; and the advent of Hans, when she would have wished to have been free to re-grab Verisschenzko, was most unfortunate. It had not been altogether pleasant, his turning up at Bridgeborough, but at any rate that one evening was quite enough! She really could not be wearied with him more!

His new instructions to her from the higher command were most annoyingly difficult too--coming at a time when her whole mind was given to consolidating her position in England,--it was really too bad!

If only the tiresome bothers of these stupid old quarrelsome countries did not upset matters, she just meant to make Stanislass shut up his ugly old Polish home, and settle in some splendid country house like this, only nearer London. Now that she had seen what life was in England, she knew that this was her goal. No bothersome old other language to be learned! Besides, no men were so good-looking as the English, or made such safe and prudent lovers, because they did not boast. If any information she had been able to collect for Hans in the last year had helped his Ober-Lords to stir up trouble, she was almost sorry she had given it--unless indeed, ructions between those ridiculous southern countries made it so that she could remain in England, then it was a good thing. And Hans had assured her that England could not be dragged in. Then she laughed to herself as she always did if Hans coerced her--when she recollected how she had given his secrets away to Verisschenzko and that no matter how he seemed to compel her obedience, she was even with him underneath!

She looked now at the Russian standing there, so tall and ugly, and weirdly distinguished, and a wild passionate desire for him overcame her, as primitive as one a savage might have felt. At that moment she almost hated her late husband, for she dared not speak to Verisschenzko with Hans there. She must wait until Verisschenzko spoke to her. Hans could not prevent that, nor accuse her of disobeying his command. So that it was with joy that she saw the Russian approach her. She did not know that he was leaving suddenly, and she was wondering if some meeting could not be arranged for later on, when Hans would be gone.

"Good evening, Madame!" Verisschenzko said suavely. "May I not have the pleasure of a turn with you; it is delightful to meet you again."

Harietta slipped her hand out of Hans' arm and stood still, determined to secure Stepan at once since the chance had come.

Verisschenzko divined her intention and continued, his voice serious with its mock respect:

"I wonder if I could persuade you to come with me and find your husband. You know the house and I do not. I have something I want to talk to him about if you won't think me a great bore taking you from your partner," and he bowed politely to Hans.

Harietta introduced them casually, and then said archly:

"I am sure you will excuse me, Captain von Pickelheim. And don't forget you have the first one-step after supper!" So Hans was dismissed with a ravishing smile.

Verisschenzko had watched the German covertly and saw that with all his forced stolidity an angry gleam had come into his eyes.

"They have certainly met before--and he knows me--I must somehow make time," then, aloud:

"You are looking a dream of beauty to-night, Harietta," he told her as they walked across the hall. "Is there not some quiet corner in the garden where we can be alone for a few minutes. You drive me mad."

Harietta loved to hear this, and in triumph she raised her head and drew him into one of the sitting-rooms, and so out of the open windows on into the darkness beyond the limitations of the lawn.

Twenty minutes afterwards Verisschenzko entered the house alone, a grim smile of satisfaction upon his rugged countenance. Jealousy, acting on animal passion, had been for once as productive of information as a ruby ring or brooch--and what a remarkable type Harietta! Could there be anything more elemental on the earth! Meanwhile this lady had gained the ball-room by another door, delighted with her adventure, and the thought that she had tricked Hans!

"Have you seen our hostess, Madame?" the Russian asked, meeting Lady de la Paule. "I have been looking for her everywhere. Is not this a charming sight?"

They stayed and talked for a few minutes, watching the joyous company of dancers, among whom Amaryllis could now be seen. Verisschenzko wished to say farewell to her when the one-step should be done. They would all be going into supper, and then would be his chance. He could not delay longer--he must be gone.

He was paying little attention to what Lady de la Paule was saying--her fat voice prattled on:

"I hope these tiresome little quarrels of the Balkan peoples will settle themselves. If Austria should go to war with Servia, it may upset my Carlsbad cure."

Then he laughed out suddenly, but instantly checked himself.

"That would be too unfortunate, Madame, we must not anticipate such preposterous happenings!"

And as he walked forward to meet Amaryllis his face was set:

"Half the civilised world thinks thus of things. The sinister events in the Balkans convey no suggestions of danger, and only matter in that they could upset a Carlsbad cure! Alas! how sound asleep these splendid people are!"

He met Amaryllis and briefly told her that he must go. She left her partner and came with him to the foot of the staircase, which led to his room.

"Good-bye, and God keep you," she said feelingly, but she noticed that he did not even offer to take her hand.

"All blessings, my Star," and his voice was hoarse, then he turned abruptly and went on up the stairs. But when he reached the landing above he paused, and looked down at her, moving away among the throng.

"Sweet Lady of my Soul," he whispered softly. "After Harietta I could not soil--even thy glove!"

CHAPTER VIII

Events moved rapidly. Of what use to write of those restless, feverish days before the 4th of August, 1914? They are too well known to all the world. John, as ever, did his duty, and at once put his name down for active service, cajoled a medical board which would otherwise probably have condemned him and trained with the North Somerset Yeomanry in anticipation of being soon sent to France. But before all this happened, the night War was declared; he remained in his own sitting-room at Ardayre, and Amaryllis wondered, and towards dawn crept out of bed and listened in the passage, but no sound came from within the room.

How very unsatisfactory this strange reserve between them was becoming! Would she never be able to surmount it? Must they go on to the end of their lives, living like two polite friendly acquaintances, neither sharing the other's thoughts? She hardly realised that the War could personally concern John. The Yeomanry, she imagined, were only for home defence, so at this stage no anxiety troubled her about her husband.

The next day he seemed frightfully preoccupied, and then he talked to her seriously of their home and its traditions, and how she must love it and understand its meaning. He spoke too of his great wish for a child--and Amaryllis wondered at the tone almost of anguish in his voice.

"If only we had a son, Amaryllis, I would not care what came to me. A true Ardayre to carry on! The thought of Ferdinand here after me drives me perfectly mad!"

Amaryllis knew not what to answer. She looked down and clasped her hands.

John came quite close and gazed into her face, as if therein some comfort could be found; then he folded her in his arms.

"Oh! Amaryllis!" he said, and that was all.

"What is it? Oh! what does everything mean?" the poor child cried. "Why, why can't we have a son like other people of our age?"

John kissed her again.

"It shall be--it must be so," he answered--and framed her face in his hands.

"Amaryllis--I know you have often wondered whether I really loved you. You have found me a stupid, unsatisfactory sort of husband--indeed, I am but a dull companion at the best of times. Well, I want you to know that I do--and I am going to try to change, dear little girl. If I knew that I held some corner of your heart it would comfort me."

"Of course, you do, John. Alas! if you would only unbend and be loving to me, how happy we could be."

He kissed her once more. "I will try."

That afternoon he went up to London to his medical board, and Amaryllis was to join him in Brook Street on the following day.

She was stunned like every one else. War seemed a nightmare--an unreality--she had not grasped its meaning as yet. She thought of Verisschenzko and his words. What was her duty? Surely at a great crisis like this she must have some duty to do?

The library in Brook Street was a comfortable room and was always their general sitting-room; its windows looked out on the street.

That evening when John Ardayre arrived he paced up and down it for half an hour. He was very pale and lines of thought were stamped upon his brow.

He had come to a decision; there only remained the details of a course of action to be arranged.

He went to the telephone and called up the Cavalry Club. Yes, Captain Ardayre was in, and presently Denzil's voice said surprisedly:

"Hullo!"

"I heard by chance that you were in town. I suppose your regiment will be going out at once. It is your cousin, John Ardayre, speaking, we have not met since you were a boy. I have something rather vital I want to say to you. Could you possibly come round?"

The two voices were so alike in tone it was quite remarkable, each was aware of it as he listened to the other.

"Where are you, and what is the time?".

"I am in our house in Brook Street, number 102, and it is nearly seven. Could you manage to come now?"

There was a second or two's pause, then Denzil said:

"All right. I will get into a taxi and be with you in about five minutes," and he put the receiver down.

John Ardayre grew paler still, and sank into a chair. His hands were trembling, this sign of weakness angered him and he got up and rang the bell and ordered his valet who had come up with him, to bring him some brandy.

Murcheson was an old and valued servant, and he looked at his master with concern, but he knew him too to make any remark. If there was any one in the world beyond the great surgeon, Lemon Bridges, who could understand the preoccupations of John Ardayre, Murcheson was the man.

He brought the old Cognac immediately and retired from the room a moment or two before Denzil arrived. Very little trace of emotion remained upon the face of the head of the family when his cousin was shown in, and he came forward cordially to meet him. Standing opposite one another, they might have been brothers, not cousins, the resemblance was so strong! Denzil was perhaps fairer, but their heads were both small and their limbs had the same long lines. But where as John Ardayre suggested undemonstrative stolidity, every atom of the younger man was vitally alive.

His eyes were bluer, his hair more bronze, and exuberant perfect health glowed in his tanned fresh skin.

Both their voices were peculiarly deep, with the pronunciation of the words especially refined. John Ardayre said some civil things with composure, and Denzil replied in kind, explaining how he had been most anxious to meet John and Amaryllis and heal the breach the fathers had made.

John offered him a cigar, and finally the atmosphere seemed to be unfrozen as they smoked. But in Denzil's mind there was speculation. It was not for just this that he had been asked to come round.

John began to speak presently with a note of deep seriousness in his voice. He talked of the war and of his Yeomanry's going out, and of Denzil's regiment also. It was quite on the cards that they might both be killed--then he spoke of Ferdinand, and the old story of the shame, and he told Denzil of his boyhood and its great trials, and of his determination to redeem the family home and of the great luck which had befallen him in the city after the South African War--and how that the thought of worthily handing on the inheritance in the direct male line had become the dominating desire of his life.

At first his manner had been very restrained, but gradually the intense feeling which was vibrating in him made itself known, and Denzil grew to realise how profound was his love for Ardayre and how great his family pride.

But underneath all this some absolute agony must be wringing his soul.

Denzil became increasingly interested.

At last John seemed to have come to a very difficult part of his narration; he got up from his chair and walked rapidly up and down the room, then forced himself to sit down again and resume his original calm.

"I am going to trust you, Denzil, with something which matters far more than my life." John looked Denzil straight in the eyes. "And I will confide in you because you are next in the direct line. Listen very carefully, please, it concerns your honour in the family as well as mine. It would be too infamous to let Ardayre go to the bastard, Ferdinand, the snake-charmer's son, if, as is quite possible, I shall be killed in the coming time."

Denzil felt some strange excitement permeating him. What did these words portend? Beads of perspiration appeared on John's forehead, and his voice sunk so low that his cousin bent forward to be certain of hearing him.

Then John spoke in broken sentences, for the first time in his life letting another share the thoughts which tortured him, but the time was not for reticence. Denzil must understand everything so that he would consent to a certain plan. At length, all that was in John's heart had been made plain, and exhausted with the effort of his innermost being's unburdenment, he sank back in his chair, deadly pale. The quiet, waiting attitude in Denzil had given way to keenness, and more than once as he listened to the moving narration he had emitted words of sympathy and concern, but when the actual plan which John had evolved was unfolded to him, and the part he was to play explained, he rose from his chair and stood leaning on the high mantelpiece, an expression of excitement and illumination on his strong, good-looking face.

"Do not say anything for a little," John said. "Think over everything quietly. I am not asking you to do anything dishonourable--and however much I had hated his mother I would not ask this of you if Ferdinand were my father's son. You are the next real heir--Ferdinand could not be; my father had never met the woman until a month before he married her, and the baby arrived five months afterwards, at its full time. There was no question of incubators or difficulties and special precautions to rear him, nor was there any suggestion that he was a seven months' child. It was only after years that I found out when my father first saw the woman, but even before this proof there were many and convincing evidences that Ferdinand was no Ardayre."

"One has only to look at the beast!" cried Denzil. "If the mother was a Bulgarian, he's a mongrel Turk, there is not a trace of English blood in his body!"

"Then surely you agree with me that it would be an infamy if he should take the place of the head of the family, should I not survive?"

Denzil clenched his hands.

"There is no moral question attached, remember," John went on anxiously before he could reply. "There is only the question of the law, which has been tricked and defamed by my father, for the meanest ends of revenge towards me--and now we--you and I--have the right to save the family and its honour and circumvent the perfidy and weakness of that one man. Oh!--can't you understand what this means to me, since for this trust of Ardayre that I feel I must faithfully carry on, I am willing to--Oh!--my God, I can't say it. Denzil, answer me--tell me that you look at it in the same way as I do! You are of the family. It is your blood which Ferdinand would depose--the disgrace would be yours then, since if Ferdinand reigned I would have gone."

The two men were standing opposite one another, and both their faces were pale and stern, but Denzil's blue eyes were blazing with some wonderful new emotion, as they looked at John.

"Very well," he said, and held out his hand. "I appreciate the tremendous faith you have placed in me, and on my word of honour as an Ardayre, I will not abuse it, nor take advantage of it afterwards. My regiment will go out at once, I suppose, the chances are as likely that I shall be killed as you--"

They shook hands silently.

"We must lose no time."

Then John poured out two glasses of brandy, and the toast they drank was unspoken. But suddenly Denzil remembered as a strange coincidence that he was drinking it for the third time.

*   *   *   *   *

Amaryllis arrived from Ardayre the next afternoon, after John's medical board had been squared into pronouncing him fit for active service--and he met his wife at the station and was particularly solicitous of her well-being. He seemed to be unusually glad to see her, and put his arm round her in the motor driving to Brook Street. What would she like to do? They could not, of course, go to the theatre, but if she would rather they could go out to a restaurant to dine--there were going to be all kinds of difficulties about food. Amaryllis, who responded immediately to the smallest advance on his part, glowed now with fond sweetness. She had been so miserable without him; so crushed and upset by the thought of war, and his possible participation in it. All the long night, alone at Ardayre, she had tried to realise what it all would mean. It was too stupendous, she could not grasp it as yet, it was just a blank horror. And now to be in the motor and close to him, and everything ordinary and as usual seemed to drive the hideous fact further and further away. She would not face it for to-night, she would try to be happy and banish the remembrance. No one knew what was happening, nor if the Expeditionary Force had or had not crossed to France. John asked her again what she would like to do.

She did not want to go out at all, she told him; if the kitchenmaid and Murcheson could find them something to eat she would much rather dine alone with him, like a regular old Darby and Joan pair--and afterwards she would play nice things to him, and John agreed.

When she came down ready for dinner, she was radiant; she had put on a new and ravishing tea-gown and her grey eyes were shining with a winsome challenge, and her beautiful skin was brilliant with health and freshness. A man could not have desired a more delectable creature to call his own.

John thought so and at dinner expanded and told her so. He was not a practised lover; women had played a very small part in his life--always too filled with work and the one dominating idea to make room for them. He had none of the tender graciousness ready at his command which Denzil would very well have known how to show. But he loved Amaryllis, and this was the first time he had permitted the expression of his emotion to appear.

She became ever more fascinating, and at length unconscious passion grew in her glance. John said some rather clumsy but loving things, and when they went back to the library he slipped his arm round her, and drew her to his side.

"I love to be near you, John," she whispered; "I like your being so tall and so distinguished-looking. I like your clothes--they are so well made--" and then she wrinkled her pretty nose--"and I adore the smell of the stuff you put on your hair! Oh! I don't know--I just want to be in your arms!"

John kissed her. "I must give you a bottle of that lotion--it is supposed to do wonders for the hair. It was originally made by an old housekeeper of my mother's family in the still room, and I have always kept the receipt--there are cloves in it and some other aromatic herbs."

"Yes, that is what I smell, like a clove carnation--it is divine. I wonder why scents have such an effect upon one--don't you? Perhaps I am a very sensuous creature--they can make me feel wicked or good--some scents make me deliciously intoxicated--that one of yours does--when I get near you--I want you to hold me and kiss me--John."

Every fibre of John Ardayre's being quivered with pain. The cruel, ironical bitterness of things.

"I've never smelt this same scent on any one else," she went on, rubbing her soft cheek up and down against his shoulder in the most alluring way. "I should know it anywhere for it means just my dear--John!"

He turned away on the pretence of getting a cigarette; he knew that his eyes had filled with tears.

Then Murcheson came into the room with the coffee, and this made a break-- and he immediately asked her to play to him, and settled himself in one of the big chairs. He was too much on the rack to continue any more love-making then; "what might have been" caused too poignant anguish.

He watched her delicate profile outlined against the curtain of green silk. It was so pure and young--and her long throat was white as milk. If this time next year she should have a child--a son--and he, not killed, but sitting there perhaps watching her holding it. How would he feel then? Would the certainty of having an Ardayre carry on heal the wild rebellion in his soul?

"Ah, God!" he prayed, "take away all feeling--reward this sacrifice--let the family go on."

"You don't think you will have really to go to the war, do you, John?" Amaryllis asked after she left the piano. "It will be all over, won't it, before the New Year, and in any case the Yeomanry are only for home defence, aren't they?" and she took a low seat and rested her head against his arm.

John stroked her hair.

"I am afraid it will not be over for a long time, Amaryllis. Yes, I think we shall go out and pretty soon. You would not wish to stop me, child?"

Amaryllis looked straight in front of her.

"What is this thing in us, John, which makes us feel that--yes, we would give our nearest and dearest, even if they must be killed? When the big thing comes even into the lives which have been perhaps all frivolous like mine--it seems to make a great light. There is an exaltation, and a pity, and a glory, and a grief, but no holding back. Is that patriotism, John?"

"That is one name for it, darling."

"But it is really beyond that in this war, because we are not going to fight for England, but for right. I think that feeling that we must give is some oblation of the soul which has freed itself from the chains of the body at last. For so many years we have all been asleep."

"This is a rude awakening."

They were silent for a little while, each busy with unusual thoughts.

There was a sense of nearness between them--of understanding, new and dangerously sweet.

Amaryllis felt it deliciously, sensuously, and took joy in that she was touching him.

John thrust it away.

"I must get through to-night," he thought, "but I cannot if this hideous pain of knowledge of what I must renounce conquers me--I must be strong."

He went on stroking her hair; it made her thrill and she turned and bit one of his fingers playfully with a wicked little laugh.

"I wish I knew what I am feeling, John," she whispered, and her eyes were aflame, "I wish I knew--"

"I must teach you!" and with sudden fierceness he bent down and kissed her lips.

Then he told her to go to bed.

"You must be tired, Amaryllis, after your journey. Go like a good child."

She pouted. She was all vibrating with some totally new and overmastering emotion. She wanted to stay and be made love to. She wanted--she knew not what, only everything in her was thrilling with passionate warmth.

"Must I? It is only ten."

"I have a frightful lot of business things to write tonight, Amaryllis. Go now and sleep, and I will come and wake you about twelve!" He looked lover-like. She sighed.

"Ah! if you would only come now!"

He kissed her almost roughly again and led her to the door. And he stood watching her with burning eyes as she went up the stairs.

Then he came back and rang the bell.

"I shall be very late, Murcheson--do not sit up, I will turn out the lights. Good-night."

"Very good, Sir John."

And the valet left the room.

But John Ardayre did not write any business letters; he sank back into his great leather chair--his lips were trembling, and presently sobs shook him, and he leaned forward and buried his face in his hands.

Just before twelve had struck, he went out into the hall, and turned off the light at the main. The whole house would now be in absolute darkness but for an electric torch he carried. He listened--there was not a sound.

Then he crept quietly up to his dressing room and returned with a bottle of the clove-scented hair lotion.

"What a mercy she spoke of it," his thoughts ran. "How sensitive women are--I should never have remembered such a thing."

Yes--now there was a sound.

*   *   *   *   *

Midnight had struck--and Amaryllis, sleeping peacefully, had been dreaming of John.

"Oh! dearest," she whispered drowsily, as but half awakened, she felt herself being drawn into a pair of strong arms--"Oh!--you know I love that scent of cloves--Oh!--I love you, John!"

CHAPTER IX

When Amaryllis awoke in the morning her head rested on John's breast, and his arm encircled her. She raised herself on her elbow and looked at him. He was still asleep--and his face was infinitely sad. She bent over and kissed him with shy tenderness, but he did not move, he only sighed heavily as he lay there.

Why should he look so sad, when they were so happy?

She thought of loving things he had said to her at dinner--and then the afterwards!--and she thrilled with emotion. Life seemed a glorious thing and--But John was sad, of course, because he must go away. The recollection of this fact came upon her suddenly like a blast of cold air. They must part. War hung there with its hideous shadow, and John must be conscious of it even in his dreams, that was why he sighed.

The irony of things--now--when--Oh! how cruel that he must go.

Then John awoke with a shudder, and saw her there leaning over him with a new soft love light in her eyes, and he realised that the anguish of his calvary had only just begun.

She was perfectly exquisite at breakfast, a fresh and tender graciousness radiated in her every glance; she was subtle and captivating, teasing him that he had been so silent in the night. "Why wouldn't you talk to me, John? But it was all divine, I did not mind." Then she became full of winsome ways and caresses, which she had hitherto been too timid to express; and every fond word she spoke stabbed John's heart.

Could she not come and stay somewhere near so as to be with him while he was in training? It was unbearable to remain alone.

But he told her that this would be impossible and that she must go back to Ardayre.

"I will get leave, if there is a chance, dear little girl."

"Oh! John, you must indeed."

After he had gone out to the War Office, she sang as she undid a bundle of late roses he had sent her from Soloman's, on his way.

She must herself put them in water; no servant should have this pleasing task. Was it the thought of the imminence of separation which had altered John into so dear a lover? She went over his words there in the library. She relived the joy of his sudden fierce kiss, when he had said that he must teach her as to what her emotions meant.

Ah! how good to learn, how all glorious was life and love!

"Sweetheart," the word rang in her ears. He had never called her that before! Indeed, John rarely ever used any term of endearment, and never got beyond "Dear" or "Darling" before. But now it was an exquisite remembrance! Just the murmured word "Sweetheart!" whispered softly again and again in the night.

John came back to lunch, but two of the de la Paule family dropped in also, and the talk was all of war, and the difficulty of getting money at the banks, and how food would go on, and what the whole thing would mean.

But over Amaryllis some spell had fallen--nothing seemed a reality, she could not attend to ordinary things, she felt that she but moved and spoke as one still in a dream.

The world, and life, and death, and love, were all a blended mystery which was but beginning to unravel for her and drew her nearer to John.

The days went on apace.

John in camp thanked God for the strenuous work of his training that it kept him so occupied that he had barely time to think of Amaryllis or the tragedy of things. When he had left her on the following afternoon, the seventh of August, she had returned to Ardayre alone and began the knitting and shirt-making and amateurish hospital committees which all well-meaning English women vaguely grasped at before the stern necessities brought them organised work to do. Amaryllis wrote constantly to John--all through August--and many of the letters contained loving allusions which made him wince with pain.

Then the awful news came of Mons, then the Marne--and the Aisne--awful and glorious, and a hush and mourning fell over the land, and Amaryllis, like every one else, lost interest in all personal things for a time.

A young cousin had been killed and many of her season's partners and friends, and now she knew that the North Somerset Yeomanry would shortly go out and fight as they had volunteered at once. She was very miserable. But when September grew, in spite of all this general sorrow, a new horizon presented itself, lit up as if by approaching dawn, for a hope had gradually developed--a hope which would mean the rejoicing of John's heart.

And the day when first this possibility of future fulfilment was pronounced a certainty was one of almost exalted beatitude, and when Doctor Geddis drove away down the Northern Avenue, Amaryllis seized a coat from the folded pile of John's in the hall, and walked out into the park hatless, the wind blowing the curly tendrils of her soft brown hair, a radiance not of earth in her eyes. The late September sun was sinking and gilding the windows of the noble house, and she turned and looked back at it when she was far across the lake.

And the whole of her spirit rose in thankfulness to God, while her soul sang a glad magnificat.

She, too, might hand on this great and splendid inheritance! She, too, would be the mother of Ardayres!

And now to write to John!

That was a fresh pleasure! What would he say? What would he feel? Dear John! His letters had been calm and matter of fact, but that was his way. She did not mind it now. He loved her, and what did words matter with this glorious knowledge in her heart?

To have a baby! Her very own--and John's!

How wonderful! How utterly divine--!

Her little feet hardly touched the moss beneath them, she wanted to skip and sing.

Next May! Next May! A Spring flower--a little life to care for when war, of course, would have ended and all the world again could be happy and young!

And then she returned by the tiny ancient church. She had the key of it, a golden one which John had given her on their first coming down. It hung on her bracelet with her own private key.

The sun was pouring through the western window, carpeting the altar steps in translucent cloth of gold.

Amaryllis stole up the short aisle, and paused when she came between the two tall canopied tombs of recumbent sixteenth century knights, which made so dignified a screen for the little side aisles--and then she moved on and knelt in the shaft of the sunlight there at the carved rails.

And no one ever raised to God a purer or more fervent prayer.

She stayed until the sun sunk below the window, and then she rose and went back to the house, and up to her cedar room. And now she must write to John!

She began--once--twice--but tore up each sheet. Her news was a supreme happiness, but so difficult to transmit!

At last she finished three sides of her own rather large sized note-paper, but as she read over what she had written, she was not quite content; it did not express all that she desired John to know.

But how could a mere letter convey the wordless gladness in her heart?

She wanted to tell him how she would worship their baby, and how she would pray that they should be given a son--and how she would remember all his love words spoken that last time they were together, and weave the joy of them round the little form, so that it should grow strong and beautiful and radiant, and come to earth welcomed and blessed!

Something of all this finally did get written, and she concluded thus:

"John, is it not all wonderful and blissful and mysterious, this coming proof of our love? And when I lie awake I say over and over again the sweet name you called me, and which I want to sign! I am not just Amaryllis any longer, but your very own 'Sweetheart'!"

John received this letter by the afternoon post in camp. He sat down alone in his tent and read and re-read each line. Then he stiffened and remained icily still.

He could not have analysed his emotions. They were so intermixed with thankfulness and pain--and underneath there was a fierce, primitive jealousy burning.

"Sweetheart!" he said aloud, as though the word were anathema! "And must I call her that 'Sweetheart'! Oh! God, it is too hard!" and he clenched his hands.

By the same post came a letter from Denzil, of whose movements he had asked to be kept informed, saying that the 110th Hussars were going out at once, so that they would probably soon meet in France.

Then John wrote to Amaryllis. The very force of his feelings seemed to freeze his power of expression, and when he had finished he knew that it was but a cold, lifeless thing he had produced, quite inadequate as an answer to her tender, exalted words.

"My poor little girl," he sighed as he read it. "I know this will disappoint her. What a hideous, sickening mockery everything is."

He forced himself to add a postscript, a practice very foreign to his usual methodical rule. "Never forget that I love you, Amaryllis--Sweetheart!" he said.

And then he went to his Colonel and asked for two days' leave, and when it was granted for the following Saturday and Monday he wired to his wife asking her to meet him in Brook Street.

"I must see her--I cannot bear it," he cried to himself.

And late at night he wrote to Denzil--it was just that he should do this.

"My wife is going to have a baby--if only it should be a son, then it will not so much matter if both of us are killed, at least the family will be saved, and be able to carry oh."

He tried to make the letter cordial. Denzil had behaved with the most perfect delicacy throughout, he must admit, and although they had met once and exchanged several letters, not the faintest allusion to the subject of their talk in the library at Brook Street had ever been made by him.

Denzil had indeed acted and written as though such knowledge between them did not exist. He--Denzil--in these last seven weeks had been extremely occupied, and while his forces were concentrated upon the exhilarating preparations for war, it would happen in rare moments before sleep claimed him at night that he would let his thoughts conjure a waking dream, infinitely, mystically sweet. And every pulse would thrill with ecstasy, and then his will would banish it, and he would think of other subjects.

He could not face the marvel of his emotions at this period, nor dwell upon the romantically exciting aspect of some things.

He was up in London upon equipment business on the very Saturday that John got leave, and he was due to dine at the Carlton with Verisschenzko who had that day arrived on vital matters bent.

As they came into the hall, a man stopped to talk to the Russian, and Denzil's eyes wandered over the unnumerous and depressed looking company collected waiting for their parties to arrive. War had even in those early Autumn days set its grim seal upon this festive spot. People looked rather ashamed of being seen and no one smiled. He nodded to one or two friends, and then his glance fell upon a beautiful, slim, brown-haired girl, sitting quietly waiting in an armchair by the restaurant steps.

She wore a plain black frock, but in her belt one huge crimson clove carnation was unostentatiously tucked.

"What a lovely creature!" his thoughts ran, and Verisschenzko turning from his acquaintance that moment, he said to him as they started to advance:

"Stepan, if you want to see something typically English and perfectly exquisite, look at that girl in the armchair opposite where the band used to be. I wonder who she is?"

"What luck!" cried Verisschenzko. "That is your cousin, Amaryllis Ardayre--come along!"

And in a second Denzil found himself being introduced to her, and being greeted by her with interested cordiality, as befitted their cousinly relationship.

But Verisschenzko, whose eyes missed nothing, remarked that under his sunburn, Denzil had grown suddenly very pale. Amaryllis was enchanted to see her friend, the Russian. John had gone to the telephone, it appeared--and yes, they were dining alone--and, of course, she was sure John would love to amalgamate parties, it was so nice of Verisschenzko to think of it! There was John now.

The blood rushed back to Denzil's heart, and the colour to his face--he had only murmured a few conventional words. Mercifully John would decide the matter--it was not his doing that he and Amaryllis had met.

John caught sight of the three as he came along the balcony from the telephone, so that he had time to take in the situation; he saw that the meeting was quite *imprevu*, and he had, of course, no choice but to accept Verisschenzko's suggestion with a show of grace. At that very moment, before they could enter the restaurant, and re-arrange their tables, Harietta Boleski and her husband swept upon them--they were staying in the hotel. Harietta was enraptured.

What a delightful surprise meeting them! Were they all just together, would they not dine with her?

She purred to John, while her eyes took in with satisfaction Denzil's extraordinary good looks--and there was Stepan, too! Nothing could be more agreeable than to scintillate for them both.

John hailed their advent with relief: it would relax the intolerable strain which both he and Denzil would be bound to have to experience. So looking at the rest of the party, he indicated that he thought they would accept. It suited Verisschenzko also for his own reasons. And any suggestion to enlarge the intimate number of four would have been received by Denzil with graciousness.

He had not imagined that he would feel such profound emotion on seeing Amaryllis, the intensity of it caused him displeasure. It was altogether such a remarkable situation. He knew that it would have been of thrilling interest to him had it not been for the presence of John. His knowledge of what John must be suffering, and the knowledge that John was aware of what he also must be feeling, turned the whole circumstance into discomfort.

As soon as he recalled himself to Madame Boleski they all went into the restaurant to the Boleski table, just inside the door, by the window on the right. Harietta put John on one side of her and Denzil at the other, and beyond were Verisschenzko and her husband, with Amaryllis between, who thus sat nearly opposite Denzil, with her back to the room.

Harietta, when she desired to be, was always an inspiriting hostess, making things go. She intended to do her best to-night. The turn affairs had taken, England being at war, was quite too tiresome. It had spoilt all her country house visits and nullified much of the pleasure and profit she was intending to reap from her now secured position in this promised land.

Stanislass, too, had been difficult, he had threatened to go back to Poland immediately, which he explained was his obvious duty to do--but she had fortunately been able to crush that idea completely with tears and scenes. Then he suggested Paris, but information from Hans gave her occasion to think this might not be a comfortable or indeed quite a safe spot, and in all cases if the Frenchmen were fighting for dear life they would not have leisure to entertain her, therefore, dull and gloomy as England had become, she preferred to remain.

Hans, too, had given her orders. For the present London must be her home, and the lease of the Mount Lennard house in Grosvenor Square having expired, they had moved to the Carlton Hotel.

The misery of war, the holocaust of all that was noblest, left her absolutely cold. It was certainly a pity that those darling young guardsmen she had danced with should have had to be killed, but there was never any use in crying over spilt milk--better look out for new ones coming on. She was quite indifferent as to which country won. It was still a great bother collecting information for her former husband, but he threatened terrible reprisals if she refused to go on, and as in her secret heart she thought that there was no doubt as to who would be victor, she felt it might be wiser to remain on good terms with the power she believed would win!

Ferdinand Ardayre had been very helpful all the summer--he had moved from the Constantinople branch of his business to one in Holland and had just returned to England now; he was, in fact, coming to see her later on when she should have packed Stanislass safely off to the St. James' Club.

Harietta had no imagination to be inflamed by terrible descriptions of things. She saw no actual horrors, therefore war to her was only a nuisance--nothing ghastly or to be feared. But it was a disgusting nuisance and caused her fatigue. She had continually to remember to simulate proper sympathy, and concern and to subdue her vivacity, and show enthusiasm for any agreeable war work which could divert her dull days. If she had not been more than doubtful of her reception in America, even as a Polish magnate's wife, she would have gone over there to escape as far as possible from the whole situation, and she had been bored to death now for several days. People were too occupied and too grieved to go out of their way now to make much of her, and she had been left alone to brood. Thus the advent of Verisschenzko, who thrilled her always, and a possible new admirer in Denzil, seemed a heaven-sent occurrence. Amaryllis and John were undesired but unavoidable appendages who had to be swallowed.

Denzil's type particularly attracted her. There was an insouciance about him, a ***debonnair sans gene*** which increased the charm of his good looks; he had everything of attraction about him which John Ardayre lacked.

Amaryllis, against her will, before the end of the dinner, was conscious of the fact also, though Denzil studiously avoided any conversation with her beyond what the exigencies of politeness required. He devoted himself entirely to Harietta, to her delight, and Verisschenzko and Amaryllis talked while John was left to Stanislass. But the very fact of Denzil's likeness to John made Amaryllis look at him, and she resented his attraction and the interest he aroused in her.

His voice was perhaps even deeper than John's, and how extraordinarily well his bronze hair was planted on his forehead; and how perfectly groomed and brushed and soldierly he looked!

He seemingly had taken the measure of Madame Boleski, too, and was apparently enjoying with a cultivated subtlety the drawing of her out. He was no novice it seemed, and there was a whimsical light in his eyes and once or twice they had inadvertently met hers with understanding when Verisschenzko had made some especially cryptic remark. She knew that she would very much have liked to talk to him.

Verisschenzko was observing Amaryllis carefully. There was a new expression in her eyes which puzzled him. Her features seemed to be drawn with finer lines and pale violet shadows lay beneath her grey eyes. Was it the gloom of the war which oppressed her? It could not be altogether that, because her regard was serene and even happy.

"Did I not know that nothing could be more unlikely, I should say she was going to have a child. What is the mystery?" He found himself very much interested. Especially he was anxious to watch what impression Denzil made upon her. He saw, as the dinner went on, that Amaryllis was aware that he was an attractive creature.

"There is the beginning of a chapter of necessary and expedient--romance--here," he decided. "If only Denzil is not killed." But what did his growing so pale on learning that she was his cousin mean...? that was not a natural circumstance--some deep undercurrents were stirred. And in what way was all this going to affect the lady of his soul?

They could not have any intimate conversation at dinner; they spoke of ordinary things and the war and the horror of it. Russia was moving forward, but Verisschenzko did not appear to be very optimistic in spite of this. There were things in his country, he told Amaryllis, which might handicap the fighting.

Stanislass Boleski looked extremely depressed. He had a hang-dog, strained mien and Verisschenzko's contemptuously friendly attitude towards him wounded him deeply. Once he had shone as a leader and chief in Stepan's life, and now after the stormy scene in the smoking-room at Ardayre, that he could greet him casually and not turn from him in anger, showed, alas! to where he had sunk in Verisschenzko's estimation--a thing of nought--not even worth his disapproval. The dinner to him was a painful trial.

John also was far from content. He had been longing to see Amaryllis, and yet the sight of her and her fond and insinuating words and caresses had caused him exquisite suffering. His emotions were so varied and complex. His prayer had been answered, but apart from his natural loathing for all subterfuge, every new tenderness towards himself which Amaryllis displayed aroused some indefinable jealousy. She had been so glad to see him and he had been conscious himself that he had been even unusually stolid and self-contained towards her. He knew that she grew disappointed and that probably the exalted sentiment which her letter had indicated that she was feeling had been chilled before she could put it into words.

All this distressed him, and yet he could not break through the reserve of his nature.

And now to crown unfortunate things, there was Denzil brought by fate and no one's manoeuvring into Amaryllis' company! Of all things he had hoped that they need not meet before he and his cousin should go to the Front. And it was all brought about by his own action in insisting that they had better dine at a restaurant, as the kitchenmaid, who always remained at Brook Street, had gone to see a wounded brother.

Amaryllis had sighed a little as she had consented, with the faint protest that they could have eaten something cold.

But on their drive to the Carlton she had become fondly affectionate again, nestling close to him, and then she had pulled out the carnation from her belt and held it for him to smell.

"I picked it in the greenhouse this morning, the last of them; I have had them all around me while there were any, because they remind me of you, dearest--and of everything divine."

John felt that he should always now hate that clove stuff for the hair and could no longer bear to use it.

He was perfectly aware that Denzil on his hostess' other hand was looking everything that a woman could desire, and that his easy casualness of manner would be likely to charm. He saw that Amaryllis, too, observed him with unconscious interest, and a feeling akin to despair filled his heart.

Life for him had always been difficult, and he was accustomed to blows, but this one was particularly hard to bear, because he really loved Amaryllis and desired happiness with her which he knew could never really be attained.

Only Harietta of the whole party was quite content. She intended to annex Stepan when they should be drinking coffee in the hall. She looked upon Denzil's conquest now as almost an accomplished fact, and so felt that she might let him talk to Amaryllis, since the Russian was her real object. His ugly rugged face and odd Calmuck eyes always attracted her.

"Why aren't you staying in the hotel, darling Brute?'" she whispered to him as they left the restaurant. "If you had been--"

"I am," said Verisschenzko, and leaving her for a moment he went and telephoned to his not unintelligent Russian servant at the Ritz to arrange about the transference of his rooms.

"She requires the most careful watching--I must waste no time."

And then he returned to the party in the hall.

CHAPTER X

Denzil Ardayre took up his letters which had been forwarded to him from the depot where he was stationed. He and Verisschenzko were passing through the hall of his mother's house, for a talk and a smoke in his sitting-room, after leaving the Carlton.

The house was in St. James' Place, a small, old building, the ground floor of which was given over to Denzil whenever he was in London. His mother was absent at Bath, where she spent a long autumn cure.

John's letter lay on the top, and Verisschenzko caught the look of interest which came into Denzil's face.

"Don't mind me, my dear chap," he remarked, "read your letters." And they went on into the sitting-room.

"I want just to look at this one--it is from John Ardayre whom we met to-night," and Denzil opened it casually--"I wonder what he is writing to me about, he did not say anything at dinner."

He read the short communication and exclaimed: "Good God!" and then checked himself. He was obviously stirred, and Verisschenzko watched him narrowly. Anything to do with John must concern Amaryllis, and therefore was of profound interest to himself.

"No bad news, I hope?" he said.

Denzil was gazing into the fire, and there was a look of wonderment and even rapture upon his face.

"Oh! No--rather splendid--" He felt quite the strangest emotion he had ever experienced in his life. His usual serene self-confidence and easy flow of words deserted him, and Verisschenzko, watching him, began to link certain things in his mind.

"Tell me, what did you think of your cousin, Lady Ardayre?" he asked casually, as though the subject was irrelevant.

"Amaryllis?" and Denzil almost started from a reverie. "Oh, yes, of course, she is a lovely creature, is not she, Stepan?"

Verisschenzko narrowed his eyes.

"I have told you that I adore her--but with the spirit--if it were not so, she would appeal very strongly to the flesh--Yes?--Did you not feel it?"

"I did."

"Well?"

"Well--"

"She is longing to understand life, she is groping; why do you not set about her education, Denzil?"

"That is the husband's business."

"Not in this case. I consider it is yours; you are the right mate for her. John Ardayre is a good fellow, but he stands for nothing in the affair. Why did you waste your time upon Harietta, when time is so short?"

"I was given no choice."

"But afterwards, in the hall?"

It was quite evident to Verisschenzko that the mention of Amaryllis was causing his friend some unexplainable emotion.

"You did not even exert yourself, then. Why, Denzil?"

Denzil lit a cigarette.

"I thought her awfully attractive--it is the first time I have ever seen her--as you know."

"And that was a reason for remaining silent and as stiff as a poker in manner! You English are a strange race!"

Denzil smiled--if Stepan only knew everything, what would he say!

"You were made for each other. If I were you, I would not lose a second's time!"

"My dear old boy, you seem quite to forget that the girl has a husband of her own!"

"Not at all, it is for that reason--just because of that husband. I shall say no more, you are quite intelligent enough to understand."

"You think it is all right then for a woman to have a lover?" Denzil smiled as he curled rings of smoke. "It is curious how the most honourable among us has not much conscience concerning such things."

Verisschenzko knocked off his cigarette ash and spoke contemplatively:

"The world would be an insupportable place for women, if he had! But whatever the moral aspect of the matter is in general, circumstances arise which alter the point, and that is where the absurd ticketing system hampers suitable action. A thing is ticketed 'dishonourable.' Pah! it is sometimes, and it is not at others--there is no hard and fast rule."

Denzil stretched himself--he was always interested in Verisschenzko's reasonings and prepared to listen with enjoyment:

"The general idea is that a man should not make love to another man's wife. Man professes this as a creed, and the law enforces it and punishes him if he is found out doing so. And if he acted up to this creed as he does about stealing goods and behaving like a gentleman over business matters, all might be well, but unfortunately that seldom occurs, because there is that strong; instinct which is the base of all things working in him, and which does not work in regard to any other point of honour--i.e., the unconscious desire to re-create his, species, so that this one particular branch of moral responsibility cannot be measured, judged, or criticised from the same standpoint as any other. No laws can. alter human nature, or really control a man's actions when a natural force is prompting him unless stern self-analysis discovers the truth to the man, and so permits his spirit to regain dominion. The best chance would be to resist the first feeling of attraction which a woman belonging to another man aroused before it had actually obtained a hold upon his senses--but the percentage of men who do this must be very small. Some resist--or try to resist the actual possession of the woman from moral motives, but many more from motives of expediency and fear of consequences. Then to salve conscience the mass of men ride a high moral stalking horse, and write and speak condemnation of every back-sliding, while their own behaviour coincides with the behaviour they are criticising. The hypocrisy of the thing sickens me; no one ever looks any question straight in the face, denuded of its man-made sophistries. And few realise that a woman is a creature to be fought for--it is prehistoric instinct, and if she can't be obtained in fair fight then you secure her by strategy. And if a man cannot keep her once he has secured her, it is up to him. If I had a wife, I should take good care that she *desired* no other man--but if I bored her, or was a cold and bad lover, I should not expect the other men not to try and take her from me--because I should know this was a natural instinct with them--like taking food. It would probably be no temptation to most of us to steal gold lying about in a room, even if we were poor, but a hideous temptation to refrain from eating a tempting dish if we were starving with hunger and it was before us--and if a woman did succumb to some new passion I should blame myself, not her."

Denzil agreed.

"Jealousy is a natural instinct, though," he said, "and although there would be not much profit in trying to hold a woman who no longer cared, one could not help being mad about it."

"Of course not--that is the sense of personal possession which is affronted. Vanity is deeply wounded, and so the power to analyse cause and result sleeps. But this attitude which men take up of neglecting a woman and then expecting her to be faithful still is quite ridiculous, and without logic; they are as usual fogged by convention and can't see straight."

Verisschenzko's rough voice was keen--compelling.

Denzil smiled.

"Another of your windmills to fight!"

"I am always fighting convention and shams. Get down to the meaning of a thing, and if its true significance coincides with the convention which surrounds it, then let that hold, but if convention is a super-imposed growth, then amputate it and study the thing without it."

"I suppose a man marries a woman nine times out of ten because he cannot obtain her in any other way; then when he has become indifferent by possession, he still thinks that she should remain devoted to him. You are right, Stepan, it is very illogical."

"Club the creature, or keep her in a cage if you want fidelity through fear, but don't expect it if you allow her to remain at large and neglected, and don't be such an ass as to imagine that your friends won't act just as you yourself would act were she some one's else wife. If a woman has that quality in her which arouses sex, married or single, I never have observed that men refrained from making love to her."

"All this means that you consider I am quite at liberty to make love to Amaryllis Ardayre!"

"Quite."

Denzil threw his cigarette end into the fire:

"Well, for once you are wrong, Stepan, in your usually perfect deductions," he got up from his chair. "There is a reason in this case which makes the thing an absolute impossibility; under no possible circumstance while John is alive could I make the smallest advance towards Amaryllis! There is another point of honour involved in the affair."

Verisschenzko felt that here was some mystery which he had yet to elucidate, the links in the chain were visible up to a point, but he then became baffled by the incontestable fact that Denzil had seen Amaryllis that evening for the first time!

"If this is so, then it is a very great pity," he announced, after a moment or two's thought. "Were the times normal, we might leave all to Fate and trust to luck, but if you are killed and John is killed, it will be a thousand pities for Ferdinand to be the head of the family. A creature like that will not enlist, he will be safe while you risk your lives."

Denzil went over to the window, apparently to get out a fresh box of cigars which were in a cabinet near.

"John writes to-night that there is the chance of an heir after all--so perhaps we need not worry," he said, his voice a little hoarse with feeling. "I was so awfully glad to hear this--we all loathe the thought of Ferdinand."

Verisschenzko actually was startled, and also he was strangely moved.

"When I saw my lady Amaryllis to-night that idea came to me, only as I believed it was quite an impossibility--I dismissed it--It is a war miracle then?" and he smiled enquiringly.

"Apparently."

The cigar box was selected and Denzil had once more resumed his seat in a big chair before either of them spoke again.

"I perfectly understand that there is some mystery here, Denzil--and that you cannot tell me--and equally I cannot ask you any questions, but it may be that in the days that are coming I could be of assistance to you. I have some very curious information which I am holding concerning Ferdinand Ardayre in his activities. You can always count on me--" Verisschenzko rose from his chair, stirred deeply with the thoughts which were coursing through his brain.

"Denzil--I love that woman--I am absolutely determined that I shall not do so in any way but in spirit--I long for her to be happy--protected. She has an exquisite soul--I would have given her to you with contentment. You are her counterpart upon this plane--"

Denzil remained silent, he had never seen Stepan so agitated. The situation was altogether very unusual. Then he asked:

"Do you think Ferdinand will make some protest then?"

"It is possible."

"But there is absolutely nothing to be said, the fact of there being a child refutes all the old rumours."

"In law--"

"In every way," a flush had mounted to Denzil's forehead.

"You know Lemon Bridges?" Verisschenzko suggested.

"Yes--why do you ask?"

"He is a remarkably clever surgeon. It is said that he is also a gentleman; if this news surprises him he will not express his feelings probably."

Stepan was observing his friend with the minutest scrutiny now, while he spoke lazily once more as though upon a casual topic bent, and he saw that a lightning flash of anxiety passed through Denzil's eyes.

"I do not see how any one can have a word to say about the matter," and he lit his cigar deliberately. "John is awfully pleased--"

"And so am I--and so are you, and so will be the lady Amaryllis. Thus we can only wish for general happiness, and not anticipate difficulties which may never occur. When is the event to happen?"

"The beginning of next May," Denzil announced, without hesitation, and then the flush deepened, for he suddenly remembered that John had not mentioned any date in his letter!

The subject was growing embarrassing, and he asked, so as to change it:

"What is your friend, Madame Boleski, doing now, Stepan?"

"She is receiving news from Germany which I shall endeavour to have her transmit to me, and I have some suspicion that she is transmitting any information which she can pick up here to Germany, but I cannot yet be sure. When I am, then I shall have no mercy. She would betray any country for an hour's personal pleasure or gain. I have not yet discovered who the man was at the Ardayre ball--I told you about it, did I not? Just then more important matters pressed and I could not follow up the clue."

"She is certainly physically attractive, and all the things she says are so obvious and easy, she is quite a rest at a dinner, but Lord! think of spending one's life with a woman like that!" and Denzil smiled.

"There are very few women whom it would be possible to contemplate in calmness spending one's life with, because one's own needs change, and the woman's also. The tie is a galling bond unless it can be looked at with common sense by both--but I think men are quite as illogical as women over it, and of such an incredible vanity! It is because we have mixed so much sentiment into such a simple nature-act that all the bothers arise, and men are unjust over every thing to do with women. All men think, for instance, that a woman must not deceive her lover and, at the same time that she is appearing to be his faithful mistress, take another for her pleasure and diversion in secret. A man would look upon this and rightly as a dishonourable betrayal because it would wound his vanity and lower his personal prestige. But the illogical part is that he would not hesitate to do the same thing himself, and would never see the matter in the light of a betrayal, because the Creator has happily equipped him with a rhinoceros hide which enables him never to feel stings of self-contempt when viewing his own actions towards the other sex."

Denzil laughed aloud.

"You are hard on us, Stepan, but I dare say you are right."

"It is just custom and convention which make us think ourselves such gods. Had woman had the same chance always, who knows what she might not have become by now! Everything is ticketed, it is called by a name and put down under such and such a heading--women are 'weak' and 'illogical' and 'unreliable' and men are 'brave' and 'sound' and 'to be trusted'--tosh! in quantities of cases--and if so, why so? Women are wonderful beings in many ways--of a courage! The way they bear things so gladly for men--think of their suffering when they have children. You don't know about it probably, men take all this as a matter of course--but I saw my sister die--after hours of it--"

Denzil moved his arm rather suddenly and upset the glass of lemon squash on a little table near.

Verisschenzko observed this, but went on without a break:

"It is agony for them under the best conditions, and sometimes they become divine over it. Amaryllis will be divine--I hope John will take care of her--"

A look of concern came into Denzil's face, and Verisschenzko watched him. Could any one be more attractive as a splendid mate for Amaryllis, he thought. He crushed down all feeling of human jealousy. His intuition would probably reveal all the mystery to him presently, and meanwhile if he could forward any scheme which would be for the good of Amaryllis and the security of the family, he would do so.

"I must leave you now, old man," he said, looking at his watch. "I have a rendezvous with Harietta. I shall have to play the part of an ardent lover and cannot yet wring her neck."

When Denzil was alone, he stood gazing into the fire.

"That John should take care of her?"--but John was going out to fight--and so was he--and they might both be killed--What then?

"Stepan knows, I am certain," he thought, "and he is true as steel; he must stand by her if we don't come back."

And then his thoughts flew to the vision of her sitting opposite him at the table, with her sweet eyes turned to his now and then, the faint violet shadows beneath them and the transparent exquisiteness of her skin telling their own story by the added, fragile beauty. Oh! what unutterable joy to hold her in his arms and whisper passionate love words in her little ears, to live again the dream of her dainty head lying prone there on his breast. Every pulse in his being throbbed to bursting, seeming almost to suffocate him.

"Amaryllis--Sweetheart!" he whispered aloud, and then started at his own voice.

He paced up and down the room, clenching his hands. The family might go on, but the two members of it must endure the pain of renunciation.

Which was the harder to bear, he wondered--his part of hopeless memory and regret, or John's of forced denial and abstinence?

In all the world, no situation could be more strange or more cruel.

He had felt deeply about it before he had seen Amaryllis. He thought of the myth of Eros and Psyche. His emotions had been much as Psyche's before she lit the lamp. And now the lamp had been lighted--his eyes had seen what his arms had clasped, the reality was more lovely than his dream, and passion was kindled a hundredfold. It swept him off his feet.

He forgot war and the horror of the time, he forgot everything except that he longed for Amaryllis.

"She is mine, absolutely mine," he said wildly. "Not John's."

And then he remembered his promise, given before any personal equation had entered into the affair.

Never to take advantage of the situation--afterwards!

And what would the child be like? A true Ardayre, of course--they would say that it had harked back, perhaps, to that Elizabethan Denzil whom his father had told him was his exact portrait in the picture gallery at Ardayre.

He could have laughed at the sardonic humour of everything if he had not been too overcome with passionate desire to retain any critical sense.

Then he sat down and forced himself to realise what it meant--parenthood. Not much to a man, as a rule. He had looked upon those occult stirrings of the spirit of which he had read as romantic nonsense. It was a natural thing and all right if a man had a place for him to wish to have a son--but otherwise, sentimentality over such things was such rot!

And yet now he found himself thrilling with sentiment. He would like to talk to Amaryllis all about it, and listen to her thoughts, too. And then he remembered the many discussions with Verisschenzko upon the theory of re-birth and of the soul's return again and again until its lessons are learned on this plane of existence, and he wondered what soul would animate the physical form of this little being who would be his and hers.

And suddenly in his mental vision the walls of the room seemed to fade, and he was only conscious of a vastness of space, and knew that for this brief moment he was looking into eternity and realising for the first time the wonder of things.

    *   *   *   *   *

Meanwhile Verisschenzko had returned to the Carlton and was softly walking down the passage towards the Boleskis' rooms. The ante-room door was at the corner, and as he was about ten yards from it a man came out and strode rapidly towards the lift down the corridor at right angles, but the bright light fell upon his face for an instant, and Verisschenzko saw that it was Ferdinand Ardayre.

He waited where he was until he heard the lift doors shut, and even then he paced up and down for a time before he entered the sitting-room. There must be no suspicion that he had encountered the late visitor.

"Darling Brute, here you are!" Harietta cried delightedly, rising from her sofa and throwing herself into his arms. "I've packed Stanislass off to the St. James' to play piquet. I have been all alone waiting for you for the last hour--I began to fear you would not come."

Verisschenzko looked at her, with his cynical, humorous smile, whose meaning never reached her. He took in the transparent garments which hardly covered her, and then he bent and picked up a man's handkerchief which lay on a table near.

"*Tiens*! Harietta!" he remarked lazily. "Since when has Stanislass taken to using this very Eastern perfume?" and he sniffed with disgust.

The wide look of startled innocence grew in Madame Boleski's hazel eyes.

"I believe Stanislass must have got a mistress, Stepan. I have noticed lately these scents on his things--as you know, he never used any before!"

"The handkerchief is marked with 'F.A.' I suppose the *blanchisseuse* mixes them in hotels. Let us burn the memento of a husband's straying fancies then; the taste in perfumes of his inamorata is anything but refined," and Verisschenzko tossed the bit of cambric into the fire which sparkled in the grate.

"I've lots of news to tell you, Darling Brute--but I shan't--yet! Have you come to England to see that bit of bread and butter--or--?"

But Verisschenzko, with a fierce savagery which she adored, crushed her in his arms.

CHAPTER XI

On the Tuesday morning after the Carlton dinner, fate fell upon Denzil and Amaryllis in the way the jade does at times, swooping down upon them suddenly and then like a whirlwind altering the very current of their destiny. It came about quite naturally, too, and not by one of those wildly improbable situations which often prove truth to be stranger than fiction.

Amaryllis was settled in an empty compartment of the Weymouth express at Paddington. She had said good-bye to John the evening before, and he had returned to camp. She was going back to Ardayre, and feeling very miserable. Everything had been a disillusion. John's reserve seemed to have augmented, and she had been unable to break it down, and all the new emotions which she was trembling with and longing to express, had grown chilled.

Presumably John must be pleased at the possibility of having a son since it was his heart's desire; but it almost seemed as though the subject embarrassed him! And all the beautiful things which she had meant to say to him about it remained unspoken.

He was stolidly matter-of-fact.

What could it all mean?

At last she had become deeply hurt and had cried with a tremour in her voice the morning before he left her:

"Oh! John, how different you have become; it can't be the same you who once called me 'Sweetheart' and held me so closely in your arms! Have I done anything to displease you, dearest? Aren't you glad that I am going to have a baby?"

He had kissed her and assured her gravely that he was glad--overjoyed. And his eyes had been full of pain, and he had added that he was stupid and dull, but that she must not mind--it was only his way.

"Alas!" she had answered and nothing more.

She dwelt upon these things as she sat in the train gazing out of the window on the blank side.

Yes. Joy was turning into dead sea fruit. How moving her thoughts had been when coming up to meet him!

The marvel of love creating life had exalted her and she had longed to pour her tender visionings into the ears of--her lover! For John had been thus enshrined in her fond imagination!

The whole idea of having a child to her was a sacred wonder with little of earth in it, and she had woven exquisite sentiment round it and had dreamed fair dreams of how she would whisper her thoughts to John as she lay clasped to his heart; and John, too, would be thrilled with exaltation, for was not the glorious mystery his as well--not hers alone?

Now everything looked grey.

Tears rose in her eyes. Then she took herself to task; it was perhaps only her foolish romance leading her astray once more. The thought might mean nothing to a man beyond the pride of having a son to carry on his name. If the baby should be a little girl John might not care for it at all!

The tears brimmed over and fell upon a big crimson carnation in her coat, a bunch of which John had ordered to be sent her, and which were now safely reposing in a card-board box in the rack above her head.

Fortunately she had the carriage to herself. No one had attempted to get in, and they would soon be off. To be away from London would be a relief.

Then her thoughts flew to Verisschenzko; he had told her that circumstances in his country might require his frequent presence in England for the next few months.

She would see him again. What would he tell her to do now? Conquer emotion and look at things with common sense.

The picture of the dinner at the Carlton then came back to her, and the face of

Denzil across the table, so like, and yet so unlike John!

If Denzil had a wife would he be cold to her? Was it in the nature of all Ardayres?

At the very instant the train began to move the carriage was invaded by a man in khaki who bounded in and almost fell by her knees, and with a cheery 'Just done it, Sir!' the guard flung in a dressing-bag and slammed the door, and she realised with conscious interest that the intruder was Denzil Ardayre!

"How do you do? By Jove. I am awfully sorry," and he held out his hand. "I nearly lost the train and I am afraid I have bundled in without asking leave. I am going down to Bath to say good-bye to my mother. I say, do forgive me if I startled you," and he looked full of concern.

Amaryllis laughed; she was nervous and overstrung.

"Your entrance was certainly sudden and in this non-stop to Westbury we shall have to put up with each other till then--shall you mind?"

"Awfully--Must I say that the truth would be that I am enchanted!"

Fortune had flung him these two hours. He had not planned them, his conscience was clear, and he could not help delight rushing through him. Two hours with her--alone!

There are some blue eyes which seem to have a spark of the devil lurking in them always, even when they are serious. Denzil's were such eyes. Women found it difficult to resist his charm, and indeed had never tried very hard. Life and its living, knowledge to acquire, work to do, beasts to hunt, had not left him too much time to be spoiled by them fortunately, and he had passed through several adventures safely and had never felt anything but the most transient emotion, until now looking at Amaryllis sitting opposite him he knew that he was in love with this dream which had materialised.

Amaryllis studied him while they talked of ordinary things and the war news and when he would go out. She felt some strong attraction drawing her to him. Her sense of depression left her. She found herself noticing how the sun which had broken through a cloud turned his immaculately brushed hair into bronze. She did a little modelling to amuse herself, and so appreciated balance and line.

Everything in Denzil was in the right place, she decided, and above all he looked so peculiarly alive. He seemed, indeed, to be the reality of what her imagination had built up round the personality of John in the weeks of their separation. Denzil believed that he was talking quite casually, but his glance was ardent, and atmosphere becomes charged when emotions are strong no matter how insignificant words may be. Amaryllis *felt* that he was deeply interested in her.

"You know my friend Verisschenzko well, it seems," she said presently. "Is not he a fascinating creature? I always feel stimulated when I am with him, and as if I must accomplish great things."

"Stepan is a wonder--we were at Oxford together--he can do anything he desires. He is a musician and an artist and is chock full of common sense, and there's not a touch of rot. He would have taken honours if he had not been sent down."

Amaryllis wanted to know about this, and listened amazedly to the story of the mad freak which had so scandalised the Dons.

She had recovered from her nervousness, she was natural and delightful, and although the peculiar situation was filling Denzil with excitement and emotion, he was too much a man of the world to experience any *gene*. So they talked for a while with friendliness upon interesting things. Then a pause came and Amaryllis looked out of the window, and Denzil had time to grow aware that he must hold himself with a tighter hand, a sense almost of intoxication had begun to steal over him.

Suddenly Amaryllis grew very pale and her eyelids flickered a little; for the first time in her life she felt faint.

He bent forward in anxiety as she leaned her head against the cushioned division.

"Oh! what is it, you poor little darling! what can I do for you?" he exclaimed, unconscious that he had used a word of endearment; but even though things had grown vague for her Amaryllis caught the tenderly pronounced 'darling' and, physically ill as she felt, her spirit thrilled with some agreeable surprise. He came nearer and pushing up the padded divisions between the seats, he lifted her as though she had been a baby and laid her flat down. He got out his flask from his dressing bag and poured some brandy between her pale lips, then he rubbed her hands, murmuring he knew not what of commiseration. She looked so fragile and helpless and the probable reason of her indisposition was of such infinite solicitude to himself.

"To think that she is feeling like that because--Ah!--and I may not even kiss her and comfort her, or tell her I adore her and understand." So his thoughts ran.

Presently Amaryllis sat up and opened her eyes. She had not actually fainted, but for a few moments everything had grown dim and she was not certain of what had happened, or if she had dreamed that Denzil had spoken a love word, or whether it was true--she smiled feebly.

"I did feel so queer," she explained. "How silly of me! I have never felt faint before--it is stupid"--and then she blushed deeply, remembering what certainly must be the cause.

"I am going to open the window wide," he said, appreciating the blush, and let it down. "You ought not to sit with your back to the engine like that, let us change sides."

He took command and drew her to her feet, and placed her gently in his vacant seat; then he sat down opposite her and looked at her with anxious eyes.

"I sit that way as a rule because of avoiding the dust, but, of course, it was that. I am not generally such a goose though--it is the nastiest feeling that I have ever known."

"You poor dear little girl," his deep voice said. "You must shut your eyes and not talk now."

She obeyed, and he watched her intently as she lay back with her eyes closed, the long lashes resting upon her pale cheeks. She looked childish and a little pathetic, and every fibre of his being quivered with desire to protect her. He had never felt so profoundly in his life--and the whole thing was so complicated. He tried to force himself to remember that he was not travelling with *his* wife whom he could take care of and cherish because she was going to have *his* child, but that he was travelling with John's wife whom he hardly knew and must take no more interest in than any Ardayre would in the wife of the head of the family!

He could have laughed at the extraordinary irony of the thing, if it had not been so moving.

Verisschenzko, had he been there and known the circumstances, would have taken joy in analysing what nature was saying to them both!

Amaryllis was only conscious that Denzil seemed the reality of her dream of John, and that she liked his nearness--and Denzil only knew that he loved her extremely and must banish emotion and remember his given word. So he pulled himself together when she sat up presently and began talking again, and gradually the atmosphere of throbbing excitement between them calmed. They spoke of each other's tastes and likings and found many to be the same. Then they spoke of books, and each discovered that the other was sufficiently well read to be able to discuss varied favourite authors.

An understanding and sympathy had grown up between them before they reached Westbury, and yet Denzil was really trying to keep his word in the spirit as well as the letter.

Amaryllis felt no constraint--she was more friendly than she would have been with any other man she knew so slightly. Were they not cousins, and was it not perfectly natural!

They talked of Oxford and of the effect it had upon young men, and again they spoke of Stepan and of the dream he and Denzil shared.

"You will go into Parliament, I suppose, when you come back from the war?" she remarked at last. "If you have dreams they should become realities...."

"That is what I intend to do. The war may last a long time though--but it ought to teach one something, and England will be a vastly different place after it, and perhaps the younger men who have fought may have a greater chance."

"You have pet theories, of course."

"I suppose so--I believe that the first great step will be to give the people better homes--the housing question is what I am going to devote my energy to. I am sure it is the root of nearly every evil. Every man and woman who works should have the right to a good home. I have two supreme interests--that is one, and the other is elimination of the wastrels and the unfit. I am quite ruthless, perhaps, you will think. But there is such a sickening lot of mawkish sentiment mixed up with nearly every scheme to benefit workers. I agree with Stepan who always preaches: Get down to the commonsense point of view about a thing. Prune the convention and religion and sentimentality first and then you can judge."

Amaryllis thought for a moment; her eyes became wide and dreamy, and her charmingly set head was a little thrown back. Denzil took in the line of her white throat and the curve of her chin--it was not weak. Why was it that women with the possibilities of this one always seemed to be some other man's property! He had never come across such charm in girls. Or was it that marriage developed charm?

They neither of them spoke for a minute or two, each busy with speculation.

"I want to do something," Amaryllis said at last, "not, only just make shirts and socks," and then the pink flushed her cheeks again suddenly as she remembered that she would not be fit for more strenuous work for quite a long time--and then the war would be over, of course.

Denzil thought the same thing without the last qualification. He was under no delusions as to the speedy end of strife.

He could not help visioning the wonderful interest the hope of a son would be to him if she really were his wife--how filled with supreme sympathy and tenderness would be the months coming on. How they would talk together about their wishes and the mystery and the glory of the evolution of life. And here she had blushed at some thought concerning it, and no words must pass between them about this sacred thing. He longed to ask her many questions--and then a pang of jealousy shook him. She would confide to John, not to him, all the emotions aroused by the thought of the child--then. He wondered what she would do in the winter all alone. Had she relations she was fond of? He wished that she knew his Mother, who was the kindest sweetest lady in the world. He said aloud:

"I would like you to meet my Mother. She is going to be at Bath for a month. She is almost an invalid with rheumatism in her ankle where she broke it five years ago. I believe you would get on."

"I should love to--it is not an impossible distance from us. I will go over to see her, if you will tell her about me--so that she won't think some stranger is descending upon her some day!"

"She will be so pleased," and he thought that he would be happier knowing that they were friends.

"Does she mean a great deal to you? Some mothers do," and she sighed--her own was less than emptiness--they had never been near, and now her stepfather and the step-family claimed all the affection her mother could feel.

"She is a great dear--one of my best friends," and his eyes beamed. "We have always been pals--because I have no brothers and sisters I suppose she spoilt me!"

"I daresay you were quite a nice little boy!" Amaryllis smiled--"and it must be divine to have a son--I expect it would be easy to spoil one."

Denzil clasped his hands rather tightly--she looked so adorable as she said that, her eyes soft with inward knowledge of her great hope. How impossible it all was that they must remain strangers--casual cousins and nothing more.

"It must be an awful responsibility to have children," he said, watching her. "Don't you think so?"

The pink flared up again as she answered a rather solemn "Yes."

Then she went on, a little hurriedly:

"One would try to study their characters and lead them to the highest good, as gardeners watch over and train plants until they come to perfection. But what funny, serious things we are talking about," and she gave a little, nervous laugh--"Like two old grandfather philosophers."

"It is rather a treat to talk seriously; one so seldom has the chance to meet any one who understands."

"To understand!" and she sighed. "Alas--How quite perfect life would be--" and then she stopped abruptly. If she continued her words might contain a reflection upon John.

Denzil bent forward eagerly--what had she been going to say?

She saw his blue attractive eyes gazing at her so ardently and some delicious thrill passed through her. But Denzil recovered himself, and leaned back in his seat--while he abruptly changed the conversation by remarking casually:

"I have never seen Ardayre. I would love to look at our common ancestors. My father used to say there was an Elizabethan Denzil who was rather like me. I suppose we are all stamped with the same brand."

"I know him!" Amaryllis cried delightedly. "He is up at the end of the gallery in puffed white satin and a ruff. Of course, you must come and see him; he has exactly the same eyes."

"The whole family are alive I believe--we were a tenacious lot!"

"If you and John both get leave at Christmas you must come with him and spend it at Ardayre--I shall have made your Mother's acquaintance by then, and we must persuade her too."

He gave some friendly answer--while he felt that John might not endorse this invitation. If the places were reversed, how would he himself act? Difficult as the situation was for him, it was infinitely harder for John. Then the train stopped at Westbury.

CHAPTER XII

Denzil had got out to get some papers which he had been to hurried to secure at Paddington tipping the guard on the way, so that an old gentleman who showed signs of desiring to enter was warded off to another compartment. Thus when the train re-started, they were again left alone.

Amaryllis had partially recovered and was looking nearly her usual self, but for the violet shadows beneath her eyes. She glanced at the papers which he handed to her, and Denzil retired behind the Times. He wanted to think; he must not let himself slip out of hand. He must resolutely stamp out all the emotion that she was causing him; he despised weakness of any sort.

He thought of Verisschenzko's words about laws being powerless to control a man's actions, when a natural force is prompting him, unless he uses self-analysis, and so by gaining knowledge permits the spirit to conquer. He recollected that he had transgressed often without a backward thought in past days with other women, but now his honour was engaged even apart from his firm belief in Stepan's favourite saying, that a man must never sully the wrong thing. Then the argument they had often had about indulgences came to him, and the truth of the only possibility of their enjoyment being while they remained servants, not masters.

He had had his indulgences in the two hours to Westbury, and had very nearly let it conquer him, more than once, and now he must not only curb all friendly words and delightful dalliance with forbidden topics, but he must *feel* no more passion.

He made himself read the war news and try to visualize the grim reality behind the official phrasing of the communiques. And gradually he became calm, and was almost startled when Amaryllis, who had been watching him furtively and had begun to wonder if he was really so interested in his paper, said timidly:

"Will you pull the window up a little? It seems to be growing cold."

She noticed that his lips were set firmly and that an abstracted expression had grown in his eyes.

Then Denzil spoke, now quite naturally and about the war, and deliberately kept the conversation to this subject, until Amaryllis lay back again in her corner and closed her eyes.

"I am going to have a little sleep," she said.

She too had begun to realise that in more personal investigation of mutual tastes there lay some danger. She had become conscious of the fact that she was very interested in Denzil--and there he was, not really the least like John!

They were silent for some time, and were nearing Frome when he spoke. He had been deliberating as to what he ought to do? Get out and leave her, to catch his connection to Bath, or sacrifice that and see her safely to her destination and perhaps hire a motor from Bridgeborough?

This latter was his strong desire and also seemed the only chivalrous thing to do when she still looked so pale, but--

"Here we are almost at Frome," he said.

Her eyes rounded with concern. It would be horrid to be alone. She had left her maid in London for a few days' holiday.

"You change here for Bath," she faltered a little uncertainly.

He decided in a second. He could not be inhuman! Duty and desire were one!

"Yes--but I am coming on with you. I shall not leave you until I see you safely into your own motor. I can hire one perhaps then, to take me on the rest of the way."

She was relieved--or she thought it was merely relief, which made a sudden lifting in her heart!

"How kind of you. I do feel as if I did not like the thought of being by myself, it is so stupid of me--But you can't hire a motor from Bridgeborough which would get you to Bath before dark! They are wretched things there. You must come with me to Ardayre; it is on the Bath road, you know--and we can have a late lunch, and and then I'll send you on in the Rolls Royce. You will be there in an hour--in time for tea."

This was a tremendous fresh temptation. He tried to look at it as though it did not in reality matter to him more than the appearance suggested. Had there been no emotion in his interest in Amaryllis, he would not have hesitated, he knew.

Then it was only for him to conquer emotion and behave as he would do under ordinary circumstances--it would be a good test of his will.

"All right--that's splendid, and I shall be able to see Ardayre!"

It was when they were in Amaryllis's own little coupe very close to each other that strong temptation assailed Denzil. He suddenly felt his pulses throbbing wildly and it was with the greatest difficulty he prevented himself from clasping her in his arms. He tried to look out of the window and take an interest in the park, which was entered very soon after leaving the station. He told himself Ardayre was something which deserved his attention and he looked for the first view of the house, but all his will could only keep his arms from transgressing, it could not control the riot of his thoughts.

Amaryllis was conscious in some measure that he was far from calm, and her own heart began to beat unaccountably. She talked rather fast about the place and its history, and both were relieved when the front door came in sight.

There was a welcoming smell of burning logs in the hall to greet them, and the old butler could not restrain an expression of startled curiosity when he saw Denzil, the likeness to his master was so great.

"This is Captain Ardayre, Filson," Amaryllis said, "Sir John's cousin," and then she gave the order about the motor to take Denzil on to Bath.

They went through the Henry VII inner hall, and on to the green drawing-room, with its air of home and comfort, in spite of its great size and stateliness.

There were no portraits here, but some fine specimens of the Dutch school, and the big tawny dogs rose to welcome their mistress and were introduced to their "new relation."

She was utterly fascinating, Denzil thought, playing with them there on the great bear skin rug.

"We shall lunch at once," she told him, "and then rush through the pictures afterwards before you start for Bath."

They both tried to talk of ordinary things for the few moments before that meal was announced, and then some kind of devilment seemed to come into Amaryllis--nothing could have been more seductive or alluring than her manner, while keeping to strict convention. The bright pink colour glowed in her cheeks and her eyes sparkled. She could not have accounted for her mood herself. It was one of excitement and interest.

Denzil had the hardest fight he had ever been through, and he grew almost gruff in consequence. He was really suffering.

He admired the way she acted as hostess, and the way the home was done. He hardly felt anything else, though apart from her he would have been interested in his first view of Ardayre, but she absorbed all other emotions, he only knew that he desired to make passionate love to her, or to get away as quickly as he could.

"Are you going to remain here all the winter?" he asked her presently, as they rose from the table, "or shall you go to London? You will be awfully lonely, won't you, if you stay here?"

"I love the country and I am growing to love and understand the place. John wants me to so much, it means more to him than anything else in the world. I shall remain until after Christmas anyway. But come now, I want just to take you into the church, because there are two such fine tombs there of both our ancestors, yours and mine. We can go out of the windows and come back for coffee in the cedar parlour."

Denzil acquiesced; he wished to see the church. They reached it in a minute or two and Amaryllis opened the door with her own key and led him on up the aisle to the recumbent knights--and then she whispered their history to him, standing where a ray of sunlight turned her brown hair into gold.

"I wonder what their lives were," Denzil said, "and if they lived and loved and fought their desires--as we do now--the younger one's face looks as though he had not always conquered his. Stepan would say his indulgences had become his masters, not his servants, I expect."

"Verisschenzko is wonderful--he makes one want to be strong," and Amaryllis sighed. "I wonder how many of us even begin to fight our desires--"

"One has to be strong always if one wants to attain--but sometimes it is only honour which holds one--and weaklings are so pitiful."

"What is honour?" Her eyes searched his face wistfully. "Is it being true to some canon of the laws of chivalry, or is it being true to some higher thing in one's own soul?"

Denzil leaned against the tomb and he thought deeply: then he looked straight into her eyes:

"Honour lies in not betraying a trust reposed in one, either in the spirit or in the letter."

"Then, when, we say of a man 'he acted honourably,' we mean that he did not betray a trust placed in him, even if it was only perhaps by circumstance and not by a person."

"It is simply that'--keeping faith. If a man stole a sum of money from a friend, the dishonour would not be in the act of stealing, which is another offence--but in abusing his friend's trust in him by committing that act."

"Dishonour is a betrayal then--"

"Of course."

"Why would this knight"--and she placed her hand on the marble face, "have said that he must kill another who had stolen his wife, say, to avenge his 'honour'?"

"That is the conventional part of it--what Stepan calls the grafting on of a meaning to suit some idea of civilisation. It was a nice way of having personal revenges too and teaching people that they could not steal anything with impunity. If we analysed that kind of honour we would find it was principally vanity. The dishonour really lay with the wife, if she deceived her husband--and with the other man if he was the husband's friend--if he was not, his abduction of the woman was not 'dishonourable' because he was not trusted, it was merely an act of theft."

"What then must we do when we are very strongly tempted?" Her voice was so low he could hardly hear it.

"It is sometimes wisest to run away," and he turned from her and moved towards the door.

She followed wondering. She knew not why she had promoted this discussion. She felt that she had been very unbalanced all the day.

They went back to the house almost silently and through the green drawing-room window again and up the broad stairs with Sir William Hamilton's huge decorative painting of an Ardayre group of his time, filling one vast wall at the turn.

And so they reached the cedar parlour, and found coffee waiting and cigarettes.

There was a growing tension between them and each guessed that the other was not calm. Amaryllis began showing him the view from the windows across the park, and then the old fireplace and panelling of the room.

"We sit here generally when we are alone," she said. "I like it the best of all the rooms in the house."

"It is a fitting frame for you."

They lit cigarettes.

Denzil had many things he longed to say to her of the place, and the thoughts it called up in him--but he checked himself. The thing was to get through with it all quickly and to be gone. They went into the picture gallery then, and began from the end, and when they came to the Elizabethan Denzil they paused for a little while. The painted likeness was extraordinary to the living splendid namesake who gazed up at the old panel with such interested eyes.

And Amaryllis was thinking:

"If only John had that something in him which these two have in their eyes, how happy we could be."

And Denzil was thinking:

"I hope the child will reproduce the type." He felt it would be some kind of satisfaction to himself if she should have a son which should be his own image.

"It is so strange," she remarked, "that you should be exactly like this Denzil, and yet resemble John who does not remind me of him at all, except in the general family look which every one of them share. This one might have been painted from you."

He looked down at her suddenly and he was unable to control the passionate emotion in his eyes. He was thinking that yes, certainly, the child must be like him--and then what message would it convey to her?

Amaryllis was disturbed, she longed to ask him what it was which she felt, and why there seemed some illusive remembrance always haunting her. She grew confused, and they passed on to another frame which contained the Lady Amaryllis who had had the sonnets written to her nut brown locks. She was a dainty creature in her stiff farthingale, but bore no likeness to the present mistress of Ardayre.

Denzil examined her for some seconds, and then he said reflectively:

"She is a Sweetheart--but she is not you!"

There was some tone of tenderness in his voice when he said the word "Sweetheart" and Amaryllis started and drew in her breath. It recalled something which had given her joy, a low murmur whispered in the night. "Sweetheart!"--a word which John, alas! had never used before nor since, except in that one letter in answer to her cry of exaltation--her glad Magnificat. What was this echo sounding in her ears? How like Denzil's voice was to John's--only a little deeper. Why, why should he have used that word "Sweetheart"?

No coherent thought had yet come to her, it was as though she had looked for an instant upon some scene which awakened a chord of memory, and then that the curtain had dropped before she could define it.

She grew agitated, and Denzil turning, saw that her face was pale, and her grey eyes vague and troubled.

"I am quite sure that it is tiring you, showing me all the house like this, we won't look at another picture--and really I must be getting on."

She did not contradict him.

"I am afraid that you ought to go perhaps, if you want to arrive by daylight."

And as they returned to the green drawing-room she said some nice things about wanting to meet his mother, and she tried to be natural and at ease, but her hand was cold as ice when he held it in saying good-bye before the fire, when Filson had announced the motor.

And if his eyes had shown passionate emotion in the picture gallery, hers now filled with question and distress.

"Good-bye, Denzil--"

"Good-bye, Amaryllis--" He could not bring himself to say the usual conventionalities, and went towards the door with nothing more.

Her brain was clearing, terror and passion and uncertainty had come in like a flood.

"Denzil--?"

He turned to her side fearfully. Why had she called him now?

"Denzil--?" her face had paled still further, and there was an anguish of pleading in it. "Oh, please, what does it all mean?" and she fell forward into his arms.

He held her breathlessly. Had she fainted? No--she still stood on her feet, but her little face there lying on his breast was as a lily in whiteness and tears escaped from her closed eyes.

"For God's sake, Denzil, have you not something to tell me? You cannot leave me so!"

He shivered with the misery of things.

"I have nothing to tell you, child." His voice was hoarse. "You are overwrought and overstrung. I have nothing to say to you but just good-bye."

She held his coat and looked up at him wildly.

"--Denzil--It was you--not--John!"

He unclasped her clinging arms:

"I must go."

"You shall not until you answer me--I have a right to know."

"I tell you I have nothing to say to you," he was stern with the suffering of restraint.

She clung to him again.

"Why did you say that word 'Sweetheart' then? It was your own word. Oh! Denzil, you cannot be so frightfully cruel as to leave me in uncertainty--tell me the truth or I shall die!"

But he drew himself away from her and was silent; he could not make lying protestations of not understanding her, so there only remained one course for him to follow--he must go, and the brutality of such action made him fierce with pain.

She burst into passionate sobs and would have fallen to the ground. He raised her in his arms and laid her on the sofa near, and then fear seized him. What if this excitement and emotion should make her really ill--?

He knelt down beside her and stroked her hair. But she only sobbed the more.

"How hideously cruel are men. Why can't you tell me what I ask you? You dare not even pretend that you do not understand!"

He knew that his silence was an admission, he was torn with distress.

"Darling," he cried at last in torment, "for God's sake, let me go."

"Denzil--" and then her tears stopped suddenly, and the great drops glistened on her white cheeks. Weeping had not disfigured her--she looked but as a suffering child.

"Denzil--if you knew everything, you could not possibly leave me--you don't know what has happened--But you must, you will have to since--soon--"

He bowed his head and placed her two hands over his face with a despairing movement.

"Hush--I implore you--say nothing. I do know, but I love you--I must go."

At that she gave a glad cry and drew him close to her.

"You shall not now! I do not care for conventions any more, or for laws, or for anything! I am a savage--you are mine! John must know that you are mine! The family is all that matters to him, I am only an instrument, a medium for its continuance--but Denzil, you and I are young and loving and living. It is you I desire, and now I know that I belong to you. You are the man and I am the woman--and the child will be our child!"

Her spirit had arisen at last and broken all chains. She was transfigured, transformed, translated. No one knowing the gentle Amaryllis could have recognised her in this fierce, primitive creature claiming her mate!

Furious, answering passion surged through Denzil; it was the supreme moment when all artificial restrictions of civilisation were swept away. Nature had come to her own. All her forces were working for these two of her children brought near by a turn of fate. He strained her in his arms wildly--he kissed her lips, and ears, and eyes.

"Mine, mine," he cried, and then "Sweetheart!"

And for some seconds which seemed an eternity of bliss they forgot all but the joy of love.

But presently reality fell upon Denzil and he almost groaned.

"I must leave you, precious dear one--even so--I gave my word of honour to John that I would never take advantage of the situation. Fate has done this thing by bringing us together; it has overwhelmed us. I do not feel that we are greatly to blame, but that does not release me from my promise. It is all a frightful price that we must pay for pride in the Family. Darling, help me to have courage to go."

"I will not--It is shameful cruelty," and she clung to him, "that we must be parted now I am yours really--not John's at all. Everything in my heart and being cries out to you--you are the reality of my dream lover, your image has been growing in my vision for months. I love you, Denzil, and it is your right to stay with me now and take care of me, and it is my right to tell you of my thoughts about the--child--Ah! if you knew what it means to me, the joy, the wonder, the delight! I cannot keep it all to myself any longer. I am starving! I am frozen! I want to tell it all to my Beloved!"

He held her to him again--and she poured forth the tenderest holy things, and he listened enraptured and forgot time and place.

"Denzil," she whispered at last, from the shelter of his arms. "I have felt so strange--exalted, ever since--and now I shall have this ever present thought of you and love women in my existence--But how is it going to be in the years which are coming? How can I go on pretending to John?--I cannot--I shall blurt out the truth--For me there is only you--not just the you of these last days since we saw each other with our eyes--but the you that I had dreamed about and fashioned as my lover--my delight--Can I whisper to John all my joy and tenderness as I watch the growing up of my little one? No! the thing is monstrous, grotesque--I will not face the pain of it all. John gave you to me--he must have done so--it was some compact between you both for the family, and if I did not love you I should hate you now, and want to kill myself. But I love you, I love you, I love you!" and she fiercely clasped her arms once more about his neck. "You must take the consequences of your action. I did not ask to have this complication in my life. John forced it upon me for his own aims, but I have to be reckoned with, and I want my lover, I claim my mate." Her cheeks were flaming and her eyes flashed.

"And your lover wants you," and Denzil wildly returned her fond caress, "but the choice is not left to me, darling, even if you were my wife, not John's. You have forgotten the war--I must go out and fight."

All the warmth and passion died out of her, and she lay back on the pillows of the sofa for a moment and closed her eyes. She had indeed forgotten that ghastly colossus in her absorption in their own two selves.

Yes--he must go out and fight--and John would go too--and they might both be killed like all those gallant partners of the season and her cousin, and those who had fallen at Mons and the battle of the Marne.

No--she must not be so paltry as to think of personal things, even love. She must rise above all selfishness, and not make it harder for her man. Her little face grew resigned and sanctified, and Denzil watching her with burning, longing eyes, waited for her to speak.

"It is true--for the moment nothing but you and my great desire for you was in my mind. But you are right, Denzil; of course, I cannot keep you. Only I am glad that just this once we have tasted a brief moment of happiness, and--Denzil, I believe our souls belong to each other, even if we do not meet again on earth."

And when at last they had parted, and Amaryllis, listening, heard the motor go, she rose from the sofa and went out through the window to the lawn, and so to the church again, and there lay on the steps of the young knight's tomb, sobbing and praying until darkness enveloped the land.

CHAPTER XIII

A day or two before Denzil sailed for France he dined with Verisschenzko. The intense preoccupation of the last war preparations had left him very little time for grieving. He was unhappy when he thought of Amaryllis, but he was a man, and another primitive instinct was in action in him--the zest of going out to fight!

Verisschenzko was depressed, his country was not yet giving him the opportunity to fulfil his hopes, and he fretted that he must direct things from so far.

They sat in a quiet corner of the Berkeley and talked in a desultory fashion all through the **hors d'ouvres** and the soup.

"I am sick of things, Denzil," Verisschenzko said at last. "I feel inclined to end it all sometimes."

"And belie the whole meaning of your whole beliefs. Don't be a fool, Stepan. I always have told you that there is one grain of suicide in the composition of every Russian. Now it has become active with you. Have another glass of champagne, old boy, and then you'll talk sense again. It is sickening to be killed, or maimed, or any beastly thing if it comes along with duty, but to court it is madness pure and simple. It's just rot."

"I'm with you," and he called the waiter and ordered a fine champagne, while he smiled, showing his strong, square teeth.

"They don't have decent vodka--but the brandy will do the trick," and in an instant his mood changed even before the cognac had come.

"It is the lingering trace of some other life of folly, when I talk like that--I know it, Denzil. It is the harking back to long months of gloom and darkness and snow and the howling of wolves and the fear of the knout. This is not my first Russian life, you know!"

"Probably not; but you've had some more balanced intervening ones, or I should have found you dead with veronal, or some other filthy thing before this, with your highly strung nerves! I am not really alarmed about you though, Stepan--you are fundamentally sane."

"I am glad you think that--very few English understand us--"

"Because you don't understand yourselves. You seem to have every quality and fault crammed into your skins with no discrimination as to how to sort them. You are not self-conscious like we are and afraid of looking like fools--so whatever is uppermost bursts out. If one of us had half your brains he would never have said an idiot thing completely contrary to his whole natural bent like that, just because he felt down on his luck for the moment."

Verisschenzko laughed outright.

"Go ahead, Denzil--let off steam! I'm done in!"

"Well, don't be such a damned fool again!"

"I won't--how is my Lady Amaryllis?"

Denzil looked at him keenly.

"Why do you ask?"

"Because she has written to me, and I am going down to see her--"

"Then you know how she is?"

"I guess. Look here, Denzil, do try and be frank with me. You are acquainted with me and know whether I am to be trusted or not. You are aware that I love her with the spirit. You and the worthy husband are off to be killed, and yet just because you are so damned reserved English, you can't bring yourself to do the sensible thing and tell me all about it so that if you go to glory I could look after her rights and--the child's--and take care of her. It is you who are a fool really, not I! Because I get a little drunk with my moods and talk about suicide, that is froth, but I should not bottle up a confidence because it's 'not the thing' to talk about a woman--even though it's for her benefit and protection to do so. I've more common sense. Some difficult questions might crop up later with Ferdinand Ardayre, and I want to have the real truth made plain to myself so that I can crush him. If you've some cards up your sleeve that I don't know of, I can't defend Amaryllis so well."

Denzil put down his knife and fork for a moment; he realised the truth of what his friend said, but it was very difficult for him to speak all the same.

"Tell me what you know, Stepan, and I'll see what I can do. It is not because I don't trust you, but it is against everything in me to talk."

"Convention again, and selfishness. You are thinking more about the English-man's point of view than the good of the woman you love--because I feel partly from her letter that you do love her and that she loves you--and I surmise that the child is yours, not John's, though how this miracle has been accomplished, since it was clear that you had never seen her until the night at the Carlton, I don't pretend to guess!"

Denzil drank down his champagne, and then he made Verisschenzko under-stand in a few words--the Russian's imagination filled in the details.

He lit a cigarette between the course and puffed rings of smoke.

"So poor John devised this plan, and yet he loves her--he must indeed be ob-sessed by the family!"

"He is--he is a frightfully reserved person too, and I am sure has frozen Ama-ryllis from the first day."

"My idea was always for this, directly I went to Ardayre. I felt that mysterious pull of the family there in that glorious house. I thought she would probably simpli-fy things by just taking you for a lover, when you met, as you are her counterpart--a perfect mate for her. I had even made up my mind to suggest this to her, and influ-ence her as much as I could to this end--but lo! the husband takes the matter out of our hands and devises a really unique accomplishment of our wishes. Gosh! Denzil! it's John who's got the common sense and the genius, not we!"

"Yes, he has--so far, but he did not reckon with human emotion. He might have known that directly I should see Amaryllis I should fall in love with her, and he ought to have understood that that extraordinary thing, nature, might make her draw to me afterwards. Now the situation is tragic, however you look at it. John will have the hell of a life if he comes back; he can't help feeling jealous every time he sees the child, and the tension between him and Amaryllis, now that she knows, will be great. Amaryllis is wretched--she is passionate and vivid as a humming bird. Every hair of her darling head is living and quivering with human power for joy and union, and she will lead the famished life of a nun! I absolutely worship her. I am frantically in love, so my outlook, if I come back is not gay either. I wonder if we did well, after all, John and I, and if the family makes all this suffering worth while? Perhaps it would have been better to leave it to fate!" Denzil sighed and forgot to notice a dish the waiter was handing.

"It is perfectly certain," and Verisschenzko grew contemplative, "that the result of deliberately turning the current of events like that must have some momentous consequence. Mind you, I think you were right. I should have advised it as I have told you, because of that swine of a Turk, Ferdinand--but it may have deranged some plan of the Cosmos, and if so some of you will have to pay for it. I hate that it should be my lady Amaryllis. All her sorrow comes from your dramatically honourable promise. You can't make love to her now--because a man who is a gentleman does not break his word. Now if my plan had been followed, you would not have had this limitation and you could have had some joy--but who knows! A false position is a gall in any case, and it would have soiled my star, which now shines purely. So perhaps all is for the best. But have you analysed, now that we are on the subject, what it is 'being in love,' old boy?"

"It is divine--and it is hell--"

"All that! Amaryllis is the exact opposite to Harietta Boleski--in this, that she attracts as strongly as Harietta could ever do physically, and will be no disappointment in soul in the *entre actes*. *Being in love* is a physical state of exaltation; *loving* is the merging of spirit which in its white heat has glorified the physical instinct for re-creation into a godlike beatitude not of earth. A man could be in love with Harietta, he could never love her. A man could always love Amaryllis, so much that he would not be aware that half his joy was because he was *in love* with her also."

"You know, Stepan, men, women and every one talk a lot of nonsense about other interests in life mattering more, and there being other kinds of really better happiness, but it is pure rot; if one is honest one owns that there is no real happiness but in the satisfaction of love. Every other kind is second best. It is jolly good often, but only a *pis aller* in comparison to the real thing.

"And when people deny this, believing they are speaking honestly, it is simply because the real thing has not come their way, or they are too brutalised by transient indulgences to be able to feel exaltation.

"So here's to love!" and Denzil emptied his glass. "The supreme God--"

"Ainsi soit il," and Stepan drank in response. "Our toast before has always been to the Ardayre son, and now we drink to what I hope has been his creator!"

They were silent for some moments, and then Verisschenzko went on:

"When the state of being in love is waning, affection often remains, but then one is at the mercy of a new emotion. I'd be nervous if a woman who had loved me subsided into feeling affection!"

"Then define loving?"

"Loving throbs with delight in the flesh; it thrills the spirit with reverence. It glorifies into beauty commonplace things. It draws nearer in sickness and sorrow, and is not the sport of change. When a woman loves truly she has the passion of the mistress, the selfless tenderness of the mother, the dignity and devotion of the wife. She is all fire and snow, all will and frankness, all passion and reserve, she is authoritative and obedient--queen and child."

"And a man?"

"He ceases to be a brute and becomes a god."

"Can it last, I wonder?" and again Denzil sighed.

"It could if people were not such fools--they nearly always deliberately destroy the loved one's emotion by senseless stupidity--in not grasping the fact that no fire burns without fuel. They disillusionise each other. The joy once secured, they take no pains to keep it. A woman will do things when the lover is an acknowledged possession, which she would not have dreamed of doing while desiring to attract the man--and a man likewise--neither realising that the whole state of being in love is an intoxication of the senses, and that the senses are very easily wearied or affronted."

"Stepan--what am I going to do about Amaryllis? If I come back, it will be hell--a continual longing and aching, and I want to accomplish something in life; it was never my plan to have the whole thing held and bounded by passion for a woman. A hopeless passion I can understand facing and crushing, but one which you know that the woman returns, and that it is only the law and promises you have made which separate you, is the most awful torment." He covered his eyes with his hand for a moment. His face was stern. "And her life too--how sickening. You say you are going down to Ardayre to see Amaryllis--you will tell me how you find her. I have not written--I am trying not to feel."

"Are you interested about the coming child? I am never quite certain how much it matters to a man, whether we deceive ourselves and feel sentiment simply because we love the woman, whether the emotion is half vanity, or whether there is something in the actual state called parenthood? How do you feel?"

Denzil thought of his musings upon this subject after he had seen Amaryllis at the Carlton.

"It is hard to describe," he answered now, "it is all so interwoven with love for Amaryllis that I cannot distinguish which is which, or how I feel about the state in the abstract. Women have these mysterious emotions, I believe, but I do not think that they come to the average man, but if he loves it seems a fulfilment."

"I have two children scattered in Russia, begotten before I had begun to think of things and their meanings. I have them finely educated--I loathe them. I sicken at the memory of the mothers; I am ashamed when I see in them some chance physical likeness to myself. But how will you feel presently when you see the child, adoring the mother as you do? What will it say to you, looking at you with your own eyes, perhaps? You'll long to have some hand in the training of it. You'll desire to watch the budding brain and the expanding soul. You'll be drawn closer and closer to Amaryllis--it will all pull you with an invisible nature chain--"

"I know it,--that is the tragedy of the whole thing. Those delights will be John's--and I hate to think that Amaryllis will be alone for all these months--and yet I believe I would prefer that to her being with John. I am jealous when I remember that he has rights denied to me--so what must he feel, poor devil, when he remembers about me?"

"It is quite a peculiar situation. I wonder what the years will develop it into."

"If the child is a girl, the whole thing is in vain."

"It won't be a girl--you will see I am right. When will you and John get leave, do you suppose?"

"I don't know, but about Christmas, perhaps, if we are alive--"

"Do you want to see her again, then?"

"I long always to see her--but by Christmas--it would be nearly five months. I don't think I could keep my word and not make love to her--if I saw her--then."

"You will wish to hear about her--?"

"Always."

After this they were both silent while the cheese was being removed. Verisschenzko was thinking profoundly. Here was a study worthy of his highest intuitive faculties. What possible solution could the future hold? Only one--that of death for either of the men concerned. Well, death was busy with England's best--it was no unlikely possibility--and as he looked at Denzil he felt a stab of pain. Nothing more splendid and living and strong could be imagined than his six foot one of manhood, crowned with the health of his twenty-nine years.

"I hope to God he comes through," he prayed. And then he became cynical, as was his habit, when he found himself moved.

"I am on the track of Harietta, Denzil. She has a new lover--Ferdinand Ardayre."

"What a combination!"

"Yes, but who the officer was at the Ardayre ball I cannot yet trace. Stanislass is quite a *gaga*--he spends his time packed off to play piquet at the St. James'--he has no *bosse des cartes*,--it is his burdensome duty."

"He does not feel the war?"

"He is numb."

"What will you do if you catch her red-handed?"

"I shall have her shot without a moment's compunction. It would be a fitting end."

"I don't know that I should have the nerve to shoot a woman--even a spy."

Verisschenzko laughed, and a savage light grew in his Calmuck eyes.

"My want of civilisation will serve me--if ever that moment comes."

Then their talk turned to fighting, and women were forgotten for the time.

CHAPTER XIV

Amaryllis came up to London the following week to say good-bye to John, so Verisschenzko did not go down to Ardayre to see her.

John's leave-taking was characteristic. He could not break through the iron band of his reserve, he longed to say something loving to her, but the more deeply he felt things the greater was his difficulty in self-expression. And the knowledge of the secret he hid in his heart made him still more ill at ease with Amaryllis. She too was changed--he felt it at once. Her grey eyes were mysterious--they had grown from a girl's into a woman's. She did not mention the coming child until he did--

and then it was she who showed desire to change the conversation. All this pained John, while he felt that he himself was the cause--he knew that he had frozen her. He thought over his marriage from the beginning. He thought of the night when he had sat on the bench outside her window until dawn, of the agony he suffered, realising at last that the axe had indeed fallen, and that some day she must know the truth. And would she reproach him and say that he should have warned her that this possibility might occur? He remembered his talk with Lemon Bridges. He had been going to give him a definite answer that morning, but John had missed the appointment, so they spoke at the ball.

Would it have been better if he had let himself go and fondly kissed and netted Amaryllis? Or would that have been misleading and still more unkind? It was too late now, in any case. He must learn to take the only satisfaction which was left to him, the knowledge that there was the hope of a true Ardayre to carry on.

He talked long to his wife of his desires for the child's education, should it prove a boy, and he should not return, and Amaryllis listened dutifully.

Her mind was filled with wonder all the time. She had been through much emotion since the passionate outburst after Denzil had gone, but was quite calm now. She had classified things in her mind. She felt no resentment against John. He ought not to have married her perhaps, but it might be that at the time he did not know. Only she wondered when she looked at him sitting opposite her, talking gravely about the baby, in the library of Brook Street, how he could possibly be feeling. What an immense influence the thought of the family must have in his life. She understood it in a great measure herself. She remembered Verisschenzko's words upon the occasions when he had spoken to her about it, and of her duties towards it, and how she must uphold it. She particularly remembered that which he had said when they walked by the lake, and he had seemed to be transmitting some message to her, which she had not understood at the time. Did Verisschenzko know then that John must always be heirless and had he been suggesting to her that the line should go on through her? Some of the pride in it all had come to her before she had left the dark church after parting with Denzil. Perhaps she was fulfilling destiny. She must not be angry with John. She did not try to cease from loving Denzil. She had not knowingly been unfaithful to John--and now, she would be faithful to Denzil, he was her love and her mate. Indeed, even in the fortnight which elapsed between her farewell to him, and now when she was going to say farewell to John, she had many months of tender consolation in the thought of the baby--Denzil's son. She could revive and revel in that exquisite exaltation which she had experienced at first and which John had withered. Denzil far surpassed even the imagined lover into which she had turned John. So now Denzil had become the reality, and John the dream.

She felt sorry for her husband too. She was fine enough to understand and divine his difficulties.

She found that she felt just nothing for him but a kindly affection. He might have been Archie de la Paule--or any of her other cousins. She knew that her whole being was given to Denzil--who represented her dream.

She tried to be very kind to John, and when he kissed her before starting, the tears came to her eyes.

Poor good, cold John!

And when he had departed--all the de la Paule family had been there at Brook Street also--Lady de la Paule wondered at her niece's set face. But what a mercy it was the marriage was such a success after all and that there might be a son!

So both Denzil and John went to the war--and Amaryllis was alone. Verisschenzko had returned to Paris without seeing her--and it was the beginning of December before he was in England again and rang her up at Brook Street where she had returned for a week, asking if he might call.

"Of course!" she said, and so he came.

The library was looking its best. Amaryllis had a knack of arranging flowers and cushions and such things--her rooms always breathed an air of home and repose, and Verisschenzko was struck by the sweet scent and the warmth and cosiness when he came in out of the gloomy fog.

She rose to greet him, her face more ethereal still than when he had dined with her.

"You are looking like an angel," he said, when she had given him some tea and they were seated on the big sofa before the fire. "What have you to tell me? I know that you are going to have a child; I am very interested about it all."

Amaryllis blushed a soft pink--he went on with perfect calm.

"You blush as though I had said something unheard of! How custom rules you still! For a blush is caused by feeling some sort of shame or discomfort, or agitating surprise at some discovery. We may get red with anger, or get pale, but that bright, sudden flush always has some self-conscious element of shame in it. It is just convention which has wrapped the most natural and divine thing in life round with discomfort in this way. You are deeply to be congratulated that you are going to have a baby, do you not think so?"

"Of course I do--" and Amaryllis controlled her uneasy bashfulness. She really wished to talk to her friend.

"Who told you about it?" she asked.

"Denzil."

Amaryllis drew in her breath suddenly. Verisschenzko's eyes were looking her through and through.

"Denzil--?"

"Yes,--he is glad that there may be the possibility of a son for the family."

"How do you feel about it? It is an enormous responsibility to have children."

"I feel that--I want to do the wisest things from the beginning--"

"You must take great care of yourself, and always remain serene. Never let your mind become agitated by speculation as to the *presently*, keep all thoughts fixed upon the now."

Amaryllis looked at him a little troubled. What did he know? Something tangible, or were these views of his just applicable to any case? Her eyes were full of question and pleading.

"What do you want to ask me?" His eyes narrowed in contemplating her.

"I--I--do not know."

"Yes, you want to hear of Denzil--is it not so?"

She clasped her hands.

"Yes--perhaps--"

"He is well--I heard from him yesterday. He asked me to come to you. His mother is still at Bath--he wishes you to meet."

Suddenly the impossibleness of everything seemed to come over Amaryllis. She rose quickly and threw out her hands:

"Oh! if I could only understand the meaning of things, my friend! I am afraid to think!"

"You love Denzil very much--yes?"

"Yes--"

"Sit down and let us talk about it, lady of my soul. I am your mother now."

She sank into her seat beside him, among the green silk pillows--and he leaned back and watched her for a while.

"He fulfils some imaginary picture, **hein?** You had not seen him really until we all dined?"

"No."

"You were bound to be drawn to him--he is everything a woman could desire--but it was not only that--tell me?"

"He was what I had hoped John would be--the likeness is so great--"

"It is much deeper than that--nature was drawing you unconsciously."

She covered her face with her hands. It seemed as if Verisschenzko must know the truth. Had Denzil told him, or was it his wonderful intuition which was enlightening him now, or was it just her sensitive conscience?

"You see custom and convention and false shames have so distorted most natural things that no one has been taught to understand them. Men were intended in the scheme of things to love women and to have children; women were meant to love men and to desire to be mothers. These instincts are primordial, the life of the world depends upon them. They have been distorted and abused into sins and vices and excesses and every evil by civilisation, so that now we rule them out of every calculation in judging of a circumstance; if we are 'nice' people they are taboo. Supposing we so suppressed and distorted and misused the other two primitive instincts, to obtain food and to kill one's enemy, the world would have ended long ago. We have done what we could to distort those also, but nothing to the extent to which we have debased the nobility of the recreative instinct!"

Amaryllis listened attentively, and he went on:

"It is admitted that we require food to live--and that if we are threatened with death from an enemy we have the right to kill him in self-defence. But it is never admitted that it is equally natural that we desire to recreate our species. Under certain circumstances of vows and restrictions, we are permitted to take one partner for life--and--if this person turns out to be a fraud for the purpose for which we made the promise, we may not have another. Supposing hungry savages were given covered dishes purporting to contain food, and upon lifting the cover one of them discovered his dish was empty--what would happen? He would bear it as long as he could, but when he was starving he would certainly try to steal some food from his neighbour--and might even knock him on the head and obtain it! Civilisation has controlled primitive instincts, so that a civilised man might perhaps prefer to die himself from starvation rather than kill or steal. He is master of his actions, ***but he is not master of the effects of his abstinence--Nature wins these,*** and whatever would be the natural physical result of his abstinence occurs. Now you can reason this thought out in all its branches, and you will see where it leads to--"

Amaryllis mused for some moments--and she saw the justice of his reflections.

"But for hundreds of years there have been priests and nuns and companies of ascetics," she remarked tentatively.

"There have been hundreds of lunatics also--and madness is not on the decrease. When you destroy nature you always produce the abnormal, when life survives from your treatment."

"You think that it is natural that one should have a mate then?"--she hesitated.

"Absolutely."

"It is more important than the keeping of vows?"

"No, the spirit is degraded by the knowledge of broken vows--only one must have intelligence to realise what the price of keeping them will be, and then summon strength enough to carry out whatever course is best for the soul, or best for the ideal one is living for. Sometimes that end requires ruthlessness, and sometimes that end requires that we starve in one way or another, so ***we must*** be prepared for sacrifice perhaps of life, or what makes life worth living, if we are strong enough to keep vows which we have been short-sighted enough to make too hastily."

Amaryllis gazed in front of her--then she asked softly:

"Do you think it is wicked of me to be thinking of Denzil--not John?"

"No--it is quite natural--the wickedness would be if you pretended to John that you were thinking of him. Deception is wickedness."

"Everything is so sad now. Both have gone to fight. I do not dare to think at all."

"Yes, you must think--you must think of your child and draw to it all the good forces, so that it may come to life unhampered by any weakness of balance in you. That must be your constant self-discipline. Keep serene and try to live in a world of noble ideals and serenity. Now I am going to play to you--"

Amaryllis had never heard Verisschenzko play. He arranged the sofa cushions and made her lie comfortably among them, then he went to the piano--and presently it seemed to her that her soul was floating upward into realms of perfect content. She had never even dreamed of such playing. It was like nothing she had ever heard before, the sounds touched all the highest chords in her spirit. She did not ask whose was the music. She seemed to know that it was Verisschenzko's own, which was just talking to her, telling her to be calm and brave and true.

He played for a whole hour--and at last softly and yet more softly, and when he finished he saw that she was quietly asleep.

A smile as tender as a mother's came into his rugged face, and he stole from the room noiselessly, breathing a blessing as he passed.

And somewhere in France, Denzil and John were thinking of her too, each with great love in his heart.

CHAPTER XV

Harietta Boleski was growing dissatisfied with her life. England was of no amusement to her, and yet Hans insisted upon her staying on. She wanted to go to Paris. The war altogether was a supreme bore and upset her plans!

She had been so successful in her obvious stupid way that Hans had been enabled to transmit the most useful information to his country, which had assisted to foil more than one Allied plan. Harietta saw numbers of old gentlemen who pulled strings in that time, and although they wearied her, she found them easier to extract news from than the younger men. Her method was so irresistible: a direct appeal to the senses, and it hardly ever failed. If only Hans would consent to her returning to Paris, with the help of Ferdinand Ardayre, who was now her slave, she promised wonderful things.

Hans, as a Swedish philanthropic gentleman, had been over to give her instructions once or twice, and at last had agreed to her crossing the Channel.

She told this good news to Ferdinand one afternoon just before Christmas, when he came in to see her in London.

"I'm going to Paris, Ferdie, and you must come too. There's no use in your pretending that England matters to you, and you are of such use to us with your branch business in Holland like that. If I'd thought in the beginning that there was a chance to knock out Germany, I would have been right on this side, because there's no two ways about it, England's the place to have a good time in, but I've information which makes it certain that we shall take Calais in the Spring, and so I guess it's safer to cling to Kaiser Bill--and get it all done soon, then we can enjoy ourselves again. I do pine for a tango! My! I'm just through with this dull time!"

Ferdinand was a rest to her, almost as good as Hans. She had not to be over-refined--she knew that he was on the same level as herself. He amused her too in several ways.

He looked sulky now. It did not suit his plans to go to Paris yet. He was trying to collect information for a game of his own. But where Harietta went he must go, he was besotted about her, and knew that he could not trust her a yard.

He protested a little that they were very well where they were, but as she never allowed any one's wishes to interfere with her plans she only smiled.

"I'm going on Saturday. We have secured a suite at the Universal this time, now that the Rhin is shut up, and it is such a large hotel, you can quite well stay there; Stanislass won't notice you among the crowd."

Ferdinand agreed unwillingly--and just then Verisschenzko came in. He had not seen Madame Boleski since the night at the Carlton, having taken care not to let her know of his further visits to England since.

He looked at Ferdinand Ardayre as though he had been some bit of furniture, and he took up Fou-Chow who was cowering beneath a chair. He did not speak a word.

Harietta talked for every one for a little while, and then she began to feel nervous.

Verisschenzko smiled lazily--he was trying an experiment. The interview could not go on like this; Ferdinand Ardayre would certainly have to go.

Now that Verisschenzko had come, Harietta ardently wished that he would.

The most venomous hate was arising in Ferdinand's resentful soul. He felt that here was a rival to be dreaded indeed. He saw that Harietta was nervous; he had never seen her so before. He shut his teeth and determined to stay on.

Verisschenzko continued his disconcerting silence. Harietta felt that she should presently scream! She took Fou-Chow from Stepan and pinched him cruelly in her exasperation. He gave a feeble squeak and she pushed him roughly down. Animals to her were a nuisance. She disliked them if she had any feeling at all. But Fou-Chow was an adjunct to her toilet sometimes, and was a coveted possession, envied by her many female friends. His tiny, cringing body irritated her though extremely when she was not using him for effect, and he was often kicked and cuffed out of her way.

He showed evident fear of her and ran from her always, so that when she wanted to make a picture with him, she was obliged to carry him in her arms.

Verisschenzko raised one bushy eyebrow, and a sardonic smile came into his eyes.

Madame Boleski saw that she had made a mistake in showing her temper to the dog; it would have given her pleasure then to wring its neck!

The two men sat on. She began to grow so uncomfortable that she could endure it no more.

"You are coming back to dinner, Mr. Ardayre," she remarked at length, "and I want you to get me gardenias to wear, if you will be so kind, and I am afraid you will have to hurry as the shops close soon."

Ferdinand Ardayre rose, rage showing in his mean face, but as he had no choice he said good-bye. Harietta accompanied him to the door, pressing his hand stealthily, then she returned to the Russian with flaming eyes. He had not uttered a word.

"How dare you make me so nervous, sitting there like a log! I won't stand for such treatment--you Bear!"

"Then sit down. Why do you have that Turk with you at all?"

"He is not a Turk; he's an Englishman and a friend of mine. Why, he is the brother of your precious John Ardayre--and they have behaved shamefully to him, poor dear boy."

She was still enraged.

"He is not even a pure Turk--some of them are gentlemen. He is just the scum of the earth, and no blood relation to John Ardayre."

"He will let them know whether he is or not some day! I hear that your bit of bread and butter is going to have a child, and as Ferdie says it can't be John's, I suppose it is yours!"

Verisschenzko's face looked dangerous.

"You would do well to guard your words, Harietta. I do not permit you to make such remarks to me--and it would be more prudent if you warned your friend that he had better not make such assertions either--do you understand?"

Harietta felt some twinge of fear at the strange tone in the Russian's voice, but she was too out of temper to be cowed now.

"Puh!" and she tossed her head. "If the child is a boy Ferdie will have something to say--and as for Amaryllis--I hate her! I'd like to kill her with my own hands."

Verisschenzko rose and stood before her--and there was a look in his eyes which made her suddenly grow cold.

"Listen," he said icily. "I have warned you once and you know me well enough to decide whether I ever speak lightly. I warn you again to be careful of your words and your deeds. I shall warn you no more--if you transgress a third time--then I will strike."

Harietta grew pale to her painted lips.

How would he strike? Not with a stick as Hans would have done, but in some much more deadly way. She changed her manner instantly and began to laugh.

"Darling Brute!"

Verisschenzko knew that he had alarmed her sufficiently, so he sat down in his chair again and lit a cigarette calmly--then he sniffed the air.

"Your mongrel friend uses the same perfume as Stanislass' mistress!"

"Stanislass' mistress?" she had forgotten for the moment.

"Yes--don't you remember we burnt his scented handkerchief the last time we met, because we did not like her taste in perfumes?"

Harietta's ill humour rose again; she was annoyed that she had forgotten this incident. Her instinct of self-preservation usually preserved her from committing any such mistakes. She felt that it was now advisable to become cajoling; also there was something in the face of Verisschenzko and his fierceness which aroused renewed passion in her--it was absurd to waste time in quarrelling with him when in an hour Stanislass might be coming in, so she went over behind his chair and smoothed back his thick dark hair.

"You know that I adore you, darling Brute!"

"Of course--" he did not even turn his head towards her. "Have you had your heart's desire here in England?"

"Before this stupid war came--yes--now I'm through with it. I'm for Paris again."

"I suppose I must have been mistaken, but I thought I caught sight of your handsome German friend in the hall just now?"

"German friend--who?"

"Your *danseur* at the Ardayre ball. I have forgotten his name."

"And so have I."

At that instant Marie appeared at the door and Fou-Chow came from under the chair where he was sheltering and pattered towards her with a glad tiny whine. The maid's eyes rounded with dislike as she looked at her mistress; she realised that the little creature had been roughly treated again. She picked him up and could hardly control her voice into a tone of respectfulness as she spoke:

"Monsieur Insborg demands if he can see Madame in half an hour. He telephoned to Madame but received no reply."

For a second Harietta's eyes betrayed her; they narrowed with alarm, and then she said suavely: "I suppose the receiver was off. No, say I am dining early for the theatre--but to-morrow at five."

The maid inclined her head and left the room silently, carrying Fou-Chow, but as she did so her eyes met Verisschenzko's and their expression suggested to him several things:

"Marie loves the dog--so she hates Harietta. Good--we shall see."

Thus his thoughts ran, but aloud he asked what Harietta meant to do with her life in Paris, and who had been her lovers here?

"You do say such frightful things to me, Stepan," and she tossed her head. "You think that because I took you, I take others! Pah!--and if I do--these Englishmen are peaches, just like little school boys--they'd not harm a fly. But I only love you, Darling Brute--even though we have had a row."

"I know that, of course. I am not jealous, only you have not given me any proofs lately, so I am going to retire from the field. I came to say good-bye."

He looked adorably attractive, Harietta thought--he made her blood run. Ferdinand Ardayre was but an instructed weakling, when one had come through his intricacies there was nothing in him. As a lover he was not worth the Russian's little finger, and the more Verisschenzko eluded her, the higher her passion for him grew; and here he was after months of absence and suggesting that he would leave her for ever! This was not to be borne!

The enraging part was that she would not dare to try to keep him with Hans again upon the scene. She hated Hans once more as she had hated him at the Ardayre ball!

Verisschenzko did not attempt to caress her; he sat perfectly still, nor did he speak.

Harietta could not think how to cope with this new mood; her weariness with the gloom of England and the absence of amusement seemed to render Stepan more than ever desirable. He represented the wild, the strong, the primitive, the only thing she felt that she desired at that moment--and if she let him go to-day he was capable of never coming back to her again. It was worth using any means to keep him on. She knew that she could obtain some show of love from him if she bribed him with bits of news. It would serve Hans right too for daring to turn up so inconveniently!

So she came from behind his chair and sat down on Verisschenzko's knee and commenced to whisper in his ear.

"Now I am beginning to think that you love me again," he announced presently,--"and of course I must always pay for love!"

    *   *   *   *   *

They were seated by the fire in two armchairs when Stanislass came in from the Club before dinner at eight. Harietta had not even remembered that she must dress, so intoxicated with re-awakened passion for Verisschenzko had she become. A man for her must be in the room; her affection could not keep alight in absence. She had revelled in the joy of finding again a complete physical master. She loved him as a tigress may love her tamer, the man with the whip; and the knowledge that she was deceiving Hans and her husband and Ferdinand added a fillip to her satisfaction. But how was she going to be sure to see Stepan again--that was the question which still agitated her. Verisschenzko wished to further examine Ferdinand Ardayre, and so decided to make every one uncomfortable once more by staying on. Stanislass, very nervous with him now, talked fast and foolishly. Harietta fidgeted, and in a moment or two Ferdinand Ardayre was announced.

He reddened with annoyance to see the Russian had not gone; the flowers which he had brought were in a parcel in his hand.

Harietta took them disdainfully without a word of thanks. What a nuisance the creature was after all!--and Stanislass was--and everything and anything was which kept her from being alone with Verisschenzko!

"When are you coming to see me again, Stepan?" she asked, determined not to let him part without some definite future meeting settled.

"I will come back and take coffee with you to-night," he answered unexpectedly.

Harietta was enchanted, she had not hoped for this.

"No one bothers so much about dressing now, stay and dine as you are."

"Yes, do," chimed in Stanislass timidly in Russian, "we should be so charmed."

"Very well--I will dine--but I must change. I shall not be long though. Begin dinner without me, I will join you before the fish." And with no further waste of words he left them.

Harietta pushed Stanislass gently from the room with an injunction to be quick--and then she returned and held out her arms to Ferdinand Ardayre.

"Now you must not be jealous, Ferdie pet, about Verisschenzko," and she patted him. "It is business--I must talk to him to-night; he has an idea that you and I are not favourable to the Allies," and she laughed delightedly, "and I must get him off this notion!"

Ferdinand Ardayre looked sullen; he was burning with jealousy.

"Will you make it up to me afterwards?"

"But, of course, in the usual way!" and with one of her wonderful kisses Harietta went laughing from the room.

Left alone, the young man gave himself a morphine *piqure*, and then sat down and held his head in his hands.

He had heard, as he had told Harietta earlier in the afternoon, that his brother's wife was going to have a child, and he could find no way of proving legally that it could not be John's, so his venom had grown with his impotence.

His mother had said to him once:

"The accursed English will always beat us, my son. Thy real father would have put poison in their coffee. We can only hope for revenge some day. I fear we shall never gain our desires. The old fool whom thou callest father must be sucked dry of everything while he lives, because no quarter will be given us once the breath is out of his body."

Was this true? Must the English always beat him? He remembered his hatred of Denzil while at Eton, and the dog's life he had often led there. Well, he would hit back with an adder's sting when the chance came to him. He would like to see both Ardayres ruined and England herself in the dust, numbed and conquered. All his English life and education had never made him anything but an alien in thought and appearance.

It was his powerlessness which enraged him, but surely the day must come when he could make some of them suffer.

Harietta had not appeared in the hall when Verisschenzko returned dressed, and she even kept all three men waiting for about ten minutes, and then swept in resplendent in yellow brocade and the gardenias, when the clock had struck nine and most of the other diners were having their coffee.

The atmosphere of restraint and depression was a constant source of resentment to her. It was all very well to be dignified and refined for some definite end, like securing an unquestioned position, but it was a weariness of the flesh to have to keep up this role month after month with no excitement or reward, and every now and then she felt that she must break out even in small ways by wearing too gorgeous and unsuitable raiment. She wished that Germany would be quick about winning, then things could settle down and she could begin her social career again.

"It don't amount to a row of pins to the people who want to enjoy themselves, as I do, if their country is beaten or not; it'll all be the same six months after peace is declared, so I'm all for knocking whichever seems feeblest out quickly," she had said to Ferdinand, "and Paris will always be top of the world for clothes and things that one wants, so what do old politics matter?"

She derived some pleasure out of the sensation she created when she went into a restaurant, and she really looked extraordinarily handsome.

The dinner amused her, too; it was entertaining to make Ferdinand jealous. The emotions of Stanislass had ceased to count to her in any way whatsoever.

Verisschenzko had discovered what he required in regard to Ferdinand Ardayre before they went into the hall for coffee--there was nothing further to be gained by having another tete-a-tete with Harietta, so he sat down by Stanislass and suggested that the other two should go on to the Coliseum without them, and Harietta was obliged to depart reluctantly with Ferdinand, having arranged that Stepan should let her know, directly he arrived in Paris, whither he was going in a day or two also.

When she had left them Stanislass Boleski turned melancholy eyes to his old friend, but remained silent.

"Has it been worth it?" Verisschenzko asked, with certain feeling--they had relapsed into Russian.

Stanislass sighed deeply.

"No--far from it--I am broken and finished, Stepan, she has devoured my soul--"

"Why don't you kill her! I should."

The Pole clenched one of his transparent looking hands:

"I cannot--I desire her so--she is an obsession. I cannot work--she leaves me neither time nor brain. But I want her always, she is a burning torment, and a blast, and a sin. I see visions of the chance that I have missed, and then all is obliterated by her voluptuous kisses. I die each day with jealousy and shame. She withholds herself, and I would pay with the blood from my veins to possess her again!"

"You have no longer any delusions about her--you see her as a curse and a vampire?"

Stanislass reddened.

"I see everything, but I know only desire. Stepan, she has dragged me through every degradation. I am a witness of her unfaithfulness. She gives herself to this Turk with hardly a pretence of concealment--I know it--I burn with rage, and I can do nothing. She returns to my arms and I forget everything. I am a most unhappy man and only death can release me, and yet I wish to live because I love her. Each day is fierce longing for her--each night away from her hell--" Tears sprang to his hopeless black eyes and his voice broke with emotion.

Verisschenzko looked at him and a rough pity tempered his contempt.

Here was a case where an indulgence having become master was exacting a hideous toll. But the net was drawing closer and when all the strands were in his hands he would act without mercy.

CHAPTER XVI

When Amaryllis knew that John was going to get a few days' leave at Christmas a strange nervousness took possession of her. The personality of Denzil had been growing more real to her ever since they had parted, in spite of her endeavours to discipline her mind and control all emotion. The thought of him and the thought of the baby were inseparable and were seldom absent from her consciousness. All sorts of wonderful emotions held her, and exalted her imagination until she felt that Denzil was part of her daily life--and with the double interest her love for him grew and grew.

She had only seen John during the day when he had come to bid her good-bye before leaving for the Front, and most of the time they had been surrounded by the de la Paule family. But now she would have to face the fact of living with him again in an intimate relationship.

The thought appeared awful to her. There was something in her nature which resembled that of the bride of King Caudaules. She could not support the idea of belonging now to John; it seemed to her that he must have no rights at all. She had written to him dutifully each week letters about the place and her Committees in the County. She had not once mentioned the coming child.

Denzil's mother had been ill and the visit to Bath had been postponed, and after a fortnight alone at Ardayre she had come up to London. She had too much time to think there.

Stepan had left her a list of books to get and she had been steadily reading them.

How horribly ignorant she had been! She realised that what knowledge she had possessed had never been centralised or brought to any use. She had known isolated histories of Europe, and never had studied them collectively or contemporarily to discover their effect upon human evolution. She had learned many things, and then never employed her critical faculties about them. A whole new world seemed to be opening to her view. She had determined not to be unhappy and not to look ahead, but in spite of these good resolutions she would often dream in the firelight of the joy of being clasped in Denzil's arms.

When she thought of John it was with tolerance more than affection. What did he really mean to her, denuded of the glamour with which she herself had surrounded him?

Practically nothing at all.

She was quite aware that her state of being was rendering all her mental and emotional faculties particularly sensitive, and she did her utmost to remember all Verisschenzko's counsel to discipline herself and remain serene. The morning John was expected to arrive she had a hard fight with herself. She felt very nervous and ill at ease. Above all things, she must not be unkind.

He was bronzed and looked well, he was more expansive also and plainly very glad to see her.

He held her close to him and bent to kiss her lips; but some undefined reluctance came over her, and she moved her head aside.

Something in her resented the caress. Her lips were now for Denzil and for no other man. It was she who was recalcitrant and turned the conversation into everyday things.

The de la Paule family had been summoned for luncheon and the afternoon passed among them all, and then the evening and the tete-a-tete dinner came.

John knocked at the door of her room while she was dressing. Her maid had just finished her hair and she wondered at herself that she should experience a sense of shyness and have to suppress an inclination to refuse to let him come in. And once any of these little intimate happenings would have given her joy!

She kept Adams there, and hurried into her tea-gown and then walked towards the door.

John had not spoken much, but stood by the fire.

How changed things were! Once he had to be persuaded and enticed to stay with her at such moments, and it was he who now seemed to desire to do so, and it was she who discouraged his wishes!

In Amaryllis' mind an agitation grew. What could she say to him presently--if he suggested coming to sleep in her room?

The knowledge in her breast rose as an insurmountable barrier between them.

During dinner she kept the conversation entirely upon his life at the Front--which indeed really interested her. She was not cold or stiff in her manner, but she was unconsciously aloof.

Then they went back into the library, each feeling exceedingly depressed.

When coffee had come and they were quite alone Amaryllis felt she could not stand the strain, and went to the piano. She played for quite a long time all the things she remembered that John liked best. She wanted the music to calm her, and she wanted to gain time. John sat in one of the monster chairs and gazed into the fire. He seemed to see pictures in the glowing coals.

The strange relentless fate which had pursued him always as far as happiness was concerned!

He remembered what his mother had said to him when she lay a-dying with a broken heart.

"John, we cannot see what God means in it all. There must be some explanation because He cannot be unjust. It is because we have missed the point of some lesson, probably, and so are given it again to learn. Do not ever be rebellious, my son, and perhaps some day light will come."

He had read an article in some paper lately ridiculing the theory that we have had former lives, but, after all, perhaps there was some foundation for the belief. Perhaps he was paying in this one for sins in a previous birth. That would account for the seeming inexorableness of the misfortunes which fell upon him now, since common sense told him that in this life such cruel blows were undeserved.

Amaryllis glanced at his face from the piano as she played. It was infinitely sad.

A great pity grew in her heart. What ought she to do not to be unkind?

Presently she finished a soft chord and got up and came to his side.

They were both suffering cruelly--but John was going back to fight. She must have some explanation with him which could make him return to France at peace in a measure. It was cowardly to shirk telling him the truth, and she could not let him go again into danger with this black shadow between them.

He looked up at her and rose from his chair.

"You play so beautifully," he said hastily. "You take one out of oneself. Now it is late and the day has been long. Let us go to bed, dearest child."

Amaryllis stiffened suddenly--the moment that she dreaded had come.

"I would rather that you slept in your dressing-room. I have ordered that to be prepared--"

He looked at her startled--and then he took her hand.

"Amaryllis--tell me everything. Why are you so changed?"

"I'm trying not to be, John."

"You are trying--that proves that you are, if you must try. Please tell me what this means."

She endeavoured to remain calm and not become unhinged.

"It was you yourself who altered me. I came to you all loving and human and you froze me. There is nothing to be done."

"Yes, there is. You know that I love you."

"Perhaps you do, but the family matters more to you than I do, or anything else in the world."

"That may have been so once, but not now," his voice throbbed with feeling.

"Alas!" was all she answered and looked down. John longed to appeal to her--but he was too honest to seek to soften her through the link of the child. Indeed, the thought of it had grown hateful to him. He only knew that he had played for a stake which now seemed worthless. Amaryllis and her love mattered more than any child.

He clenched his hands tightly; the pain of things seemed hard to bear.

Why had he not broken the thongs of reserve which held him long days ago and made love to her in words? But that would have been dishonest. He must at least be true; and he realised now that he had starved her--no matter what his motive had been.

"Amaryllis, tell me everything, please," and he held out his hands and drew her to the sofa and sat down by her side.

She could not control her emotion any longer, and her voice shook as she answered him:

"I know that it was not you--but Denzil, John--and the baby is his, not yours."

His face altered. He had not been prepared to hear this thing and he was stunned.

"Ferdinand is an awful possibility to contemplate there at Ardayre, if you have no son--" She went on, trying to be calm, "but do you not think that you might have told me? Surely a woman has the right to select the father of her child."

John could not answer her. He covered his face with his hands.

"You see it is all pitiful," she continued, her voice deep and broken with almost a sob in it. "Denzil is so like you--it was an easy transition to find that I loved him--because I was only loving the imaginary you I had made for myself. I cannot explain myself and do not make any excuse. There is something in me, whenever I think of the baby, that draws me to Denzil and makes me remember that night. John, we must just face the situation and try to find some way to avoid as much pain as we can. I hate to think it is hurting you, too."

"Did Denzil tell you this?" his voice was icy cold.

"No--it came to me suddenly when I heard him say a word."

"'Sweetheart'!" and now John's eyes flashed. "He called you again 'Sweetheart'!"

"No, he did not--he used the word simply in speaking of a picture--but I recognised his voice then immediately--it is a little deeper than yours."

"When did you see Denzil?"

She told him the exact truth about their meeting and his coming to Ardayre, and how Denzil had endeavoured to keep his word.

"He would never have spoken to me--it was fate which sent him into the train, and then I made him speak--I could not bear it. After I recognised him, I made him admit that it was he. Denzil is not to blame. He left immediately and I have never seen him or heard from him since. It is I alone who must be counted with, John--Denzil will try never to see me again."

John groaned aloud.

"Oh God--the misery of it all!"

"John, I must tell you everything now while we are talking of these things. I love Denzil utterly. I thrill when I think of him; he seems to me my husband, not even only a lover. John, not long ago, when I felt the first movement of the child, I shook with longing for him--I found myself murmuring his name aloud. So you must think what it all means to me, so strongly passionate as I am. But I would never cheat you, John--I had to be honest. I could not go on pretending to be your wife and living a lie."

Tears of agony gathered in John Ardayre's blue eyes and rolled down his cheeks.

He suddenly understood the suffering, that she, too, must be undergoing.

What right had he to have taken this young and loving woman and then to have used her for his own aims, however high?

"Amaryllis--you cannot forgive me. I see now that I was wrong."

But the sympathy which she had felt when she had looked at him from the piano welled up again in Amaryllis's heart and drowned all resentment. She knew that he must be enduring pain greater than hers, so she stretched out her hands to him, and he took them and held them in his.

"Of course, I forgive you, John--but I cannot cease from loving Denzil, that is the tragedy of the thing. I am his really, not yours, even if I never see him again, and that is why we must not make any pretences. John dearest, let us be friends--and live as friends, then everything won't be so hard."

He let her hands drop and got up and paced the room. He was suffering acutely--must he renounce even the joy of holding her in his arms?

"But I love you, Amaryllis--I love you, dearest child--"

And now again she said "Alas!"--and that was all.

"Amaryllis--this is a frightful sacrifice to me--must you insist upon it?"

Then her eyes seemed to flash fire and her cheeks grew rose--and she stood up and faced him.

"I tell you, John, you do not know me. You have seen a well brought up, conventional girl--milk and water, ready to obey your slightest will--I had not found myself. I am a creature as primitive and passionate as a savage"--her breath came in little pants with her great emotion,--"I **could not** belong to two men--it would utterly degrade me, then I do not know what I should become. I love Denzil, body and soul--and while he lives no other man shall ever touch me; that is what passion means to me--fidelity to the thing I love! He is my Beloved and my darling, and I must go away from you altogether and throw off the thought of the family, and implore Denzil to take me when he comes home if you can agree to the only terms I can offer you now."

John bowed his head. Life seemed over for him and done.

Amaryllis came close to him, then she stood on tiptoe and kissed his brow. Her vehemence had died down in her sorrow for his pain.

"John," she whispered softly, "won't you always be my dearest friend? And when the baby comes it will be a deep interest to us both, and you must love it because it is mine and an Ardayre--and the comfort of that must fill our lives. I truly believe that you did everything, meaning it for the best, only perhaps it is dangerous to play with the creation of life--perhaps that is why fate forced me to know."

John drew her to him, he smoothed the soft brown hair back from her brow and kissed her tenderly, but not on the lips--those he told himself he must renounce for evermore.

"Amaryllis,"--his voice was husky still, "yes--I will be your friend, darling--and I will love your child. I was very wrong to marry you, but it was not quite hopeless then, and you were so young and splendid and living--and I was growing to love you, and for these reasons I hoped against hope--and then when I knew that everything was impossible--I felt that I must make it up to you in every other way I could. I don't know how to put things into words, I always was dull, but I thought if I gratified all your wishes perhaps--Ah!--I see it was very cruel. Darling, I would have told you the truth--presently--but then the war came, and the thought of Ferdinand here drove me mad and it forced my hand."

She looked up at him with her sweet true eyes--her one idea was now to comfort him since she need no longer fear.

"John, if you had explained the whole thing to me--I do not know, perhaps I should have agreed with you, for I, too, have much of this family pride, and I cannot bear to think of Ferdinand--or his children which may be, at Ardayre. I might have voluntarily consented--I cannot be sure. But somehow just lately I have been thinking very much about spiritual things, things I mean beyond the material, those great forces which must be all around us, and I have wondered if we are not perhaps too ignorant yet to upset any laws. Perhaps I am stupid--I don't know really. I have only been wondering--but perhaps there are powerful currents connected with laws, whether they are just or unjust, simply because of the force of people's thoughts for hundreds of years around them."

They went to the sofa then and sat down. It made John happier to hear her talk. His strong will was now conquering the outward show of his emotion at last.

"It may be so--"

"You see, supposing anything should happen to Ferdinand," she went on, "then Denzil would have been naturally the next heir--and now--if the child is a boy--"

John started.

"We neither of us thought of that."

"But nothing is likely to happen to Ferdinand; he won't enlist--it is only you, dear John, who are in danger, and Denzil, too--but surely the war cannot go on long now?"

John wondered if he should tell her what he really felt about this, or whether it were wiser to keep her quietly in this hopeful dream of a speedy end. He decided to say nothing; it was better for her health not to agitate her mind--events would speak for themselves, alas, presently.

He talked quietly then of Ardayre and of his boyhood and of its sorrows; he was determined to break down his own reserve, and Amaryllis listened interestedly, and gradually some kind of peace and calm seemed to come to them both, and they resolutely banished the thought of the future, and sought only to think of the present. And then at last John rose and took her hand:

"Go to bed now, dear girl,--and to-morrow I shall have quite conquered all the feelings which could disturb you, and just remember always that I am indeed your friend."

She understood at last the greatness of his sacrifice and the fineness of his soul, and she fell into a passion of weeping and ran from the room.

But John, left alone, sank down into the same chair as he had done once before on the night he was waiting for Denzil, and, as then, he buried his face in his hands.

CHAPTER XVII

The next day they met at breakfast. John had not slept at all and was very pale and Amaryllis's eyes still showed the deepened violet shadows from much weeping. But they were both quite calm.

She came over to John and kissed his forehead with gentle tenderness and then gave him his tea. They tried to talk in a friendly way as of old before any new emotions had come into their lives. And gradually the strain became lessened.

They arranged to go out shopping, and John bought Amaryllis a new emerald ring.

"Green is the colour of hope," she said. "I want green, John, because it will make me think of the springtime and nature, and all beautiful things."

They lunched at a restaurant and in the afternoon went down to Ardayre. John had many things to attend to and would be occupied all the following day.

There had been no Christmas feasting, but there were gifts to be distributed and various other duties and ceremonies to be gone through, although they had missed the Christmas day. Amaryllis tried in every way to be helpful to her husband, and he appreciated her stateliness and sweet manners with all the tenants and people on the estate.

So the four days passed quite smoothly, and the last night of the old year came.

"I don't think that you must sit up for it, dear," John said after dinner. "It will only tire you, and it is always a rather sad moment unless one has a party as we always had in old days."

Amaryllis went obediently to her room and stayed there; sleep was far from her eyes. What was the rest of her life going to be without Denzil? And what of John? Would they settle down into a real quiet friendship when he came back, and the child was born? Or would she have always to feel that he loved her and was for ever suffering pain?

The more she thought the less clear the issue became, and the deeper the sadness in the atmosphere.

At last she slipped down onto the big white bear-skin rug and began to pray.

But when the clock struck midnight, and the New Year bells rang out, a dreadful depression fell upon her, a sense of foreboding and fear.

She tried to tell herself that she was foolish, and it was all caused only because she was so highly strung and sensitive now, on account of her state. But the thought would persist that danger threatened some one she loved. Was it Denzil, or John?

Amaryllis tried to force herself from her unhappy impressions by thinking of what she could do presently in the summer, when she would be quite well again, though her greatest work must always be to try to make John happy, if by then he had come home.

She heard him go into his room at about one o'clock, and then she crept noiselessly to her great gilt bed.

John had waited for the New Year by the cedar parlour fire. The room was so filled with the radiance of Amaryllis that he liked being there.

And he, too, was thinking of what their new life would be should he chance to come through. The ache in his heart would gradually subside, he supposed, but how would he bear the long years, knowing that Amaryllis was thinking of Denzil--and longing for him--and if fate made them meet--what then?

How could he endure to know that these two beings were suffering?

There seemed no clear outlook ahead. But, as he knew only too well death could hardly fail to intervene, and if it should claim Denzil, then he must console Amaryllis' grief. But if happily it could be he who were taken, then their future path would be clear.

He could not forget the third eventuality, that he and Denzil might both be killed. He thought and thought over them all, and at last he decided to add a letter to his will. If he should be killed he would ask Denzil to marry Amaryllis immediately, without waiting for the conventional year. The times were too strenuous, and she must not be left unprotected--alone with the child.

He got up and began the letter to his lawyer, and so the instructions ran:

"I request my cousin Denzil Benedict Ardayre to marry Amaryllis, my wife, as soon as possible after my death, if he can get leave and is still alive. I confide her to his care and ask them both not to let any conventional idea of mourning stand in the way of these, my urgent last commands. And I ask my cousin Denzil, if he lives through the war, to take great care of the bringing up of the child."

He read thus far, and when he came to "the child" he scratched it out and wrote "my child" deliberately, and then he went on to add his wishes for its education, should it be a boy. The will had already amply provided for Amaryllis, so that she would be a rich woman for the rest of her days.

When all this was clearly copied out and sealed up in an envelope addressed to his lawyer, the clock struck twelve.

The silence in the old house was complete; there was no revelry for the first time for many years, even the servants far off in their wing had gone to rest.

It seemed to John that the shadow of sorrow was suddenly removed from him, and as though a weight of care had been lifted from his heart. He could not account for the alteration, but he felt no longer sad. Was it an omen? Was this New Year going to fulfill some great thing after all? A divine peace fell upon him, and then a pleasant sensation of sleep, and he turned out the lights and went softly to his room, and was soon in bed.

And then he slept soundly until late in the morning, and awoke refreshed and serene on New Year's day.

His leave was up on the third of January and he returned to London, but he would not let Amaryllis undergo the fatigue of accompanying him. He said good-bye to her there at Ardayre. She felt extremely sad and unhappy.

Had she done well, after all, to have told John the truth? Should she have borne things as they were and waited until the end of the war? But no, that would have been impossible to her nature. If she might not have Denzil for her lover, she would have no other man.

John's cheerfulness astonished her--it was so uniform, it could not be assumed. Perhaps she did not yet understand him, perhaps in his heart he was glad that all pretences had come to an end.

They had the most affectionate parting. John never was sentimental, and he went off with brave, cheery words, and every injunction that she was to take the greatest care of herself.

"Remember, Amaryllis, that you are the most precious thing on earth to me-- and you must think also of the child."

She promised him that she would carry out all his wishes in this respect and remain quietly at Ardayre until the first of April, when perhaps he could get leave again and then she would go to London for the birth of the baby.

John turned and waved his hand as he went off down the avenue, and Amaryllis watched the motor until it was out of sight, the tears slowly brimming over and running down her cheeks.

She noticed that at the turn in the avenue a telegraph boy passed the car and came straight on. The wire was not for John evidently, so she would wait at the door to see. It proved to be for her, and from Denzil's mother, saying that she was en route for Dorchester, motoring, and would stop at Ardayre on the chance of finding its mistress at home. Amaryllis felt suddenly excited; she had often longed for this and yet in some way she had feared it also. What new emotions might the meeting not arouse?

It was quite early after luncheon that Mrs. Ardayre was announced. Amaryllis had waited in the green drawing room, thinking that she would come. She was playing the piano at the far end to try and lighten her feeling of depression, when the door opened, and to her astonishment quite a young, slight woman came into the room. She was a little lame, and walked with a stick. For a moment Amaryllis thought she must be mistaken, and rose with a vague, but gracious look in her eyes.

Mrs. Ardayre held out her hand and smiled:

"I hope you got my telegram in time," she said cordially. "I felt I must not lose the opportunity of making your acquaintance. My son has been so anxious for us to meet."

"You--you can't be Denzil's mother, surely!" Amaryllis exclaimed. "He is much too old to be your son!"

Mrs. Ardayre smiled again--while Amaryllis made her sit down on the sofa beside her and helped her off with her furs. "I am forty-nine years old, Amaryllis--if I may call you so--but one ought never to grow old in body. It is not necessary, and it is not agreeable to the eye!"

Amaryllis looked at her carefully in the full side light. It was the shape of her face, she decided, which gave her such youth. There were no unsightly bones to cause shadows and the skin was smooth and ivory--and her eyes were bright brown; their expression was very humorous as well as kindly, and Amaryllis was drawn to her at once.

They talked about their desire to know one another and about the family, and the place, and the war--and at last they spoke of Denzil, and Mrs. Ardayre told of what his life was, and his whereabouts now, and then grew retrospective.

"He is the dearest boy in the world," she said. "We have been friends always, and now he will not allow me to be anxious about him. I really think that as far as the frightfulness of things will let him be, he is actually enjoying his life! Men are such queer creatures, they like to fight!"

Amaryllis asked what was her latest news of him, and where he was, and listened interestedly to Mrs. Ardayre's replies:

"The cavalry have not had very much to do lately, fortunately," she remarked. "My husband has just gone back, but I suppose if there is a shortage of men for the trenches, they will be dismounted perhaps."

"I expect so--then we shall have to use all our courage and control our fears."

Amaryllis turned the conversation back to Denzil again, and drew his mother out. She would like to have heard incidents of his childhood and of how he looked when he was a little boy, but she was too timid to ask any deliberate questions. She felt drawn to this lady, she looked so young and human. Perhaps she was not so wonderful in evening dress, but her figure was boyish in its slim spareness--in these serge travelling clothes she hardly looked thirty-five!

She wondered what Denzil had told his mother about her--probably that she was going to have a child, but nothing more.

They talked in the most friendly way for half an hour, and then Amaryllis asked her guest if she would like to come and see the house and especially the picture gallery and the Elizabethan Denzil hanging there.

"It is just my boy!" Mrs. Ardayre cried, when they stood in front of it. "Eyes and all, they are bold and true and so loving. Oh! my dear child, you can't think what a darling he is; from his babyhood every woman has adored him--the nurse maids were his slaves, and my old housekeeper and my maid are like two jealous cats as to who shall do things for him when he comes home. He has that queer quality which can wile a bird off a tree. I daresay I am the silliest of them all!"

Amaryllis listened, enchanted.

"You see he has not one touch of me in him," Mrs. Ardayre went on, "but I was so frantically in love with my husband when he was born, he naturally was all Ardayre. Does it not interest you, Amaryllis, to wonder what your little one, when it comes, will look like? It ought to be pronouncedly of the family, your being also an Ardayre."

"Indeed yes, I am very curious. And how we all hope that it will be a son!"

"Is there a portrait of your husband here? Denzil says they are alike."

"There is one in my sitting room; it is going to be moved in here presently, when mine is done next year. It is by Sargent, almost the last portrait he painted. Let us go there now and see it."

"But there is no likeness," Mrs. Ardayre exclaimed presently, when they had gone to the cedar parlour and were examining the picture of John. "Can you discover it?"

"I thought they were very alike once--but I do not altogether see it now."

Mrs. Ardayre smiled. "I cannot, of course, think any one can compare with my Denzil! And yet I am not a real mother at all! I am totally devoid of the maternal instinct in the abstract! Children bore me, and I am glad I have never had any more. I adore Denzil because he is Denzil. I loved my husband and delighted in being the mother of his son."

"There are the two sorts of women, are not there? The mother woman and the mate woman--we have to be one or the other, I suppose. I hardly yet know to which category I belong," and Amaryllis sighed, "but I rather think that I am like you--the man might matter even more to me than the child, and I know that the child matters to me enormously because of the man. It is all a great mystery and a wonder though."

Beatrice Ardayre looked up at the portrait of John; his stolid face did not give her the impression that he could make a woman, and such a fascinating and adorable creature as Amaryllis, passionately in love with him, or fill her with mysterious feelings of emotion about his child! Now, if it had been Denzil she could have understood a woman's committing any madness for him, but this stodgy, respectable John!

Her bright brown eyes glanced at Amaryllis furtively, and she saw that she was looking up at the picture with an expression of deep melancholy on her face.

There was some mystery here.

She went over again in her mind what Denzil had told her about Amaryllis. It was not a great deal. He had arrived at Bath that time looking very stern and abstracted, and had mentioned rather shortly that he had come down with the head of the family's wife in the train, and had gone on to Ardayre with her, after meeting them the previous night at dinner for the first time.

He had not been at all expansive, but later in the evening when they had sat by her sitting room fire, he had suddenly said something which had startled her greatly:

"Mum--I want you to know Amaryllis Ardayre. I am madly in love with her--she is going to have a baby, and she seems to be so alone."

It must be one of those sudden passions, and the idea seemed in some way to jar a little. Denzil to have fallen in love with a woman whom he knew was going to have a child!

She had said something of this to him, and he had turned eyes full of pain to her and even reproach.

"Mum--you always understand me--I am not a beast, you know--I haven't anything more to say, only I want you to be really kind to her--and get to know her well."

And he had not mentioned the subject again, but had been very preoccupied during all his three days' visit, which state she could not account for by the fact of the war--Denzil, she knew, was an enthusiastic soldier, and to be going out to fight would naturally be to him a keen joy. What did it all mean? And here was this sweet creature speaking of divine love mysteries and looking up at the portrait of her dull, unattractive husband with melancholy eyes, whereas they had sparkled with interest when Denzil was the subject of conversation! Could she, too, have fallen in love with Denzil in one night at dinner and a journey in the train!

It was all very remarkable.

They had tea together in the green drawing room, and by that time they had become very good friends.

Mrs. Ardayre told Amaryllis of the little old manor home she had in Kent--The Moat, it was called, and of her garden and the pleasure it was to her.

"I had about twelve thousand a year of my own, you know," she said, "and ever since Denzil was born I have each year put by half of it, so that when he was twenty-one I was able to hand over to him quite a decent sum that he might be independent and free. It is so humiliating for a man to have to be subservient to a woman, even a mother, and I go on doing the same every year. All the last years of his life my husband was very delicate--he was so badly wounded in the South African War, you know--so we lived very quietly at The Moat and in my tiny house in London. I hope you will let me show you them both one day."

Amaryllis said she would be delighted, and added:

"You will come and see me, won't you? I am going up to our house in Brook Street at the beginning of April, and I am praying that I may have a little son about the first week in May."

Just before Mrs. Ardayre went on to Dorchester, she asked Amaryllis if she had any message to send Denzil--she wanted to watch her face. It flushed slightly and her deep soft voice said a little eagerly:

"Yes--tell him I have been so delighted to meet you, and you are just what he said I should find you!--and tell him I sent him all sorts of good wishes--" and then she became a little confused.

"I should so love a photograph of you--would you give me one, I wonder?" the elder woman asked quickly, to avoid any pause, and while Amaryllis went out of the room to get it, she thought:

"She is certainly in love with Denzil. It could not have been the first time he had seen her--at the dinner--and yet he never tells lies." And she grew more and more puzzled and interested.

When Amaryllis was alone after the motor with Mrs. Ardayre in it had departed, an uncontrollable fit of restlessness came over her. The visit had stirred up all her emotions again; she could not grieve any more about the tragedy of John; her whole being was vibrating with thoughts of Denzil and desire for his presence--she could see his face and feel the joy of his kisses.

At that moment she would have flung everything in life away to rush into his arms!

CHAPTER XVIII

Denzil was wounded at Neuve Chapelle on March 10th, 1915, though not se-riously--a flesh wound in the side. He had done most gallantly and was to get a D.S.O. He had been in hospital for two weeks and was almost well when Amaryllis came up to Brook Street, on the first of April. She had read his name in the list of wounded, and had telegraphed to his mother in great anxiety, but had been reas-sured, and now she throbbed with longing to see him.

To know that soon he would be going back again to the Front, was almost more than she could bear. She was feeling wonderfully well herself. Her splendid consti-tution and her youth made natural things cause her little distress. She was neither nervous nor fretful, nor oppressed with fancies and moods. And she looked very beautiful with her added dignity of mien and perfectly chosen clothes.

Mrs. Ardayre came at once to see her the morning after her arrival, and sug-gested that Denzil should come when out driving that afternoon. Amaryllis tried to accept this suggestion calmly, and not show her joy, and Mrs. Ardayre left, promis-ing to bring her son about four.

Denzil had said to his Mother when he knew that Amaryllis was coming to London:

"Mum, I want to see Amaryllis--please arrange it for me. And Mum, don't ask me anything about it; just leave me there when we drive and come and fetch me when I must go in again."

Mrs. Ardayre was a very modern person, but she could not help exclaiming in a half voice while she sat by her son's bed:

"You know she is going to have a baby in a month, dear boy, perhaps she won't care to see you now."

A flush rose to Denzil's forehead: "Yes, I do know," he said a little hurriedly, "but we are not conventional in these days. I wish to see her; please, darling Moth-er, do what I ask."

And then he had turned the conversation.

So his mother had obediently arranged matters, and at about four in the afternoon left him at the Brook Street door.

Early as it was, Amaryllis had made the tea, and expected to see both Denzil and his mother. The room was full of hyacinths and daffodils, and she herself looked like a spring flower, as she sat on the sofa among the green silk cushions, wrapped in a pale parma violet tea-gown.

The butler announced "Captain Ardayre," and Denzil came in slowly, and murmured "How do you do?"

But as soon as the door was closed upon him, he started forward, forgetting his stiff side.

He covered her hands with kisses, he could not contain his joy; and then he drew back and looked at her with worship and reverence in his blue eyes.

The most mysterious, quivering emotions were coursing through him, mixed with triumph, as he took in the picture she made. This delicate, beautiful creature! And to see her--so!

Amaryllis lowered her head in a sweet confusion; her feelings were no less aroused. She was thrilling with passionate welcome and delicious shyness. Nature was indeed ruling them both, and with a glad "Darling Angel!" Denzil sat down beside her and clasped her in his arms. Then for a few seconds delirious pleasure was all that they knew.

"Let me look at you again, Sweetheart," he ordered presently, with a tone of command and possession in his very deep voice, which caused Amaryllis delight. It made her feel that she really belonged to him.

"To me you have never been so beautiful--and every scrap of you is mine."

"Absolutely yours."

"I had to come--I cannot help whether it is right or wrong. I must go back to the Front as soon as I am fit, and I could not have borne to go without seeing you, darling one."

They had a hundred things to say to each other about themselves--and about the baby, and the next hour was very sacred and wonderful. Denzil was a superlatively perfect lover and knew the immense value of tender words.

He intoxicated Amaryllis' imagination with the moving things he said.

Alas! how many worthy men miss themselves, and make their loved ones miss the best part of life's joys by their mulish silence and refusal to gratify this desire of all women to be ***told*** that they are loved, to have the fact expressed in passionate speech! No deeds make up for this omission.

Denzil had none of these limitations; he said everything which could cajole and excite the imagination. He murmured a hundred affecting tendernesses in her ears. He caressed her--he commanded and mastered her, and then assured her that he was her slave. He was arrogant and humble--arrogant when he claimed her love, humble in his worship. He spoke of the child and what it meant to him that it should be his and hers. He caused her to feel that he was strong and protective and that she was to be cherished and adored. He made pictures of how it would be if he could spend a whole day and night with her presently in June, when she would be quite well, and of how thrilled with interest he would be to see the baby, and that, of course, it ***must*** be exactly like himself! And Amaryllis' eyes, all soft and swimming with emotion answered him.

Naturally, since she loved him so passionately, it would be his image! Had not his own mother accounted for his pronounced Ardayre stamp by her having been so in love with his father--so, of course, this would re-occur! It was all dear to think about!

They spent another hour of divine intoxication, and then the clock struck six.

It sounded like a knell.

Amaryllis gave a little cry.

"Denzil, it is altogether unnatural that you should have to go. To think that you must leave me, and may not even welcome your son! To think that by the law we are sinning, because I am sitting here clasped in your arms! To think that I may not have the joy of showing you the exquisite little clothes, and the pink silk cot--all the things which have given me such pleasure to arrange.... It is all too cruel! You know that eighteenth century engraving in the series of Moreau le Jeune, of the married lovers playing with the darling, teeny cap together! Well, I have it beside my bed, and every day I look at it and pretend it is you and me!"

"Darling--Darling!"--and Denzil fiercely kissed her, he was so deeply moved.

"It is all holy and beautiful, the coming to earth of a soul. It only makes me long to be good and noble and worthy of this wonderful thing. But for us--we who love truly and purely, it has all been turned into something forbidden and wrong."

"Heart of me--I must have some news of you. I cannot starve there in the trenches, knowing that all the letters that should be mine are going to John. My mother is really trustworthy, will you let her be with you as often as you can, that she may be able to tell me how you are, precious one? When the seventh of May comes I shall go perfectly mad with suspense and anxiety. I will arrange that my mother sends me at once a telegram."

"Denzil!" and Amaryllis clung to him.

"It is an impossible situation," and he gave a great sigh. "I shall tell John that I have seen you--I cannot help it, the times are too precarious to have acted otherwise. And afterwards, when the war is over, we must face the matter and decide what is best to be done."

"*I* cannot live without you, Denzil, and that I know."

They said good-bye at last silently, after many kisses and tears, and Denzil came out into the darkening street to his mother in the motor, with white, set face.

"I am a little troubled, dearest boy," she whispered, as they went along. "I feel that there is something underneath all this and that Amaryllis means some great thing in your life--the whole aspect of everything fills me with discomfort. It is unlike your usual, sensitive refinement, Denzil, to have gone to see her--now--"

"I understand exactly what you mean, Mother. I should say the same thing myself in your place. I can't explain anything, only I beg of you to trust me. Amaryllis is an angel of purity and sweetness; perhaps some day you will understand."

She took his hand into her muff and held it:

"You know I have no conventions, dearest, and my creed is to believe what you say, but I cannot account for the situation because of your only having met Amaryllis so lately for the first time. I could understand it perfectly if you had been her lover, and the child was your child, but she has not been married a whole year yet to John!"

Denzil answered nothing--he pressed his mother's hand.

She returned the pressure:

"We will talk no more about it."

"And you will go on being kind?"

"Of course."

Before they reached the hospital door in Park Lane Mrs. Ardayre had been instructed to send an immediate telegram the moment the baby was born, and to comfort and take care of Amaryllis, and tell her son every little detail as to her welfare and about the child.

"I will try not to form any opinion, Denzil; and some day perhaps things will be made plain, for it would break my heart to believe that you are a dishonourable man."

"You need not worry, Mum dearest. Indeed, I am not that. It is just a tragic story, but I cannot say more. Only take care of Amaryllis, and send me news as often as you can."

          *   *   *   *   *

The telegram to say that Amaryllis had a little son came to John Ardayre on the night before he went into the trenches again at the second battle of Ypres on May 9th, 1915. He had been waiting in feverish impatience and expectancy all the day, and, in fact, for three days for news.

His whole inner life since that New Year's night had been strangely serene, in spite of its frightful outward turmoil and stress. He had taken the tumult of Neuve Chapelle calmly, and had come through it and all the beginning of the Ypres battle without a scratch. He had felt that he was looking upon it all from some detached standpoint, and that it in no way personally concerned him.

He had seen Denzil do the splendid thing and he had felt a distinct distress when he had seen him fall wounded.

Denzil was just back now and in the trenches again with the rest of the dismounted cavalry. They might meet in the attack at dawn.

When John read the telegram from his aunt, Lady de la Paule, his emotion was so great that he staggered a little, and a friend standing by in the billet took out his flask and gave him some brandy, thinking that he must have received bad news.

Then it seemed as though he went mad!

The repression of his life appeared to fall from him, he became as a new man. All his comrades were astonished at him, and a Scotch Corporal was heard to remark that it was "na canny--the Captain was fey."

The Ardayres were saved! The family would carry on!

Fondest love welled up in his heart for Amaryllis. If he only came through he would devote his life to showing her his gratitude and showering everything upon her that her heart could desire--and perhaps--perhaps the joy of the baby would make up for the absence of Denzil. This thought stayed with him and comforted him.

Lady de la Paule had wired:

"A splendid little son born 11:45 A.M. seventh May--Amaryllis well--all love."

And an hour or two before this Denzil had also received the news from his Mother. He, too, had grown exalted and thanked God.

So the day that the Germans were to fail at Ypres, and destiny was to accomplish itself for these two men--dawned.

*   *   *   *   *

Of what use to write of that terrible fight and of the gas and the horror and the mud? John Ardayre seemed to bear a charmed life as he led his men "over the top." For an hour wild with exaltation and gladness, he rallied them and cheered them on. The scene of blood and carnage has been too often repeated on other fateful days, and as often well described, when acts of glorious heroism occurred again and again. John had rushed forward to succour a wounded trooper when a shell crashed near them, and he fell to the ground. And then he know what the great thing was the New Year had promised him. For death was going to straighten out matters--John was going beyond. Well, he had never been rebellious, and he knew now that light had come. But the sky above seemed to be darkening curiously, and the terrible noise to be growing dim, when he was conscious that a man was crawling towards him, dragging a leg, and then his eyes opened wildly for an instant, and he saw that it was Denzil all covered with blood.

"Are we both going West, Denzil?" he demanded faintly. "At least I am--" then he gasped a little, while a stream of scarlet flowed from his shattered side.

"I've asked you in a letter to marry Amaryllis immediately--if you get home. I hope your number is not up, too, because she will be all alone. Take care of her, Denzil, and take care of the child...." His voice grew lower and lower, and the last words came in spasms: "There is an Ardayre son, you know--so it's all right. The family is saved from Ferdinand and I am very glad to die."

Denzil tried to get out his flask, but before he could reach John's lips with it he saw that it would be of no avail--for Death had claimed the head of the Family. And above his mangled body John's face wore a look of calm serenity, and his firm lips smiled.

Then things became all vague for Denzil and he remembered nothing more.

CHAPTER XIX

It was more than two months before Denzil was well enough to be brought from Boulogne, and then he had a relapse and for the whole of July was dangerously ill. At one moment there seemed to be no hope of saving his leg, and his mother ate her heart out with anxiety.

And Amaryllis, back at Ardayre with the little Benedict, wept many tears.

John's death had deeply grieved her. She realised his steadfast kindness and affection for her. He had written her a letter just before the battle had begun--a short epistle telling her calmly that the chances would be perhaps even for any man to come out of it alive--and assuring her of his greatest devotion.

"I know that Denzil went to see you, my dear little girl. He has told me about it. And I know that you love each other. There is only one chance for us in the future--and that lies with the child. It may be that when it comes to you it may fill your life and satisfy you. This is my prayer--otherwise we must see what can be arranged about things; because I cannot allow you to be unhappy. You were an innocent factor in all this, and it would be unjust that you should be hurt."

How good and generous John had always been.

And his letter to his lawyers! To make things smooth for her--and for Denzil--how marvellously kind!

Her mourning for John was real and deep, as it would have been for a brother. But during the month of intense anxiety about Denzil everything else was numbed, even her interest in her son.

By the end of August he was out of danger, although little hope was entertained that he would ever walk easily. But this was a minor thing--and gradually it began to be some consolation to the two women who loved him to know that he was safely wounded and would probably not be fit for active service again for a very long time.

They wrote letters to one another, but they decided not to meet. Six months must elapse at least, they both felt--even in spite of John's commands.

Another shell must have fallen not far off, for his body was never found--only his field glasses, broken and battered. And there would have been no actual information about his death had not Denzil seen him die.

       *   *   *   *   *

Harietta Boleski and Stanislass and Ferdinand Ardayre had remained in Paris, with visits to Fontainebleau.

When John had been killed, Harietta had been extremely perturbed.

"Now Stepan will be able to marry that odious bit of bread and butter, and he is sure to do it after the year!" This thought rankled with her and embittered everything. Nothing pleased her. She grew more than ever rebellious at the dullness she had to live in. War was an imposition which ought not to be tolerated and she often told Hans so. At last she grew to take quite an interest in her spying for lack of more agreeable things to do.

And so the months went by and November came, and a madness of jealousy was gradually augmenting in Harietta for Amaryllis Ardayre.

Verisschenzko had gone to Russia in September, and she was convinced that he loved Amaryllis and that the child was his child. She could not conceive of a spiritual devotion, and something had altered all Stepan's ways. From the moment he returned to Paris until he had left she had tried and been unable to invoke any response in him, and she had felt like a foiled tigress when another has eaten her prey.

As the impossibility of moving him forced itself upon her unwilling understanding, so the wildest passion for him grew, and when he left in September she was quite ill for a week with chagrin; then she became moody and more than ever capricious, and made Stanislass' life a hell, while Ferdinand Ardayre had little less misery to endure.

An incident late in November caused her jealousy to burst into flame.

She heard that Verisschenzko had returned from Russia and she went to his rooms to see him. The Russian servant who was accustomed to receive her was there waiting for his master who had not yet arrived. Without a word she passed the old man when he opened the door, and made her way into the sitting room, and then into the bedroom beyond. She did not believe that Stepan was not there and wanted to make sure. It was empty but a light burned before an Ikon, the doors of which were closed.

Curiosity made Harietta go close and examine it. She knew the room so well and had never seen it there before. The table beneath it was arranged like an altar, and the Ikon was let in to the carved boiserie of the wall. It must have been since he had parted with her that this ridiculous thing had been done! She had not entered his *appartement* since June. She felt angry that the shrine should be closed and that she could not look upon it, for it must certainly be something which Verisschenzko prized.

She bent nearer and shook the little doors; they resisted her, and her temper rose. Then some force seemed to propel her to commit sacrilege. She shook and shook and tore at the golden clasp, her irritation giving strength and cunning to her hands; and at last the small bolt came undone and the doors flew open--and an exquisitely painted modern picture of the Virgin disclosed itself, holding the Christ child in her arms. But for all the saintliness in the eyes of Mary, the face was an exact portrait of Amaryllis Ardayre!

A frenzy of rage seized Harietta. Her rival reigned now indeed! This was positive proof to her, not of spiritual meaning--not of the mystic, abstract aloofness of worship which lay deep in Stepan's nature and had caused him to have Amaryllis transfigured into the symbol of purity, a daily reminder that she must always be for him the lady of his soul--such things had no meaning for Harietta. The Ikon was merely a material proof that Verisschenzko loved Amaryllis--and, of course, as soon as the year of mourning should be over he would make her his wife.

She trembled with passionate resentment. Nothing had ever moved her so forcibly. She took out her pearl hatpin and stabbed out the eyes of the Virgin, almost shaking with passion, and scratched and obliterated the face of the Christ child. This done, she extinguished the little lamp and slammed to the doors.

She laughed savagely as she went back into the sittingroom.

"The Virgin indeed!--and *his* child!--well, I've taught him!" and she flung past the Russian servant with a look which was a curse, so that the old man crossed himself and quickly barred the entrance door, when she stamped off down the stairs.

Arrived in her gilded salon at the Universal, she would like to have wrung some one's neck. She had never been so full of rage in her life. She did find a little satisfaction in a kick at Fou-Chow, who fled whining to his faithful Marie who had come in to carry away her mistress' sable cloak.

The maid's face became thunderous. A look of sullen hate gleamed in her dark eyes.

"She will kick thee, my angel, just once too often," she murmured to the wee creature when she had carried him from the room. "And then we shall see, thy Marie knows that which may punish her some day soon!"

Harietta, quite indifferent to these matters, telephoned immediately to Ferdinand Ardayre.

He must come to her instantly without a moment's delay! And she stamped her foot.

A plan which might give her some satisfaction to execute had evolved itself in her brain.

He was in his room in another part of the building, and hastened to obey her command. She was livid with anger and seemed to have grown old.

She went over and kissed him voluptuously and then she began:

"Ferdie," and she whispered hoarsely, "now you have got to do something for me. You are not going to let the child of Verisschenzko be master of Ardayre! We are going to gain time and perhaps some day be able to do away with it. Now I have got a plan which will lighten your heart."

She knew that she could count upon him, for since the birth of the little Benedict and the death of John, Ferdinand had stormed with threats of vengeance, while knowing his impotency.

His life with Harietta had grown a torment and a hell--but with every fresh unkindness and pang of jealousy she caused him, his low passion for her increased. He knew that she loved Verisschenzko, whom he hated with all his might--and if she now proposed to hurt both his enemies, he would assist her joyfully.

"Tell it me," he begged.

So she drew him to the sofa and picked up a block and pencil.

"Do you possess any of the writing of your dead brother, John, or if you don't, can you get some from anywhere?"

Ferdinand's face blazed with excitement. What was she going to suggest?

"I always keep one letter--in which he ordered me never to address him and told me I was not of his blood but was a mongrel Turk."

"That is splendid--where is it? Have you got it here?"

"Yes, in my despatch box. I'll go and fetch it now."

"Very well. I will get rid of Stanislass for the evening and we can have some hours alone--and you will see if I don't help you to worry them hideously, Ferdie, even if that is all we can do!"

And when he had left her presence, she paced the room excitedly.

"It will prevent Stepan's marrying her at all events for; a long time."

The thought that she had lost Verisschenzko completely unbalanced her. It was the first time in her life that she had had to relinquish a man. She hated to have to realise how highly he must hold Amaryllis. He seemed the only thing she wanted now in life, and she knew that he was quite beyond her, and that indeed he had never been hers; the one human being whom she had attracted and yet never been able to intoxicate and draw against his will. She went over all their past meetings. With what supreme insolence he had invariably treated her--even in moments when he permitted himself to feel passion! And how she adored him! She would have crawled to him now on the ground. She had not known she could feel so much. Every animal, sensual desire made her throb with rage. She would have torn the flesh from Amaryllis' face had she been there, and thrust her hatpin into her real eyes.

But the spoke should be put in the wheel of Verisschenzko's marrying her! And perhaps some other revenge would come. Hans?--Hans should be made to carry the scheme through--Hans and Ferdinand. She dug her nails into the palms of her hands. No wild animal in its cage could have felt more rage.

Then when Ferdinand returned with John's letter, she controlled herself and sat down at the table beside him and supervised his attempts at copying the writing, while she unfolded the details of her scheme.

"You know John's body was never found," she informed him presently. "I heard all the details from a man who was there--they only picked up his glasses and his boot. He could very well have been taken prisoner by the Germans and be in hospital there, too ill to have written for all this time. Now think how he ought to word his first letter to his precious bread and butter wife!"

"There must only be the fewest words, because I don't know what terms they were on. I think a postcard, if we get one, would be the best thing."

"Of course?--I have some one who can see to that--it will be worth waiting the week for--we'll procure several, and meanwhile you must practise his hand."

At the end of half an hour a very creditable forgery had been secured, and the two jealous beings felt satisfied with their work for the time.

CHAPTER XX

It had been arranged that Denzil and his mother should spend Christmas with Amaryllis at Ardayre. Both felt that it was going to be the most wonderful moment when they should meet. There were no obstacles now to their happiness and everything promised to be full of joy. The months which had gone by since John's death had been turning Amaryllis into a more serene and forceful being. The whole burden of the estate had fallen upon her young shoulders and she had endeavoured to carry it with dignity and success--and yet have time to spare for her war organisations in the county. She had developed extraordinarily and had grown from a very pretty girl into a most beautiful young woman. What would Denzil think of her? That was her preoccupation--and what would he think of the baby Benedict?

The great rooms at Ardayre were shut up except the green drawing room, and she lived in her own apartments, the cedar parlour being her chief pleasure. It was now filled with her books and all the personal belongings which expressed her taste. The nurseries for the heir were just above.

Her guests were to be there on the twenty-third of December, and when the hour came for the motor to arrive from the station Amaryllis grew hot and cold with excitement. She had made herself look quite exquisite in a soft black frock, and her heart was beating almost to suffocation when she heard the footsteps in the hall. Then the green drawing room door opened and Colonel and Mrs. Ardayre were announced and were immediately greeted by the great tawny dogs and then by their mistress. A pang contracted her heart when she caught sight of Denzil--he was so very pale and thin, and he walked painfully and slowly with a stick. It was only a wreck of the splendid lover who had come to Ardayre before. But he was always Denzil of the ardent eyes and the crisp bronze hair!

They were people of the world, and so the welcoming speeches went off easily, and they sat round the tea-table with its singing kettle and its delectable buns and Devonshire cream, and Amaryllis was gracious and radiant and full of dignity and charm. But inwardly she felt deliciously shy and happy.

They had neither met nor written any love letters since the April day when they had parted in Brook Street, which now seemed to be an age away.

Her attraction for Denzil had increased a hundredfold. He thought as she sat there pouring out the tea, of how he would woo her with subtlety before he would claim her for his own. He was stimulated by her sweet shyness and her tender aloofness. The tea seemed to him to be interminably long and he wished for it to end.

Mrs. Ardayre behaved with admirable tact; she spoke of all sorts of light and friendly things, and then asked about the baby. Was he not wonderful, now at seven months old!

The lovely vivid pink deepened in Amaryllis' smooth velvet cheeks, and her grey eyes became soft as a doe's.

"You shall see him in the morning--he will be asleep now. Of course, to me he is wonderful, but I daresay he is only an ordinary child."

She had peeped at Denzil and had seen that his face fell a little as she said they should only see the baby the next day, and she had felt a wave of joy. She knew that she meant to take him up quietly presently--just he and she alone!

After they had finished tea, Mrs. Ardayre suggested that she should go to her room.

"I am tired, Amaryllis, my dear," she announced cheerily,--"and I shall rest for an hour before dinner."

"Come then and I will show you both your rooms."

They came up the broad staircase with her, Denzil a step at a time, slowly, and at the top she stopped and said to him:

"Perhaps you will remember that is the door of the cedar parlour at the end of the passage--you will find me there when I have installed your mother comfortably. Your room is next to hers," and she pointed to two doors through the archway of the gallery. Then she went on with Mrs. Ardayre.

Some contrary nervousness made her remain for quite a little while.

Was Cousin Beatrice sure that she was comfortable? Had she everything she wanted? Her maid was already unpacking, and all was warm and fresh scented with lavender and bowls of violets on the dressing table.

"My dear child, it is Paradise, and you are a perfect angel--I shall revel in it after the cold journey down."

So at last there was no excuse to stay longer, and Amaryllis left the room; but in the passage it seemed as though her knees were trembling, and as she passed the top of the staircase she leaned for a second or two on the balustrade.

The longed for moment had come!

When she opened the door of the cedar parlour, with its soft lamps and great glowing logs, she saw Denzil was already there, seated on the sofa beside the fire.

She ran to him before he could rise, the movement she knew was pain to him--and she sank down beside him and held out her hands.

"Beloved darling!" he whispered in exaltation, and she slipped forward into his arms.

Oh! the bliss of it all! After the months of separation, and the horrible trenches and the battles and the suffering, the days and nights of agonising pain! It seemed to Denzil that his being melted within him--Heaven itself had come.

They could not speak coherently for some moments, everything was too filled with holy joy.

"At last! at last!" he cried presently. "Now we shall part no more!"

Then he had to be assured that she loved him still.

"It is I who must take care of you now, Denzil, and I shall love to do that," she cooed.

"I have not thought much of the hurt," he answered her, "for all these months I have just been living for this day, and now it has come, darling one, and I can hardly believe that it is true, it is so absolutely divine--"

They could not talk of anything but themselves and love for an hour, they told each other of their longings and anxieties--and at last they spoke of John.

"He was so splendid," Denzil said, "unselfish to the very end," and then he described to Amaryllis how he actually had died, and of his last words, and their thought for her.

"If he could see us, I think that he would be glad that we are happy."

"I know that he would," but the tears had gathered in her eyes.

Denzil stroked her hand gently; he did not make any lover's caress, and she appreciated his understanding, and after a little she leaned against his arm.

"Denzil--when we live here together, we must always try to carry out all that John would have wished to do. It meant his very soul--and you will help me to be a worthy mother of the Ardayre son."

She had not spoken of the child before--some unaccountable shyness had restrained her, even in their fondest moments. And yet the thought had never been absent from either. It had throbbed there in their hearts. It was going to be so exquisite to whisper about it presently!

And Denzil had waited until she mentioned this dear interest. He did not wish to assume any rights, or take anything for granted. She should be queen, not only of his heart, but of everything, until she should herself accord him authority.

But his eyes grew wistful now as he leaned nearer to her.

"Darling, am I not going to be allowed to see--my son!"

Then, with a cry, Amaryllis bent forward and was clasped in his arms. All her wayward shyness melted, and she poured forth her delight in the baby--their very own!

"You will see that he is just you, Denzil,--as we knew that he would be, and now I will go and fetch him for you and bring him here, because the stairs up to the nursery are so steep they might hurt you to climb."

She left him swiftly, and was not long gone, and Denzil sat there by the fire trembling with an emotion which he could not have described in words.

The door opened again and Amaryllis returned with the tiny sleeping form, in its long white nightgown and wrapped in a great fleecy shawl.

She crept up to him very softly. The little one was sound asleep. She made a sign to Denzil not to rise, and she bent down and placed the bundle tenderly in his arms.

Then they gazed at the little face together with worshipping eyes.

It was just a round pink and white cherub like thousands of others in the world; the very long eyelashes, sweeping the sleep-flushed cheeks, and minute rings of bronze-gold hair curling over the edge of the close cambric cap; but it seemed to those two looking at it to be unique, and more beautiful than the dawn.

"Isn't he perfect, Denzil!" whispered Amaryllis, in ecstasy.

"Marvellous!" and Denzil's voice was awed.

Then the wonder and the divinity of love and its spirit of creation came over them both and a mist of deep feeling grew in both their eyes.

    *   *   *   *   *

At dinner they were all so happy together. Mrs. Ardayre was a note of harmony anywhere. She had gradually grown to understand the situation in the months of her son's recovering from his wounds and although no actual words had passed between them Denzil felt that his mother had divined the truth and it made things easier.

Afterwards, in the green drawing room, Amaryllis played to them and delighted their ears, and then they went up to the cedar parlour and sat round the fire and talked and made plans.

If it should be quite hopeless that Denzil could ever return to the front, or be of service behind the lines, he meant to enter Parliament. The thought that his active soldiering was probably done was very bitter to him, and the two women who loved him tried to create an enthusiasm for the parliamentary idea. The one certainty was that his adventurous spirit would never remain behind in the background, whatever occurred.

They would be married at the beginning of February, they decided. The whole of their world knew of John's written wishes, and no unkind comments would be likely to arise.

And when Beatrice Ardayre left them alone to say good-night to each other, Denzil drew Amaryllis back to his side!

"I think the world is going to be a totally new place, darling--after the war. If it goes on very long the gradual privation and suffering and misery will create a new order of things, and all of us should be ready to face it. Only fools and weaklings cling to past systems when the on-rolling wave has washed away their uses. Whatever seems for the real good of England must be one's only aim, even if it means abandoning what was the ideal of the Family for all these hundreds of years. You will advance with me, Sweetheart, will you not, even if it should seem to be a chasm we are crossing?"

"Denzil, of course I will."

He sighed a little.

"The old order made England great--but that cycle is over for all the world--and what we shall have to do is to stand steady and try to direct the new on-rush, so that it makes us greater and does not sweep civilisation into darkness, as when Rome fell. It may be a fairly easy matter because, as Stepan says, we have got such fundamental common sense. It would be much less hard if the people at the top were really courageous and unhampered by trying to secure votes, or whatever it is, which makes them wobble and surrender at the wrong moment. If the politicians could have that dogged, serene steadfastness which the Tommies, and almost every man has in the trenches, how supreme we should be--!"

"I hope so, but one must have vision as well so that one can look right ahead and not stumble over retained old prejudices; people so often want a thing and yet have not will enough to eliminate qualities in themselves which must obviously prevent their obtaining their desire."

Denzil was not looking at her now, he was gazing ahead with his blue eyes filled with light, and she saw that there was something far beyond the physical magnetism which drew her to him, and a pride and joy filled her. She would indeed be his helpmate in all his undertakings and striving for noble ends. They talked for some time of these things and their plans to aid in their fulfilment, and then they gradually spoke of Verisschenzko and Amaryllis asked what was the latest news--he was in Russia, she supposed.

"Stepan will be arriving in London next week. I heard from him to-day. Won't you ask him down, darling, to spend the New Year with us here--it would be so good to see the dear old boy again."

This was agreed upon, and then they drifted back to lovers' whisperings, and presently they said a fond good-night.

*   *   *   *   *

Christmas Day of 1915, and the weeks which followed were like some happy dream for Denzil and Amaryllis. Each hour seemed to discover some new aspect which caused further understanding and love to augment. They spent long late afternoons in the cedar parlour dipping into books and a delicious pleasure was for Amaryllis to be nestled in Denzil's arms on the sofa while he read aloud to her in his deep, magnetic voice.

Beatrice Ardayre at this period was like a pleased mother cat purring in the sun while her kittens gambol. Her well-beloved was content, and she was satisfied. She always seemed to be there when wanted and yet to leave the lovers principally to themselves.

Another of their joys was to motor about the beautiful country, exploring the old, old churches and quaint farmhouses and manors with which North Somerset abounds; and they went all over the estate also and saw all the people who were their people and their friends. The union was thoroughly approved of, and although the engagement was not to be officially announced until after the New Year it was quite understood, as the tenants had all heard of John's instructions in his will. But perhaps the most supreme joy of all was when they could play with the baby Benedict together alone for half an hour before he went to bed. Then they were just as foolish and primitive as any other two young things with their firstborn. He was a very fine and forward baby and already expressed a spirit and will of his own, and it always gave Denzil the very strangest thrill when he seized and clung firmly to one of his fingers with his tiny, strong, chubby hand. And over all his qualities and perfections his parents then said wonderful things together!

Every subtle and exquisite pleasure, mystical, symbolical and material, which either had ever dreamed of as connected with this living proof of love, was realised for them. And to know that soon, soon, they would be united for always--wedded--not merely engaged. Oh! that was glorious--when passion need be under no restraint--when there need be no good-night!

For in this the chivalry of Denzil never failed--and each day they grew to respect each other more.

Verisschenzko was to arrive in time for dinner on the last day of the old year. That afternoon was one of even unusually perfect happiness--motoring slowly round the park and up on to the hills in Amaryllis' little two-seater which she drove herself. They got out at the top and leaned upon a gate from which they seemed to be looking down over the world. Peaceful, smiling, prosperous England! Miles and miles of her fairest country lay there in front of them, giving no echo of war.

"If we had been born sixty years ago, Denzil, what different thoughts this view would be creating in our minds. We would have no speculation--no uncertainty--we should feel just happy that it is ours and would be ours for ever! The world was asleep then!"

"Stepan would say that it was resting before the throes of struggle must begin. Now we are going to face something much greater than the actual war in France, but if we are strong we ought to come through. We have always been saner than other peoples, so perhaps our upheaval will be saner too."

"Whatever there is to face, we shall be together, Denzil, and nothing can really matter then--and we must make our little Benedict armed for the future, so that he will be fitted to cope with the conditions of his day."

"Look there at the blue distance, darling, could anything be more peaceful? How can anyone in the country realise that not two hundred miles away this awful war is grinding on?"

Denzil put an arm round her and drew her close to him and clasped her fondly.

"But just for a little we must try to forget about it. I never dreamed of such perfect happiness as we are having, Sweetheart,--my own!"

"Nor I, Denzil,--I am almost afraid--"

But he kissed her passionately and bade this thought begone. Afraid of what? Nothing mattered since they would always be together. February would soon come, and then they would never part again.

So the vague foreboding passed from Amaryllis' heart, and in fond visionings they whispered plans for the spring and the summer and the growing years. And so at last they returned to the house and found the after-noon post waiting for them. Filson had just brought it in and Amaryllis' letters lay in a pile on her writing table.

There happened to be none for Denzil and he went over to the fireplace and was stroking the head of Mercury, the greatest of the big tawny dogs, when he was startled by a little ominous cry from his Beloved, and on looking up he saw that she had sunk into a chair, her face deadly pale, while there had fluttered to the floor at her feet a torn envelope and a foreign looking postcard.

What could this mean?

CHAPTER XXI

Verisschenzko had come straight through from Petrograd to England. He had been delayed and had never returned to Paris since September. He knew nothing of Harietta's sacrilege as yet. But he had at last accumulated sufficient proof against her to have her entirely in his hands.

He thought over the whole matter as he came down in the train to Ardayre. She was a grave danger to the Allies and had betrayed them again and again. He must have no mercy. Her last crimes had been against France, her punishment would be easier to manage there.

The strain of cruelty in his nature came uppermost as he reviewed the evil which she had done. Stanislass' haunted face seemed to look at him out of the mist of the half-lit carriage. What might not Poland have accomplished with such a leader as Boleski had been before this baneful passion fell upon him! Then he conjured up the? imaged faces of the brave Frenchmen who were betrayed by Harietta to Hans, and shot in Germany.

A spy's death in war time was not an ignoble one, and they had gone there with their lives in their hands. Had Harietta been true to that side, and had she been acting from patriotism, he could have desired to save her the death sentence now. But she had never been true; no country mattered to her; she had given to him secrets as well as to Hans! Then he laughed to himself grimly. So her *danseur* at the Ardayre ball was the first husband! The man who used to beat her with a stick--and who had let her divorce him in obedience to the higher command!

How clever the whole thing was! If it had not all been so serious, it would have been interesting to allow her to live longer to watch what next she would do, but the issues at stake were too vital to delay. He would not hesitate; he would denounce her to the French authorities immediately on his return to Paris, and without one qualm or regret. She had lived well and played "crooked"--and now it was meet that she should pay the price.

Filson announced him in the green drawing room when he reached Ardayre, but only Denzil rose to greet him and wrung his hand. He noticed that his friend's face looked stern and rather pale.

"I'm so awfully glad that you have come, Stepan," and they exchanged hand-shakes and greetings. "You are about the only person I should want to see just now, because you know the whole history. Something unprecedented has happened. A communication has come apparently from John to Amaryllis from a prisoners' camp in Germany, and yet as far as one can be certain of anything I am certain that I saw him die--"

Verisschenzko was greatly startled. What a frightful complication it would make should John be alive!

"The letter--merely a postcard enclosed in an envelope--came by this after-noon's post--and as you can understand, it has frightfully upset us all. It is a sort of thing about which one cannot analyse one's feelings. John had a right to his life and we ought to be glad--but the idea of giving up Amaryllis--of having all the suffering and the parting again--Stepan, it is cruelly hard."

Verisschenzko sat down in one of the big chairs, and Euterpe, the lesser tawny dog, came and pushed her nose into his hand. He patted her silky head absently. He was collecting his thoughts; the shock of this news was considerable and he must steady his judgment.

"John wrote to her himself, you say? It is not a message through a third person--no?"

"It appears to be in his own writing." Denzil stood leaning on the mantelpiece, and his face seemed to grow more haggard with each word. "Merely saying that he was taken prisoner by the enemy when they made the counter attack, and that he had been too ill to write or speak until now. I can't understand it--because they did not make the counter attack until after I was carried in--and even though I was unconscious then, the stretcher bearers must have seen John when they lifted me if he had been there. Nothing was found but his glasses and we concluded another shell had burst somewhere near his body after I was carried in. Stepan, I swear to God I saw him die."

"It sounds extraordinary. Try to tell me every detail, Denzil."

So the story of John's last moments was gone over again, and all the most min-ute events which had occurred. And at the end of it the two solid facts stood out incontrovertibly--John's body was never found, but Denzil had seen him die.

"How long will it take to communicate with him, I wonder? We can through the American Ambassador, I suppose, because he gives no address. It must be awful for him lying there wounded with no news. I say this because I suppose I must accept his own writing, but I, cannot yet bring myself to believe that he can be alive."

Verisschenzko was silent for a moment, then he asked:

"May I see my Lady Amaryllis?"

"Yes, she told me to bring you to her as soon as I should have explained to you the whole affair. Come now."

They went up the stairs together, and they hardly spoke a word. And when they reached the cedar parlour Denzil let Verisschenzko go in in front of him.

"I have brought Stepan to you," he told Amaryllis. "I am going to leave you to talk now."

Amaryllis was white as milk and her grey eyes were disturbed and very troubled. She held out her two hands to Verisschenzko and he kissed them with affectionate worship.

"Lady of my Soul!"

"Oh! Stepan,--comfort me--give me counsel. It is such a terrible moment in my life. What am I to do?"

"It is indeed difficult for you--we must think it all out--"

"Poor John--I ought to be glad that he is alive, and I am--really--only, oh! Stepan, I love Denzil so dearly. It is all too awfully complicated. What so greatly astonishes me about it is that John has not written deliriously, or as though he has lost his memory, and yet if we had carried out his instructions and wishes we should be married now, Denzil and I,--and he never alludes to the possibility of this! It is written as though no complications could enter into the case--"

"It sounds strange--may I see the letter?"

She got up and went over to the writing table and returned with a packet and the envelope which contained the card. It was not one which prisoners use as a rule; it had the picture of a German town on it and the postmark on the envelope was of a place in Holland. Verisschenzko read it carefully:

"I have been too ill to write before--I was taken prisoner in the counter attack and was unconscious. I am sending this by the kindness of a nurse through Holland.

Everyone must have believed that I was dead. I am longing for news of you, dearest. I shall soon be well. Do not worry. I am going to be moved and will write again with address.

"All love,--

"JOHN."

The writing was rather feeble as a very ill person's would naturally be, but the name "John" was firm and very legible.

"You are certain that it is his writing?"

"Yes"--and then she handed him another letter from the packet--John's last one to her. "You can see for yourself--it is the same hand."

Stepan took both over to the lamp, and was bending to examine them when he gave a little cry:

"Sapristi!"--and instead of looking at the writings he sniffed strongly at the card, and then again. Amaryllis watched him amazedly.

"The same! By the Lord, it is the work of Ferdinand. No one could mistake his scent who had once smelt it. The muskrat, the scorpion! But he has betrayed himself."

Amaryllis grew paler as she came close beside him.

"Stepan, oh, tell me! What do you mean?"

"I believe this to be a forgery--the scent is a clue to me. Smell it--there is a lingering sickly aroma round it. It came in an envelope, you see,--that would preserve it. It is an Eastern perfume, very heavy,--what do you say?"

She wrinkled her delicate nose:

"Yes, there is some scent from it. One perceives it at first and then it goes off. Oh, Stepan, please do not torture me. Can you be quite sure?"

"I am absolutely certain that whether it is in John's writing or not, Ferdinand, or some one who uses his unique scent, has touched that card. Now we must investigate everything."

He walked up and down the room in agitation for a few moments; talking rapidly to himself--half in Russian--Amaryllis caught bits. "Ferdinand--how to his advantage? None. What then? Harietta? Harietta--but why for her?"

Then he sat down and stared into the fire, his yellow-green eyes blazing with intelligence, his clear brain balancing up things. But now he did not speak his thoughts aloud.

"She is jealous. I remember--she imagined that it is my child. She believes I may marry Amaryllis. It is as plain as day!"

He jumped up and excitedly held out his hands.

"Let us fetch Denzil," he cried joyously. "I can explain everything."

Amaryllis left the room swiftly and called when she got outside his door: "Denzil--do come."

He joined them in a second or two--there as he was, in a blue silk dressing gown, as he had just been going to dress for dinner.

He looked from one face to the other anxiously and Stepan immediately spoke.

"I think that the card is a forgery, Denzil. I believe it to have been written by Ferdinand Ardayre--at the instigation of Harietta Boleski. She would have means to obtain the postcard, and have it sent through Holland too."

"But why--why should she?" Amaryllis exclaimed in wonderment. "What possible reason could she have for wishing to be so cruel to us. We were always very nice to her, as you know."

Verisschenzko laughed cynically.

"She was jealous of you all the same. But Denzil, I track it by the scent. I know Ferdinand uses that scent," he held out the card. "Smell."

Denzil sniffed as Amaryllis had done.

"It is so faint I should not have remarked it unless you had told me--but I daresay if it was a scent one had smelt before, one would be struck by it! But how are you going to prove it, Stepan? We shall have to have convincing proof--because I am the only witness of poor John's death, and it could easily be said that I am too deeply interested to be reliable. For God's sake, old friend, think of some way of making a certainty."

"I have a way which I can enforce as soon as I reach Paris. Meanwhile say nothing to any one and put the thought of it out of your heads. The evidence of your own eyes convinced you that John is dead; you found it difficult to accept that he was alive even when seeing what appeared to be his own writing, but if I assure you that this is forged you can be at peace. Is it not so?"

Amaryllis' lips were trembling; the shock and then this counter shock were unhinging her. She was horrified at herself that she should not catch at every straw to prove John was alive, instead of feeling some sense of relief when Verisschenzko protested that the postcard was a forgery.

Poor John! Good, and kind, and unselfish. It was all too agitating. But was just life such a very great thing? She knew that had she the choice she would rather be dead than separated now from Denzil. And if John were really to be alive--what misery he would be obliged to suffer, knowing the situation.

"Quite apart from what to me is a convincing proof, the scent," Verisschenzko went on, "the card must be a forgery because of John's seeming oblivion of the possibility that you two might have already carried out his wishes. All this would have been very unlike him. But if it is, as I think, Ferdinand's and Harietta Boleski's work, they would not be likely to know that John had desired that Denzil should marry you, Amaryllis, and so would have thought a short card with longings to see you would be a natural thing to write. Indeed you can be at rest. And now I will go and dress for dinner, and we will forget disturbing thoughts."

Amaryllis and Denzil will always remember Stepan's wonderful tact and goodness to them that evening; he kept everything calm and thrilled them all with his stories and his conversation and his own wonderfully magnetic personality. And after dinner he played to them in the green drawing room and, as Mrs. Ardayre said, seemed to bring peace and healing to all their troubled souls.

But when he was alone with Denzil late, after the two women had retired to bed, he sunk into a deep chair in the smoking room and suddenly burst into a peal of cynical laughter.

"What the devil's up?" demanded Denzil, astonished.

"I am thinking of Harietta's exquisite mistake. She believes the baby is mine! She is mad with a goat's jealousy; she supposes it is I who will marry Amaryllis-- hence her plot! Does it not show how the good are protected and the evil fall into their own traps!"

"Of course! She was in love with you!"

"In love! Mon Dieu! you call that love! I mastered her body and was unobtain- able. She was never able to draw me more than a person could to whom I should pay two hundred francs. She knew that perfectly--it enraged her always. The threads are now completely in my hands. Conceive of it, Denzil! The man at the Ardayre

ball was her first husband for whom she always retained some kind of animal affec-
tion--because he used to beat her. They married her to Stanislass just to obtain the
secrets of Poland, and any other thing which she could pick' up. Her marvellous
stupidity and incredible want of all moral restraint has made her the most brilliant
spy. No principles to hamper her--nothing. She has only tripped up through jealousy now. When she felt that she had lost me she grew to desire me with the only
part of her nature with which she desires anything, her flesh--then she became
unbalanced, and in September before I left, gave the clue into my hands. I shall not
bore you with all the details, but I have them both--she and Ferdinand Ardayre.
The first husband has gone back to Germany from Sweden, but we shall secure him,
too, presently. Meanwhile I shall hand Harietta to the French authorities--her last
exploits are against France. She has enabled the Germans to shoot six or seven brave
fellows, besides giving information of the most important kind wormed from foolish elderly adorers and above all from Stanislass himself."

"She will be shot, I suppose."

"Probably. But first she shall confess about the postcard from the prison camp.
I shall go to Paris immediately, Denzil; there must be no delay."

"You will not feel the slightest twinge because she was your mistress, if she is
shot, Stepan? I ask because the combination of possible emotions is interesting and
unusual."

"Not for an instant--" and suddenly Verisschenzko's yellow-green eyes flashed
fire and his face grew transfigured with fierce hate. "You do not know the affection
I had for Stanislass from my boyhood--he was my leader, my ideal. No paltry aims-
-a great pioneer of freedom on the sanest lines. He might have altered the history
of our two countries--he was the light we need, and this foul, loathsome creature
has destroyed not only his soul and his body, but the protector and defender of a
conception of freedom which might have been realised. I would strangle her with
my own hands."

"Stanislass must have been a weakling, Stepan, to have let her destroy him. He
could never have ruled. It strikes me that this is the proof of another of your theories. It must be some debt of his previous life that he is paying to this woman. He
was given his chance to use strength against her and failed."

The hate died out of Verisschenzko's face--and the look of calm reasoning returned.

"Yes, you are right, Denzil. You are wiser than I. So I shall not give her up, for punishment of her crimes. I shall only give her up because of justice--she must not be at large. You see, even in my case,--I who pride myself on being balanced, can have my true point of view obsessed by hate. It is an ignoble passion, my son!"

"You will catch Ferdinand too?"

"Undoubtedly--he is just a rotten little snipe, but he does mischief as Harietta's tool--and through his business in Holland."

"He loathes the English--that is his reason, but Madame Boleski has no incentive like that."

"Harietta has no country--she would be willing to betray any one of them to gratify any personal desire. If she had been a patriot exclusively working for Germany, one could have respected her, but she has often betrayed their secrets to me--for jewels--and other things she required at the moment. No mercy can be shown at all."

"In these days there is no use in having sentiment just because a spy is a woman--but I am glad it is not my duty to deliver her up."

Verisschenzko smiled.

"I cannot help my nature, Denzil,--or rather the attributes of the nation into which in this life I am born. I shall hand Harietta over to justice without a regret."

Then they parted for the night with much of the disturbance and the complex emotions removed from Denzil's heart.

CHAPTER XXII

When Verisschenzko reached Paris and discovered the desecration of the Ikon, an icy rage came over him. He knew, even before questioning his old servant, that it could only be the work of Harietta. Jealousy alone would be the cause of such a wanton act. It revealed to him the certainty of his theory that she had imagined the little Benedict to be his child. No further proof that the postcard was a forgery was really needed, but he would see her once more and obtain extra confirmation.

His yellow-green eyes gleamed in a curious way as he stood looking at the mutilated picture.

That her ridiculous and accursed hatpin should have dared to touch the eyes of his soul's lady, and scratch out the face of the child!

But he must not let this emotion of personal anger affect what he intended in any case to do from motives of justice. In the morning he would give all his proofs of her guilt to the French authorities, and let the law take its course--but to-night he would make her come there to his apartment and hear from him an indictment of her crimes.

He sat down in the comfortable chair in his own sitting room and began to think.

His face was ominous; all the fierce passions of his nation and of his nature held him for a while.

His dog, an intelligent terrier whom he loved, sat there before the fire and watched him, wagging his stump of a tail now and then nervously, but not daring to approach. Then, after half an hour had gone by, he rose and went to the telephone. He called up the Universal and asked to be put through to the apartment of Madame Boleski, and soon heard Harietta's voice. It was a little anxious--and yet insolent too.

"Yes? Is that you Stepan! Darling Brute! What do you want?"

"You--cannot you come and dine with me to-night--alone?"

His voice was honey sweet, with a spontaneous, frank ring in it, only his face still looked as a fiend's.

"You have just arrived? How divine!"

"This instant, so I rushed at once to the telephone. I long for you--come--now."

He allowed passion to quiver in the last notes--he must be sure that she would be drawn.

"He cannot have opened the doors of the Ikon," Harietta thought. "I will go--to see him again will be worth it anyway!"

"All right!--in half an hour!"

"*Soit*,"--and he put the receiver down.

Then he went again to the Ikon and examined the doors; by slamming them very hard and readjusting one small golden nail, he could give the fastening the appearance of its having been jammed and impossible to open. He ordered a wonderful dinner and some Chateau Ykem of 1900. Harietta, he remembered, liked it better than Champagne. Its sweetness and its strength appealed to her taste. The room was warm and delightful with its blazing wood fire. He looked round before he went to dress, and then he laughed softly, and again Fin nervously wagged his stump of a tail.

Harietta arrived punctually. She had made herself extremely beautiful. Her overmastering desire to see Verisschenzko had allowed her usually keen sense of self-preservation partially to sleep. But even so, underneath there was some undefined sense of uneasiness.

Stepan met her in the hall, and greeted her in his usual abrupt way without ceremony.

"You will leave your cloak in my room," he suggested, wishing to give her the chance to look at the Ikon's jammed doors and so put her at her ease.

The moment she found herself alone, she went swiftly to the shrine. She examined it closely--no the bolt had not been mended. She pulled at the doors but she could not open them, and she remembered with relief that she had slammed them hard. That would account for things. He certainly could not yet know of her action. The evening would be one of pleasure after all! And there was never any use in speculating about to-morrows!

Verisschenzko was waiting for her in the sitting-room, and they went straight in to dinner. A little table was drawn up to the fire; all appeared deliciously intimate, and Harietta's spirits rose.

To her Verisschenzko appeared the most attractive creature on earth. Indeed, he had a wonderful magnetism which had intoxicated many women before her day. He was looking at her now with eyes unclouded by glamour. He saw that she was painted and obvious, and without real charm. She could no longer even affect his senses. He saw nothing but the reality, the animal, blatant reality, and in his memory there remained the pierced out orbs of the Virgin and the scratched face of the Christ child.

Everything fierce and cunning in his nature was in action--he was glorying in the torture he meant to inflict, the torture of jealousy and unsatisfied suspicion.

He talked subtly, deliberately stirring her curiosity and arousing her apprehension. He had not mentioned Amaryllis, and yet he had conveyed to her, as though it were an unconscious admission, that he had been in England with her, and that she reigned in his soul. Then he used every one of his arts of fascination so that all Ha-rietta's desires were inflamed once more, and by the time she had eaten of the rich Russian dishes and drank of the Chateau Ykem she was experiencing the strongest emotion she had ever known in her life, while a sense of impotence to move him augmented her other feelings.

Her eyes swam with passion, as she leaned over the table whispering words of the most violent love in his ears.

Verisschenzko remained absolutely unstirred.

"How silly you were to send that postcard to Lady Ardayre," he remarked con-templatively in the middle of one of her burning sentences. "It was not worthy of your usual methods--a child could see that it was a forgery. If you had not done that I might have made you very happy to-night--for the last time--my little goat!"

"Stepan--what card? But you are going to make me happy anyway, darling Brute; that is what I have come for, and you know it!"

Her eyes were not so successfully innocent as usual when she lied. She was un-easy at his stolidity, some fear stayed with her that perhaps he meant not to gratify her desires just to be provoking. He had teased her more than once before.

Verisschenzko went on, lighting his cigarette calmly:

"It was a silly plot--Ferdinand Ardayre wrote it and you dictated it; I perceived the whole thing at once. You did it because you were jealous of Lady Ardayre--you believe that I love her--"

"I do not know anything about a card, but I *am* jealous about that hateful bit of bread and butter," and her eyes flashed. "It is so unlike you to worry over such a creature--I'm what you like!"

He laughed softly. "A man has many sides--you appeal to his lowest. Fortu-nately it is not in command of him all the time--but let me tell you more about the forgery. You over-reached yourselves--you made John ignore something which would have been his first thought, thus the fraud was exposed at once."

Her jealousy blazed up, so that she forgot herself and prudence.

"You mean about the child--your child--"

The ominous gleam came into Verisschenzko's eyes.

"My child--you spoke of it once before and I warned you--I never speak idly."

She got up from the table and came and flung her arms round his neck.

"Stepan, I love you--I love you! I would like to kill Amaryllis and the child--I want you--why are you so changed?"

He only laughed scornfully again, while he disengaged her arms.

"Do you know how I found out? By the perfume--the same as you told me must be that of Stanislass' mistress--on the handkerchief marked 'F.A.' The whole thing was dramatically childish. You thought to prove her husband was still alive, would stop my marriage with Amaryllis Ardayre!"

"Then you are going to marry her!"

Harietta's hazel eyes flashed fire, her face had grown distorted with passion and her cheeks burned beyond the rouge.

She appeared a most revolting sight to Stepan. He watched her with cold, critical eyes. As she put out her hands he noticed how the thumbs turned right back. How had he ever been able to touch her in the past! He shivered with disgust and degradation at the thought.

She saw his movement of repulsion, and completely lost her head.

She flung herself into his arms and almost strangled him in her furious embrace, while she threw all restraint to the winds and poured out a torrent of passion, intermingled with curses for one who had dared to try and rob her of this adored mate.

It was a wonderful and very sickening exhibition, Verisschenzko thought. He remained as a statue of ice. Then when she had exhausted herself a little, he spoke with withering calm.

"Control yourself, Harietta; such emotion will leave ugly lines, and you cannot afford to spoil the one good you possess. I have not the least desire for you--I find that you look plain and only bore me. But now listen to me for a little--I have something to say!" His voice changed from the cynical callousness to a deep note of gravity: "You need not even tell me in words that you sent the forgery--you have given me ample proof. That subject is finished--but I will make you listen to the recital of some of your vile deeds." The note grew sterner and his eyes held her cowed. "Ah! what instruments of the devil are such women as you--possessing the greatest of all power over men you have used it only for ill--wherever you have passed there is a trail of degradation and slime. Think of Stanislass! A man of fine purpose and lofty ideals. What is he now? A poor lifeless semblance of a man with neither brain nor will. You have used him--not even to gratify your own low lust, but to betray countries--and one of them your husband's country, which ought to have been your own."

She sank to her knees at his side; he went on mercilessly. He spoke of many names which she knew, and then he came to Ferdinand Ardayre.

"They tell me he is drinking and sodden with morphine, and raves wildly of you. Think of them all--where are they now? Dead many of them--and you have survived and prospered like a vampire, sucking their blood. Do you ever think of a human being but your own degraded self? You would sacrifice your nearest and dearest for a moment's personal gain. You are not caught and strangled because the outside good natures come easily to you. It makes things smooth to smile and com- mit little acts of showy kindness which cost you nothing. You live and breathe and have your being like a great maggot fattening on a putrid corpse. I blush to think that I have ever used your body for my own ends, loathing you all the time. I have watched you cynically when I should have wrung your neck."

She sobbed hoarsely and held out her hands.

"For all these things you might still have gone free, Harietta--and fate would punish you in time, but you have committed that great crime for which there can be no mercy. You have acted the part of a spy. A wretched spy, not for patriotism but for your own ends--you have not been faithful to either side. Have you not of- ten given me the secrets of your late husband Hans? Do you care one atom which country wins? Not you. The whole sordid business has had only one aim--some personal gratification."

He paused--and she began to speak, now choking with rage, but he motioned her to be silent.

"Do you think so lightly of the great issues which are shaking the world that you imagine that you can do these things with impunity? I tell you that soon you must pay the price. I am not the only one who knows of your ways."

She got up from the floor now and tossed her head. Important things had never been to her realities--her fear left her. What agitated her now was that Stepan, whom she adored, should speak to her in such a tone. She threw herself into his arms once more, passionately proclaiming her love.

He thrust her from him in shrinking disgust, and the cruel vein in his character was aroused.

"Love!--do not dare to desecrate the name of love. You do not know what it means. I do--and this shall always remain with you as a remembrance. I love Amaryllis Ardayre. She is my ideal of a woman--tender and restrained and true--I shall always lay my life at her feet. I love her with a love such beings as you cannot dream of, knowing only the senses and playing only to them. That will be your knowledge always, that I worship and reverence this woman, and hold you in supreme contempt."

Harietta writhed and whined on the sofa where she had fallen.

"Go," he went on icily. "I have no further use for you, and my car is waiting below. You may as well avail yourself of it and return to your hotel. In the morning the last proof of the interest I have taken in you may be given, but to-night you can sleep."

Harietta cried aloud--she was frightened at last. What did he mean? But even fear was swallowed up in the frantic thought that he had done with her, that he would never any more hold her in his arms. Her world lay in ruins, he seemed the one and only good. She grovelled on the floor and kissed his feet.

"Master, Master! Keep me near you--I will be your slave--"

But Verisschenzko pushed her gently aside with his foot and going to a table near took up a cigarette. He lighted it serenely, glancing indifferently at the dishevelled heap of a woman still crouching on the floor.

"Enough of this dramatic nonsense," and he blew a ring of smoke. "I advise you to go quietly to bed--you may not sleep so softly on future nights."

Fear overcame her again--what could he mean? She got up and held on to the table, searching his face with burning eyes.

"Why should I not sleep so softly always?" and her voice was thick.

He laughed hoarsely.

"Who knows? Life is a gamble in these days. You must ask your interesting German friend."

She became ghastly white--that there was real danger was beginning to dawn upon her. The rouge stood out like that on the painted face of a clown.

Verisschenzko remained completely unmoved. He pressed the bell, and his Russian servant, warned beforehand, brought him in his fur coat and hat, and assisted him to put them on.

"I will take Madame to get her cloak," he announced calmly. "Wait here to show us out."

There was nothing for Harietta to do but follow him, as he went towards the bedroom door. She was stunned.

He walked over to the Ikon, and slipping a paper knife under them opened wide the doors; then he turned to her, and the very life melted within her when she saw his face.

"This is your work," and he pointed to the mutilations, "and for that and many other things, Harietta, you shall at last pay the price. Now come, I will take you back to your lover, and your husband--both will be waiting and longing for your return. Come!"

She dropped on the floor and refused to move so that he was obliged to call in the servant, and together they lifted her, the one holding her up, while the other wrapped her in her cloak. Then, each supporting her, they made their way down the stairs, and placed her in the waiting motor, Verisschenzko taking the seat at her side--and so they drove to the Universal. She should sleep to-night in peace and have time to think over the events of the evening. But to-morrow he must no longer delay about giving information to the authorities.

She cowered in the motor until they had almost reached the door, when she flung her arms round his neck and kissed him wildly again, sobbing with rage and terror:

"You shall not marry Amaryllis; I will kill you both first."

He smiled in the darkness, and she felt that he was mocking her, and suddenly turned and bit his arm, her teeth meeting in the cloth of his fur-lined coat.

He shook her off as he would have done a rat:

"Never quite apropos, Harietta! Always a little late! But here we have arrived, and you will not care for your admirers, the concierge, and the lift men, to see you in such a state. Put your veil over your face and go quietly to your rooms. I will wish you a very good-night--and farewell!"

He got out and stood with mock respect uncovered to assist her, and she was obliged to follow him. The hall porter and the numerous personnel of the hotel were looking on.

He bowed once more and appeared to kiss her hand:

"Good-bye, Harietta! Sleep well."

Then he re-entered the car and was whirled away.

She staggered for a second and then moved forward to the lift. But as she went in, two tall men who had been waiting stepped forward and joined her, and all three were carried aloft, and as she walked to her salon she saw that they were following her.

"There will be no more kicks for thee, my Angel!" the maid, peeping from a door, whispered exultingly to Fou-Chow! "Thy Marie has saved thee at last!"

* * * * *

When Verisschenzko again reached his own sitting room he paced up and down for half an hour. He was horribly agitated, and angry with himself for being so.

Denzil had been right; when it came to the point, it was a ghastly thing to have to do, to give a woman up to death--even though her crimes amply justified such action.

And what was death?

To such a one as Harietta what would death mean?

A sinking into oblivion for a period, and then a rebirth in some sphere of suffering where the first lessons of the meanings of things might be learned? That would seem to be the probable working of the law--so that she might eventually obtain a soul.

He must not speculate further about her though, he must keep his nerve.

And his own life--what would it now become? Would the spirit of freedom, stirring in his beloved country, arrive at any good? Or would the red current of revolution, once let loose, swamp all reason and flow in rivers of blood?

He would be powerless to help if he let weakness overmaster him now.

The immediate picture looked black and hopeless to his far-seeing eyes.

But his place must be in Petrograd now, until the end. His activities, which had obliged him to be away from Russia, were finished, and new ones had begun which he must direct, there in the heart of things.

"The world is aching for freedom, God," his stormy thoughts ran, "but we cannot hope to receive it until we have paid the price of the aeons of greed and self-seeking which have held us, the ignorance, the low material gain. We must now reap that sowing. The divine Christ--one man--was enough as a sacrifice in that old period of the world's day--but now there must be a holocaust of the bravest and best for our purification."

He threw himself into his chair and gazed into the glowing embers. What pictures were forming themselves there? Nations arising glorified by a new religion of common sense, education universally enjoyed, the great forces studied, and Nature's fundamental principles reckoned with and understood.

To hunt his food.

To recreate his species.

And to kill his enemy.

A bright blade sheathed but ready, a clear judgment trained and used, ideals nobly striven for, and Wisdom the High Priest of God.

These were the visions he saw in the fire, and he started to his feet and stretched out his arms.

"Strength, God! Strength!" that was his prayer.

"That we may go-- Armoured and militant, New-pithed, new-souled, new-visioned, up the steeps To those great altitudes whereat the weak Live not, but only the strong Have leave to strive, and suffer, and achieve."

Then he sat down and wrote to Denzil.

"I have all the needed proofs, my friend. Marry my soul's lady in peace and make her happy. There come some phases in a man's life which require all his will to face. I hope I am no weakling. I return to Russia immediately. Events there will enable me to blot out some disturbing memories.

"The end is not yet. Indeed, I feel that my real life is only just beginning.

"Ferdinand Ardayre is deeply incriminated with Harietta; it is only a question of a little time and he will be taken too. Then, Denzil, you, in the natural course of events, would have been the Head of the Family. You will need all your philosophy never to feel any jar in the situation with your son as the years go on. You will have to look at it squarely, dear old friend, and know that it is impossible to have interfered with destiny and to have gone scott free. Then you will be able to accept title affair with common sense and prize what you have obtained, without spoiling it with futile regrets. You have paid most of your score with wounds and suffering, and now can expect what happiness the agony of the world can let a man enjoy.

"My blessings to you both and to the Ardayre son.

"And now adieu for a long time."

He had hardly written the last line when the telephone rang, and the frantic voice of Stanislass, his ancient friend, called to him!

Harietta had been taken away to St. Lazare--her maid had denounced her. What could be done?

A great wave of relief swept over Stepan. So he was not to be the instrument of justice after all!

How profoundly he thanked God!

But the irony of the thing shook him.

Harietta would pay with her life for having maltreated a dog!

Truly the workings of fate were marvellous.

CHAPTER XXIII

The days in prison for Harietta, before and after her trial, were days of frenzied terror, alternating with incredulity. She would not believe that she was to die.

Stanislass and Ferdinand, and even Verisschenzko, would save her!

She loathed the hard bed at St. Lazare, and the discomfort, and the ugliness, and the Sister of Charity!

She spent hours tramping her cell like a wild beast in a cage. She would roar with inarticulate fury, and cry aloud to her husband, and her lovers, one after another, and then she would cower in a corner, shaking with fear.

The greatest pain of all was the thought that Stepan and Amaryllis would marry and be happy. Once or twice foam gathered at the corners of her lips when she thought of this.

If she could have reached Marie, that would have given her some satisfaction--to tear out her eyes! For Ferdinand Ardayre had told her how Marie had given her up, working quietly until she had all necessary proofs, and then denouncing her.

When Stanislass had returned from the Club, whither she had despatched him for the evening, so that she might be free to dine with Verisschenzko, he found that she had already been taken away.

The shock, when he discovered that nothing could be done, had nearly killed him--he now lay dangerously ill in a Maison de Sante, happily unconscious of events.

For Ferdinand Ardayre the blow had fallen with crushing force. The one strong thing in his weak nature was his passion for Harietta--and to be robbed of her in such a way!

He battled impotently against fate, unable even to try to use any means in his possession to get the death sentence commuted, because he was too deeply implicated himself to make any stir.

He saw her in the prison after the trial, with the bars between and the warders near. And the awful change in Tier paralysed him with grief. On the morrow she was to die--the usual death of a spy.

Her hair was wild and her face without rouge was haggard and wan.

She implored him to save her.

The frightful pain of knowing that he could do nothing made Ferdinand desperate, and then suddenly he became inspired with an idea.

He could at all events remove some of the agony of terror from her, and enable her to go to her death without a hideous scene. He remembered "La Tosca"--the same method might serve again!

He managed to whisper to her in broken sentences that she would certainly be saved. The plan was all prepared, he assured her. The rifles would contain blank cartridges, and she must pretend to fall--and afterwards he would come, having bribed every one and made the path smooth.

He lied so fervently that Harietta was convinced, her material brain catching at any straw. She must dress herself and look her best, he told her, so as to make an impression upon all the men concerned; and then, when he had to leave her, he arranged with the prison doctor that she might receive a strong *piqure* of morphine, so that she would be serene. She spent the night dreaming quite happily and at four o'clock was awakened and began to dress.

The drug had calmed all her terrors and her dramatic instinct held full sway.

She arranged her toilet with the utmost care, using all her arts to beautify herself. In her ears were Stanislass' ruby earrings and she wore Stepan's ring and brooch.

Death to her was an impossibility--she had never seen any one die.

It was a wonderfully fine part she would have to play, with Ferdinand there really going to save her! That was all! She must even be sweet at last to the poor sister, whom she had snarled at hitherto.

If she could only have seen Stepan once more! Stanislass and his broken life and fond devotion never gave her a thought or troubled her at all. After she was free, she would find some means to pay out Hans! She hated him. If it had not been for Hans and his tiresome old higher command with their stupid intrigues, she would still be free. That she had betrayed countries--that she was guilty in any way never presented itself to her mind.

All Verisschenzko's passionate indictment had fallen upon unheeding ears. The morphine now left her only sufficiently conscious for fundamental instincts to act.

She felt that she was a beautiful woman going to be the chief figure in a wonderfully dramatic scene. Nothing solemn had touched her. Her brain was light and now only filled with cunning and *coqueterie*; she meant to charm her guards and executioners to the last man! And ready at length, she walked nonchalantly out of the prison and into the waiting car which was to carry her to Vincennes.

Now the end of all this is best told in the words of a young French soldier who was an eye witness and wrote the whole thing down. To pen the hideous horror I find too difficult a task.

"Sunday--11 in the evening.

"We had only returned at that moment from our day's leave, when the Lieutenant came to us to announce that we should be of the *piquet* to-morrow morning for the execution of Madame Boleski, the spy.

"He said this to us in his monotonous voice as though he had been saying 'To-morrow--*Revue d'Armes*'--but for us, after a whole day passed far from barracks, it was a rather brusque return to military realities!

"At once it became necessary that we look through our accoutrements for the show. No small affair! and for more than an hour there was brushing and polishing of straps and buckles. It was nearly two o'clock in the morning before we could turn in.

"Many of us could not sleep--we are all between eighteen and nineteen years old, and the idea to see a woman killed agitated us. But little by little the whole band dozed."

"Monday morning.

"At four o'clock--reveille. We dress in haste in the dark. Ten minutes later we all find ourselves in the courtyard.

"'*A droit alignement couvres sur deux*.'

"The Lieutenant made the call."

*   *   *   *   *

"The detachment moves off in the night, marching in slow cadence--that step which so peculiarly gives the impression of restrained force and condensed power.

"We leave the fort and gain the artillery butts--true landscape of the front! Trenches, stripped trees, abandoned wagons!

"And in the middle of all that--our silhouettes of carbines, casques and sacs.

"Absolute silence.

"We stop--we advance--and suddenly in the dawn which has begun, we arrive at our destination--the execution ground.

"'*Cannoniers--halte! Couvres sur deux. A droite alignement*.'"

"A rattle of arms. And there in front of us, at hardly fifteen yards, we catch sight of the post.

"Up till now we had scarcely felt anything--just startled impressions, almost of curiosity, but now I begin to experience the first strong sensation.

"The post! Symbol of all this sinister ceremony. A short post--not higher than one's shoulder! There it stands in front of the shooting butts. And to think that nearly every Monday--"

*   *   *   *   *

"Now the troops from the Square, which is in reality rectangular, the shooting butt constituting one of its sides. Then in the grim dawn we wait quietly for what is to come. One after another, we see several automobiles approach, and each time we ask ourselves, 'Is not this the condemned?'

"No--they are journalists--officers--*avocats*--and presently a hearse, out of which is lifted the coffin.

"The undertakers' men, who presently will proceed to the business of placing the body there, laugh and talk together as they sit and smoke. They are old *habitues!*"

"One was cold standing still! It begins to be quite light. The condemned one may arrive at any moment, because the execution has been fixed for exactly at the rising of the sun.

"The men of the platoon load their rifles. The number of them is twelve--four sergeants, four corporals, four soldiers.

"And then there are the *Chasseurs a pied*."

"All of a sudden, two more cars appear, escorted by a company of dragoons.

"This time it is She.

"They stop--out of the first one, officers descend. The Commissaire of the Government who has, condemned Madame Boleski to death and who had gone a little more than an hour ago to awake her in her cell. The Captain, reporter, and two other Captains. The door of the second auto opens, two gendarmes get out--a Sister of St. Lazare (what a terrible *metier* for her!)--and then Harietta Boleski!

"And at once, accompanied by the nun and followed by the gendarmes, she penetrates into the square of men.

"Until now we have been enduring a period of waiting, we have been asking ourselves if it will have an effect upon us--but now we have no more doubt. The effect has begun!

"'Present arms!'

"All together we render honour to the dead woman--for one considers a person condemned as already dead. And the bugles begin to play the March--*Do sol do do Sol do do, Mi mi mi*--

"They play slowly--very softly and in the minor key.

"Harietta Boleski walks quickly, the sister can hardly keep by her side. She is tall, beautiful, very elegant. A large hat with floating lace veil thrown back and splendid earrings. A dark dress--pretty shoes.

"She looks at the troops and the *piquet d'execution* a little disdainfully, and then she smiles gaily--it is almost a titter. The sister taps her gently on the shoulder, as if to recall her to a sense of order, but she makes one careless gesture and walks up to the post.

"The bugles are sounding plaintively, slowly and more slowly all the time.

"She pauses in front of us--and with us it is now, 'Does this make us feel something?' We must hold ourselves not to grow faint.

"To see this woman go by with the trumpets sounding ever. To say to ourselves that in sixty seconds she will be no more. There will be no life in that beautiful body. Ah! that is an emotion, believe me!

"Never has the great problem been brought more forcibly before my spirit.

"It is during the second when she passes before me that I receive the most profound impression, more even than at the actual moment of the firing."

     *   *   *   *   *

"Harietta Boleski is beside the post. The bugles stop their mournful sound. They tie her to it, but not tightly, only so that her fall may not be too hard. A gendarme presents her with a bandeau for her eyes, which she pushes aside with scorn.

"And when an officer reads the sentence, Harietta Boleski smiles."

     *   *   *   *   *

"At twelve yards the platoon is lined up. The sentence has been read.

"Madame Boleski embraces the Sister of Charity, who is very overcome. She even whispers a few words to comfort her. They stand back from the post. The adjutant who commands the platoon raises his sword--the rifles come in into position--two seconds--and the sword falls!"

     *   *   *   *   *

"A salute!"

     *   *   *   *   *

"Harietta Boleski is no more.

"The fair body drops to earth and immediately an Adjutant of Dragoons goes swiftly to the post, revolver pointed, and gives the ***coup de grace***.

"*'Arme sur l'epaule--Droit. A droit. En avant. Marche!'*

"And we file past the corpse while the trumpets recommence to sound.

"Harietta Boleski is lying down. She seems to be only reposing, so beautiful she looks.

"The ball had entered her heart (we knew this later) so that her death has been instantaneous.

"All the troops have defiled before her now.

"We regain our quarters.

"But as we file into the courtyard the sun gilds the highest window of the fortress. The day has begun."

     *   *   *   *   *

Thus perished Harietta Boleski in the thirty-seventh year of her age--in the midst of the zest of life. The times are to strenuous for sentiment.

So perish all spies!

THE END

The Codes Of Hammurabi And Moses
W. W. Davies

QTY

The discovery of the Hammurabi Code is one of the greatest achievements of archaeology, and is of paramount interest, not only to the student of the Bible, but also to all those interested in ancient history...

Religion   **ISBN:** *1-59462-338-4*   **Pages:132**
MSRP $12.95

The Theory of Moral Sentiments
Adam Smith

QTY

This work from 1749. contains original theories of conscience amd moral judgment and it is the foundation for systemof morals.

Philosophy **ISBN:** *1-59462-777-0*   **Pages:536**
MSRP $19.95

Jessica's First Prayer
Hesba Stretton

QTY

In a screened and secluded corner of one of the many railway-bridges which span the streets of London there could be seen a few years ago, from five o'clock every morning until half past eight, a tidily set-out coffee-stall, consisting of a trestle and board, upon which stood two large tin cans, with a small fire of charcoal burning under each so as to keep the coffee boiling during the early hours of the morning when the work-people were thronging into the city on their way to their daily toil...

Pages:84

Childrens   **ISBN:** *1-59462-373-2*   *MSRP $9.95*

My Life and Work
Henry Ford

QTY

Henry Ford revolutionized the world with his implementation of mass production for the Model T automobile. Gain valuable business insight into his life and work with his own auto-biography... "We have only started on our development of our country we have not as yet, with all our talk of wonderful progress, done more than scratch the surface. The progress has been wonderful enough but..."

Pages:300

Biographies/   **ISBN:** *1-59462-198-5*   *MSRP $21.95*

The Art of Cross-Examination
Francis Wellman

QTY

I presume it is the experience of every author, after his first book is published upon an important subject, to be almost overwhelmed with a wealth of ideas and illustrations which could readily have been included in his book, and which to his own mind, at least, seem to make a second edition inevitable. Such certainly was the case with me; and when the first edition had reached its sixth impression in five months, I rejoiced to learn that it seemed to my publishers that the book had met with a sufficiently favorable reception to justify a second and considerably enlarged edition. ..

Reference   **ISBN:** *1-59462-647-2*

Pages:412

MSRP $19.95

On the Duty of Civil Disobedience
Henry David Thoreau

QTY

Thoreau wrote his famous essay, On the Duty of Civil Disobedience, as a protest against an unjust but popular war and the immoral but popular institution of slave-owning. He did more than write—he declined to pay his taxes, and was hauled off to gaol in consequence. Who can say how much this refusal of his hastened the end of the war and of slavery ?

Law   **ISBN:** *1-59462-747-9*

Pages:48

MSRP $7.45

Dream Psychology Psychoanalysis for Beginners
Sigmund Freud

QTY

Sigmund Freud, born Sigismund Schlomo Freud (May 6, 1856 - September 23, 1939), was a Jewish-Austrian neurologist and psychiatrist who co-founded the psychoanalytic school of psychology. Freud is best known for his theories of the unconscious mind, especially involving the mechanism of repression; his redefinition of sexual desire as mobile and directed towards a wide variety of objects; and his therapeutic techniques, especially his understanding of transference in the therapeutic relationship and the presumed value of dreams as sources of insight into unconscious desires.

Psychology   **ISBN:** *1-59462-905-6*

Pages:196

MSRP $15.45

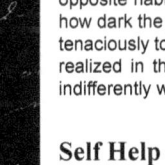

The Miracle of Right Thought
Orison Swett Marden

QTY

Believe with all of your heart that you will do what you were made to do. When the mind has once formed the habit of holding cheerful, happy, prosperous pictures, it will not be easy to form the opposite habit. It does not matter how improbable or how far away this realization may see, or how dark the prospects may be, if we visualize them as best we can, as vividly as possible, hold tenaciously to them and vigorously struggle to attain them, they will gradually become actualized, realized in the life. But a desire, a longing without endeavor, a yearning abandoned or held indifferently will vanish without realization.

Pages:360

Self Help   **ISBN:** *1-59462-644-8*

MSRP $25.45

www.bookjungle.com *email: sales@bookjungle.com fax: 630-214-0564 mail: Book Jungle PO Box 2226 Champaign, IL 61825*

QTY

The Rosicrucian Cosmo-Conception Mystic Christianity *by Max Heindel* ISBN: 1-59462-188-8 **$38.95**
The Rosicrucian Cosmo-conception is not dogmatic, neither does it appeal to any other authority than the reason of the student. It is; not controversial, but is: sent forth in the, hope that it may help to clear... New Age/Religion Pages 646

Abandonment To Divine Providence *by Jean-Pierre de Caussade* ISBN: 1-59462-228-0 **$25.95**
"The Rev. Jean Pierre de Caussade was one of the most remarkable spiritual writers of the Society of Jesus in France in the 18th Century. His death took place at Toulouse in 1751. His works have gone through many editions and have been republished... Inspirational/Religion Pages 400

Mental Chemistry *by Charles Haanel* ISBN: 1-59462-192-6 **$23.95**
Mental Chemistry allows the change of material conditions by combining and appropriately utilizing the power of the mind. Much like applied chemistry creates something new and unique out of careful combinations of chemicals the mastery of mental chemistry... New Age Pages 354

The Letters of Robert Browning and Elizabeth Barret Barrett 1845-1846 vol II ISBN: 1-59462-193-4 **$35.95**
by Robert Browning and Elizabeth Barrett Biographies Pages 596

Gleanings In Genesis (volume I) *by Arthur W. Pink* ISBN: 1-59462-130-6 **$27.45**
Appropriately has Genesis been termed "the seed plot of the Bible" for in it we have, in germ form, almost all of the great doctrines which are afterwards fully developed in the books of Scripture which follow... Religion/Inspirational Pages 420

The Master Key *by L. W. de Laurence* ISBN: 1-59462-001-6 **$30.95**
In no branch of human knowledge has there been a more lively increase of the spirit of research during the past few years than in the study of Psychology, Concentration and Mental Discipline. The requests for authentic lessons in Thought Control, Mental Discipline and... New Age/Business Pages 422

The Lesser Key Of Solomon Goetia *by L. W. de Laurence* ISBN: 1-59462-092-X **$9.95**
This translation of the first book of the "Lernegton" which is now for the first time made accessible to students of Talismanic Magic was done, after careful collation and edition, from numerous Ancient Manuscripts in Hebrew, Latin, and French... New Age/Occult Pages 92

Rubaiyat Of Omar Khayyam *by Edward Fitzgerald* ISBN:1-59462-332-5 **$13.95**
Edward Fitzgerald, whom the world has already learned, in spite of his own efforts to remain within the shadow of anonymity, to look upon as one of the rarest poets of the century, was born at Bredfield, in Suffolk, on the 31st of March, 1809. He was the third son of John Purcell... Music Pages 172

Ancient Law *by Henry Maine* ISBN: 1-59462-128-4 **$29.95**
The chief object of the following pages is to indicate some of the earliest ideas of mankind, as they are reflected in Ancient Law, and to point out the relation of those ideas to modern thought. Religion/History Pages 452

Far-Away Stories *by William J. Locke* ISBN: 1-59462-129-2 **$19.45**
"Good wine needs no bush, but a collection of mixed vintages does. And this book is just such a collection. Some of the stories I do not want to remain buried for ever in the museum files of dead magazine-numbers an author's not unpardonable vanity..." Fiction Pages 272

Life of David Crockett *by David Crockett* ISBN: 1-59462-250-7 **$27.45**
"Colonel David Crockett was one of the most remarkable men of the times in which he lived. Born in humble life, but gifted with a strong will, an indomitable courage, and unremitting perseverance... Biographies/New Age Pages 424

Lip-Reading *by Edward Nitchie* ISBN: 1-59462-206-X **$25.95**
Edward B. Nitchie, founder of the New York School for the Hard of Hearing, now the Nitchie School of Lip-Reading, Inc, wrote "LIP-READING Principles and Practice". The development and perfecting of this meritorious work on lip-reading was an undertaking... How-to Pages 400

A Handbook of Suggestive Therapeutics, Applied Hypnotism, Psychic Science ISBN: 1-59462-214-0 **$24.95**
by Henry Munro Health/New Age/Health/Self-help Pages 376

A Doll's House: and Two Other Plays *by Henrik Ibsen* ISBN: 1-59462-112-8 **$19.95**
Henrik Ibsen created this classic when in revolutionary 1848 Rome. Introducing some striking concepts in playwriting for the realist genre, this play has been studied the world over. Fiction/Classics/Plays 308

The Light of Asia *by sir Edwin Arnold* ISBN: 1-59462-204-3 **$13.95**
In this poetic masterpiece, Edwin Arnold describes the life and teachings of Buddha. The man who was to become known as Buddha to the world was born as Prince Gautama of India but he rejected the worldly riches and abandoned the reigns of power when... Religion/History/Biographies Pages 170

The Complete Works of Guy de Maupassant *by Guy de Maupassant* ISBN: 1-59462-157-8 **$16.95**
"For days and days, nights and nights, I had dreamed of that first kiss which was to consecrate our engagement, and I knew not on what spot I should put my lips..." Fiction/Classics Pages 240

The Art of Cross-Examination *by Francis L. Wellman* ISBN: 1-59462-309-0 **$26.95**
Written by a renowned trial lawyer, Wellman imparts his experience and uses case studies to explain how to use psychology to extract desired information through questioning. How-to/Science/Reference Pages 408

Answered or Unanswered? *by Louisa Vaughan* ISBN: 1-59462-248-5 **$10.95**
Miracles of Faith in China Religion Pages 112

The Edinburgh Lectures on Mental Science (1909) *by Thomas* ISBN: 1-59462-008-3 **$11.95**
This book contains the substance of a course of lectures recently given by the writer in the Queen Street Hall, Edinburgh. Its purpose is to indicate the Natural Principles governing the relation between Mental Action and Material Conditions... New Age/Psychology Pages 148

Ayesha *by H. Rider Haggard* ISBN: 1-59462-301-5 **$24.95**
Verily and indeed it is the unexpected that happens! Probably if there was one person upon the earth from whom the Editor of this, and of a certain previous history, did not expect to hear again... Classics Pages 380

Ayala's Angel *by Anthony Trollope* ISBN: 1-59462-352-X **$29.95**
The two girls were both pretty, but Lucy who was twenty-one who supposed to be simple and comparatively unattractive, whereas Ayala was credited, as her Bombwhat romantic name might show, with poetic charm and a taste for romance. Ayala when her father died was nineteen... Fiction Pages 484

The American Commonwealth *by James Bryce* ISBN: 1-59462-286-8 **$34.45**
An interpretation of American democratic political theory. It examines political mechanics and society from the perspective of Scotsman James Bryce Politics Pages 572

Stories of the Pilgrims *by Margaret P. Pumphrey* ISBN: 1-59462-116-0 **$17.95**
This book explores pilgrims religious oppression in England as well as their escape to Holland and eventual crossing to America on the Mayflower, and their early days in New England... History Pages 268

www.bookjungle.com *email: sales@bookjungle.com fax: 630-214-0564 mail: Book Jungle PO Box 2226 Champaign, IL 61825*

QTY

The Fasting Cure *by Sinclair Upton*   ISBN: *1-59462-222-1*   **$13.95**
In the Cosmopolitan Magazine for May, 1910, and in the Contemporary Review (London) for April, 1910, I published an article dealing with my experiences in fasting. I have written a great many magazine articles, but never one which attracted so much attention... New Age/Self Help/Health Pages 164

Hebrew Astrology *by Sepharial*   ISBN: *1-59462-308-2*   **$13.45**
In these days of advanced thinking it is a matter of common observation that we have left many of the old landmarks behind and that we are now pressing forward to greater heights and to a wider horizon than that which represented the mind-content of our progenitors... Astrology Pages 144

Thought Vibration or The Law of Attraction in the Thought World   ISBN: *1-59462-127-6*   **$12.95**
by William Walker Atkinson   *Psychology/Religion Pages 144*

Optimism *by Helen Keller*   ISBN: *1-59462-108-X*   **$15.95**
Helen Keller was blind, deaf, and mute since 19 months old, yet famously learned how to overcome these handicaps, communicate with the world, and spread her lectures promoting optimism. An inspiring read for everyone... Biographies/Inspirational Pages 84

Sara Crewe *by Frances Burnett*   ISBN: *1-59462-360-0*   **$9.45**
In the first place, Miss Minchin lived in London. Her home was a large, dull, tall one, in a large, dull square, where all the houses were alike, and all the sparrows were alike, and where all the door-knockers made the same heavy sound... Childrens/Classic Pages 88

The Autobiography of Benjamin Franklin *by Benjamin Franklin*   ISBN: *1-59462-135-7*   **$24.95**
The Autobiography of Benjamin Franklin has probably been more extensively read than any other American historical work, and no other book of its kind has had such ups and downs of fortune. Franklin lived for many years in England, where he was agent... Biographies/History Pages 332

Name	
Email	
Telephone	
Address	
City, State ZIP	

☐ **Credit Card**   ☐ **Check / Money Order**

Credit Card Number	
Expiration Date	
Signature	

Please Mail to: Book Jungle
PO Box 2226
Champaign, IL 61825
or Fax to: 630-214-0564

ORDERING INFORMATION
web: *www.bookjungle.com*
email: *sales@bookjungle.com*
fax: *630-214-0564*
mail: *Book Jungle PO Box 2226 Champaign, IL 61825*
or PayPal *to sales@bookjungle.com*

Please contact us for bulk discounts

DIRECT-ORDER TERMS

**20% Discount if You Order
Two or More Books**
Free Domestic Shipping!
Accepted: Master Card, Visa,
Discover, American Express

www.ingramcontent.com/pod-product-compliance
Lightning Source LLC
Chambersburg PA
CBHW080906020726
47502CB00008B/2362